"Do You Realize How Callous You Sound?"

"Success in business doesn't help a person win popularity contests," Brendan drawled. "And I'm only callous about some people and some property."

Before she realized his intentions, he had leaned across the table, taken her hand and pressed his mouth against her wrist. Her heart caught in her throat, her breathing stopped, and a tingling excitement surged along her nerves. Anger drained away, replaced by a painful, forbidden pleasure.

"I've never been callous where you're concerned, Cass," Brendan murmured. "Let me make love to you and I'll show you just how sensitive I can be."

DIANA DIXON

has always viewed the world romantically, especially when her experiences have been shared with a special man: her husband. The mountains after a snowfall, Athens, a rainbow over a Greek isle . . . all are magical. As she writes, she hopes that what is romantic for her is also romantic for other women.

Dear Reader:

There is an electricity between two people in love that makes everything they do magic, larger than life. This is what we bring you in SILHOUETTE INTIMATE MOMENTS.

SILHOUETTE INTIMATE MOMENTS are longer, more sensuous romance novels filled with adventure, suspense, glamor or melodrama. These books have an element no one else has tapped: excitement.

We are proud to present the very best romance has to offer from the very best romance writers. In the coming months look for some of your favorite authors such as Elizabeth Lowell, Nora Roberts, Erin St. Claire and Brooke Hastings.

SILHOUETTE INTIMATE MOMENTS are for the woman who wants more than she has ever had before. These books are for you.

Karen Solem
Editor-in-Chief
Silhouette Books

Lucifer's Playground

Diana Dixon

Silhouette Intimate Moments

Published by Silhouette Books New York

America's Publisher of Contemporary Romance

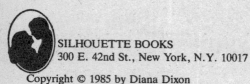 SILHOUETTE BOOKS
300 E. 42nd St., New York, N.Y. 10017

Copyright © 1985 by Diana Dixon

Distributed by Pocket Books

ISBN: 0-373-07098-5

First Silhouette Books printing June, 1985

10 9 8 7 6 5 4 3 2 1

America's Publisher of Contemporary Romance

Printed in the U.S.A.

To Gary, whose love, appreciation, and knowledge of Southern Utah taught and infected me.

Chapter 1

New York City was experiencing its first taste of spring after a cold, miserable, wet March and April. The usual hurried rushing from one warm, dry place to another had ended. That first Sunday evening in May, pedestrians strolled along the city streets in the gathering dusk, glancing with idle interest at the window displays. The shops themselves were closed and dark, but inside the substantial old brick building that housed Cassandra's House of Interiors, light streaked through the slatted blinds of a second-floor room. There, Cassandra Wells bent over a drawing table in concentration, oblivious to the pleasures of the balmy weather outside.

In fact, Cass was so absorbed in her work that she didn't hear the slam of the back door on the floor below or the sound of footsteps stomping across the showroom and up the stairs to the offices above. She swirled her brush in a splotch of burnt-orange paint on the palette and applied a color wash across the top half of the rendering. She had just completed the process and had begun rinsing out the brush in the murky jar of water at her elbow when a voice exploded in the quiet.

"Well, Cass? Do you intend to work all night?"

Cass jumped in alarm, half rose from her stool, and swiveled around to face the door. "Darin! You scared me out of my wits! What on earth are you doing here?"

Her heart was still pounding as she watched the scowl on Darin's face deepen in disapproval. Her partner was invariably tidy, and Cass's workroom at the moment was in a state of total disarray. Wadded-up sheets of art paper had missed the wastebasket and lay strewn around it. A paint-streaked cloth had fallen to the floor. A stale, half-eaten sandwich on the filing cabinet sat beside several paper cups of cold, half-finished coffee. Cass sighed inwardly as Darin's gaze finally fastened on her. His thin lips curled in displeasure at the sight of her well-worn sweater and paint-spattered cords—an almost comical contrast to the impeccably tailored evening clothes he wore.

"Why aren't you at Megan's housewarming party?" Cass asked quickly to distract his attention.

"That's exactly what I came to ask you!" Frustrated, Darin ran a hand through his expertly styled blond hair. "I've been trying to call you since noon and all I got was the answering service. Do you realize that it's nearly eight o'clock? You were supposed to have been at Megan's half an hour ago and you aren't even dressed yet."

"I may drop in later," Cass returned, her reply purposely vague. Absently she flexed her cramped fingers and rolled her head in circles to relieve the stiffness in her neck. Her concentration was broken; the adrenaline that had sustained her for the last few hours slowly ebbed and weariness seeped into every muscle. Lines of fatigue creased the corners of her mouth and added age to her usually youthful appearance. Darin frowned as she slumped against the back of the stool.

"When did you eat last, Cass?"

"I got a sandwich from the deli about three."

"And forgot to eat it," he growled. He moved behind her and began to massage the tense knots in her shoulders. "I'm sorry, baby. I didn't mean to dump on you. But you know you have to go to Megan's party."

"Mmmm," she murmured noncommittally, turning

slightly so that his fingers could reach one particularly tender spot.

"She'd be terribly hurt if you didn't show up," he suggested. It was a mild reproof, considering the circumstances.

"In that crowd, she'd never miss me." A smile of contentment curved her lips as the tension in her shoulders eased under the persuasion of his skillful fingers.

"You know she would. And so," he added casually, though there was nothing casual in his expression, "would the associate editor of *Contemporary Interiors.*" He stopped his ministrations and turned her to face him. "That's why I tried to reach you. Megan called this afternoon. Cassandra Wells has hit the big time again."

At last Cass caught his ill-concealed excitement. *"Contemporary Interiors?"*

Now Darin beamed. "Megan's house is going to be the featured article in the August issue. Their design editor has flown in from Los Angeles and wants to do an interview with you tonight. *Now* do you see why it's so important for you to show up?"

"Yes, yes, of course." She glanced distractedly at her day's work spread across the drawing table. "But I've only finished the renderings for four of the six rooms for the Nieharts, and I meet with them tomorrow at three."

Darin shrugged. "So, tell them that you've come up with a sensational idea, but you need two or three more days to make sure the materials are available. That will keep 'em happy."

Cass smiled affectionately at him. Darin Summerhays was not only her business partner but her friend. "I will tell them that, but only because it happens to be the truth."

"Just count on old Darin to solve all your problems."

"Can old Darin solve the problem of my being three days behind schedule on Mason Trent's beachhouse?" Cass sighed.

"Not unless you can teach me to design by computer."

Cass appeared to give the idea serious consideration. "Now there's a thought. I'm a high-tech idiot myself, of course, but surely *you* could write a program. Just imagine.

First, you work out a personality chart for a client; you know, the kind they have for computer dating—hobbies, likes and dislikes, color preferences . . ."

"Sexual habits," he added knowledgeably, playing the game.

"Naturally," she agreed, undaunted. After four years of working with Darin, she had become inured to his professional-bachelor's pose. "Then you punch in a room's size and function, press a few of those magic computer keys and . . . presto! There on the screen, in living color, appears the ideal design." A spark of mischief in her dark eyes gave animation to her tired face. "Come to think of it, I'm not so sure that some of the more sterile hotel rooms I've stayed in lately weren't designed just that way—" Cass broke off abruptly as she saw his start of surprise. "What is it, Darin? What did I say? You didn't think I was serious, did you?"

"No, no! Of course not, but you did just happen to hit on a subject that I want to discuss with you."

"Designing by computer?" she scoffed.

"No, hotel rooms."

"What?"

"I don't have time to explain now," he said, putting her off. "We'll talk on our way to Megan's. First, however, I'm going to run you by your apartment and give you exactly ten minutes to change out of those Salvation Army rejects you're wearing and into something ravishing. Now, come on!"

Out on the loading dock in back of the shop, Cass stopped and stared at the white Porsche standing in Darin's parking space. "Darin, you have a new car!"

"Like it?" He ran a proud hand over the fender. "You should see it under the hood, and it handles like a million bucks."

And cost a bundle too, Cass knew. Often she had wondered how Darin made his income stretch the way it did to include expensive clothes, cars, and an apartment on the Upper East Side. As partners in Cassandra's, they shared equally in the firm's profits, and while Cass was never really strapped for money, her half didn't keep her in such luxuries.

Perhaps, she concluded ruefully, that was why Darin handled the financial side of the business and she the artistic end. Darin couldn't tell a Chippendale chair from a Hepplewhite, and Cass wouldn't have recognized a debit if it bit her on the leg. He was a financial wizard.

"I wish I knew how you did it, Darin," she sighed, settling into the plush seat. "My car is just about on its last leg—or last bald tire, to be more exact."

"Cass baby, I offered to introduce you to my bookie."

She studied him curiously as he took his place behind the wheel. "You're not serious, are you? About betting, I mean?"

"Last week at Belmont I put a thousand on the nose of a forty-to-one long shot who won by a length and a half. It helps in choosing my horses," he admitted with a grin, "that I owned my own thoroughbred by the time I was sixteen. He won fourteen races before he was sold along with the rest of the family's disposable assets. Daddy," he said wryly, "should have kept his horses and left oil speculation to the suckers."

Cass, of course, had heard Darin's story of the loss of the Summerhays family fortune before, but this time she noted the absence of rancor in his voice. Perhaps, she decided, he had finally found that he *liked* working for a living. As well he should, she concluded. The partnership they had formed certainly suited his needs and qualifications. The paperwork wasn't so arduous that it put a crimp in his hedonistic life-style. But more important, he had been born to the public relations part of his job. As one of *the* New York Summerhayses, Darin had entree into the fashionable social world that recognized quality and originality in decorating and was willing to pay for it. What was more, he was blessed with both a facile charm and a knack for conjuring up business.

They had been introduced by a mutual acquaintance shortly after the Summerhays's financial disaster. The meeting had been a stroke of good fortune. Cass had just opened her own small shop, and combining Darin's business and social acumen with Cass's artistic gifts, they had created a highly successful partnership. In just four years, they had grown from a two-person, makeshift operation to a recognized, increasingly respected New York interior design house. Cassandra's was now one of the 'in" places for the wealthy, fashionable, and socially prominent. They had now expanded their staff to include an associate designer, a head seamstress and four assistants, and sales and clerical help.

Why, then, Cass couldn't help wondering, as Darin left the garment district and drove the few blocks to a renovated brownstone in Chelsea, was she finding her work less and less satisfying? When was it, she asked herself uneasily, that the work had ceased to be a labor of love and had become just a labor?

"Need any help?" Darin offered hopefully as Cass opened the door of her apartment. "I make a terrific ladies' maid."

"Thanks, but no thanks," she said dryly. "I think I can manage nicely on my own."

Their easy banter was routine, with no lurking undercurrent of sexual tension. They both knew that the partnership had been so successful because their relationship was based on nothing more personal between them than mutual respect for the other's talents and undemanding friendship.

Twenty minutes later, Cass emerged from her bedroom looking a far cry from the disheveled woman who had entered. She had left her medium-length black hair loose and her thick black lashes untouched. Her only cosmetic aids were a dash of blusher on her high, well-defined cheekbones and a touch of lustrous red lipstick on her soft, full mouth.

She had traded her cords and sweater for a long, tight strapless sheath of mint green satin. Worn alone, the dress was blatantly sexy, displaying every curve of her petite but nicely endowed figure. But that wasn't the image she presented to the world. To complete the outfit, she added a loose, long-sleeved chiffon overblouse, lavishly ornamented with sequins. The neckline was designed to drape artistically off one shoulder and the hemline cut to reach the top of the sheath's long side slit. The effect the ensemble created was chic and sophisticated rather than overtly sexy.

"Ravishing, Darin?" she asked throatily, striking a pose against the door frame.

"Definitely ravishing! I haven't seen that outfit before. Who designed it for you?"

"One of the best," she tossed off lightly. He naturally assumed that all her clothes were custom designed, just as his sisters' had once been. He was right in a way. What she had never told him was that she was her own clothes designer. Not only that, she made all of them herself. He would be even more horrified, she thought with a private smile, to know that the sheath had been cut from a mill-end length of heavy drapery satin and that the matching chiffon had come from a bolt of fabric used for sheer curtains. Cass had found both tucked away in the back of the storeroom at the shop. As much as she liked Darin and as well as they worked together, she had recognized early in their partnership that he was a snob. She couldn't see that the disintegration of his family's fortune had had any humbling effect on him whatsoever. He might be forced to work for his money now, but in his book, blue blood was blue blood. His snobbery was ingrained.

It took her a moment to notice that Darin was eyeing her with a different kind of speculation than she had ever noticed before. A slow smile widened his thin lips.

"What's going on in that opportunistic head of yours, Darin?" she asked suspiciously as they headed for the door. "I don't trust that smile."

"Oh, not much. I was just wondering what Brendan Cahill is going to think when he gets a load of you tonight."

"Brendan Cahill? Is he the man from *Contemporary Interiors?*"

"You don't know who Brendan Cahill is?" he asked in disbelief.

"Remember, I live a very sheltered life, Darin darling," she drawled, "chained to my drawing table, sewing machine, and loom. You're the social butterfly. Now, who is he?"

"Never mind now. I'll explain while we drive."

When they had settled in the car and he finally answered, she was sorry she'd asked. "Brendan Cahill," he told her smugly, "is only the best opportunity to come our way in a long time. Have you ever been in a Monarch Hotel?"

Cass frowned. "Yes, as a matter of fact. I stayed in one in Houston last year when I was on a buying trip."

"Well, Monarch Hotels is a division of Monarch Enterprises. They specialize in huge convention centers—hotel, meeting rooms, restaurants, exclusive shopping malls—the whole works under one roof. Lately they've put big money into strategically located resort condominiums."

Cass eyed his profile warily. "This is all very edifying, Darin, but what does it have to do with us?"

"I've been thinking," he offered casually—too casually— "that there's no reason why we shouldn't get a piece of Monarch Enterprises' decorating action."

Cass's artistic soul shuddered at the thought.

"Well?" Darin prompted impatiently when she made no reply.

"In a word—no."

"Look, Cass, I've been checking into it. Monarch is just finishing construction on a huge resort complex in Miami. The right suggestion at the right time to the right man could put us in the running."

"I said no, Darin!"

His enthusiasm was undampened. "Give me one good reason why not."

"I'll give you a whole fistful. First of all, you're talking about wholesale expansion of Cassandra's—for which I haven't the time, energy, or inclination—"

"I could handle the mechanics of the expansion, if that's all that's worrying you," he interjected quickly.

"It's not. Have you ever been *in* a Monarch Hotel?"

"Well, no . . ."

"I didn't think so." She sniffed. "If the Houston hotel is a fair sample of the corporation's idea of interior decoration —and I'm pretty certain it is—we want no part of it. Gaudy and tasteless are the first adjectives that come to mind when I think of the lobby," she continued relentlessly, warming indignantly to her theme. "Twelve stories open to a bubble dome, floor space the size of a football field and done up like an overdecorated Christmas tree. Little lights twinkle all over horseshoe-shaped room dividers. The chandeliers are enormous brass wagon wheels with hanging lanterns, and the stools at the bar in the middle of all this glittering splendor are western saddles! I won't offend your sensibilities with a description of the room I stayed in—in what was quaintly called the Bunkhouse Wing, as I recall. Let's just say that some of the worst mass-reproduced western furniture I've ever seen was set off by mural wallpaper of a cattle roundup. Have you ever tried to sleep with the image of a rearing horse hovering over you?"

Darin laughed uncertainly. "You're joking."

"I am *not* joking!"

"Well, all the hotels and condominiums can't be like that," he insisted, trying to retrieve lost ground.

"Oh, I don't imagine so. I'm sure that what Monarch would want in Miami would be lights twinkling in pink and silver plastic palm trees and patrons drinking at the bar from the backs of stuffed porpoises."

"Please, Cass," Darin said coaxingly, undeterred. "Before you make up your mind, at least talk to Cahill."

"Cahill?" She frowned. She had forgotten that he had been the original subject under discussion. "What exactly does he have to do with all this?"

"Cass, darling, Brendan Cahill *is* Monarch Enterprises. At least, he's president and chairman of the board."

"And he's going to be at Megan's tonight?"

"Of course." He sounded so surprised that Cass frowned. "Why 'of course'?"

"Dammit, Cass," he exclaimed in exasperation, "sometimes I don't believe you even live in the same world with the rest of us. You go through life with your head in the clouds."

In all honesty, she couldn't argue with that. She had been raised too much of a loner, and after eight years in New York, she really preferred furniture and fabrics to people.

Darin didn't say any more as he slowed and turned through a pair of stone gates. A huge red brick and white-pillared mansion loomed ahead of them. Darin, however, bore left, into the drive leading to the back of the estate. Megan's newly remodeled home was an exquisite, now converted carriage house that stood in a copse of woods, out of sight of the main house.

"Why is Brendan Cahill sure to be here tonight, Darin?" she persisted. "Is he Megan's latest obsession?"

"You seriously mean to tell me that Megan never mentioned the small fact that Cahill did the renovation of the house?"

"She may have, but it didn't mean anything to me if she did. Why on earth would Monarch take on a little job like that, anyway?" Cass asked skeptically.

"I didn't say Monarch. I said Cahill did it. He drew up the plans and personally supervised the reconstruction. I understand that's how he got his start, renovating old houses. Megan told me in an indiscreet moment . . ."

Cass recognized this particular tone of voice as the one Darin adopted when he was about to divulge a particularly snide piece of gossip. He might hustle decorating commissions from the nouveau riche, but the snob in him basically despised them.

". . . that she and Cahill grew up together in a slum section of Baltimore. So much for the airs she puts on. Also, if they grew up together, that would make her close to ten years older than she claims to be," he concluded triumphantly.

Cass made no reply. Darin's hypocrisy certainly wasn't an endearing trait, but she had become used to it, and for the sake of harmony she ignored it. To her relief they were now approaching the carriage house, and Darin's attention turned to the cars lining the road, filling the drive in front, overflowing the gravel parking space, and pulled off into the trees.

"She must have invited half the world," he murmured in satisfaction. A big party meant potential business. "I'll drop you off at the door and look for a place to park. Find Megan and let her know you're here. She's set up the interview with the design editor."

Megan was apparently back in favor now, Cass concluded dryly as she climbed out of the car. At least talking of their hostess had diverted his attention so that he had neglected to worm a promise out of Cass to talk with Brendan Cahill.

Darin was out of his mind even to consider a project like the Monarch complex! Concern brought a pinched look to Cass's face. More and more often, the past few months, she had had to temper his ambition with what she felt was the amount of work Cassandra's could realistically handle.

The party was in full swing when Cass slipped unobtrusively through the open front door. From the entryway she surveyed the room. Her interest, though, was in the decor, not in the guests. She savored the moment, the elation of knowing she was looking at some of her best work. But then, she had had wonderful spaces and unusual architectural features to work with.

The natural beams in the walls and ceiling had been left exposed. The oversized fireplace had been constructed out of massive, rough-hewn native rock. A circular staircase of solid oak led to the bedrooms above—once the servants' quarters. The interior walls had been stripped down to their natural brick, a perfect background for the individually designed and handwoven wall hangings that were Cassandra's decorating signature.

All this stained wood and natural old brick had given her the inspiration to create an interior design that blended old-style warmth and comfort with a more modern feeling of light and space. . . .

The thought gave her pause. According to Darin, she had Brendan Cahill to thank for the tasteful physical renovation that had provided her decorating inspiration. She didn't want to think about that. She would look for Megan.

The task wasn't as easy as she had thought it would be. Ordinarily, screen star Megan Cooke stood out in any crowd, but Cass saw no sign of her flaming red hair in the packed room. She sidled along the wall until she found herself an unoccupied corner and waited. Basically, Cass detested parties like this. She had so much better use for her time than standing around drinking and making idle chit-chat. It bewildered her that Darin thrived on such entertainment. By now he would have been on a first-name basis with half the guests. In fact, through a break in the crowd, she saw that he had arrived and was already deep in conversation near the fireplace.

The grizzled-haired man with Darin was probably in his early forties, round-faced, fatuously smiling, and wearing an appalling red and gold sculptured velvet dinner jacket. If Cass were a betting person, she would have laid odds that the man was Brendan Cahill. No matter how tasteful his renovation of the carriage house, a man who decorated a hotel lobby with twinkling horseshoes would have no qualms about wearing a jacket that looked as though the fabric had once upholstered a Victorian loveseat.

Cass leaned wearily against the wall behind her. At least the man was so conspicuous that she should have no trouble avoiding him. She wasn't up to any kind of business discussion that night—especially one that would be fruitless and could prove unpleasant if she were tired enough to lose her discretion and speak her mind. Once again she searched the room for Megan. She would say a quick hello, talk briefly with the man from *Contemporary Interiors,* and make a quick exit.

"You're looking for someone," a voice said near her right ear. "Will I do?"

Slowly Cass turned her head and met a pair of startlingly blue eyes, heavily fringed with black lashes. A swath of hair as dark as the lashes cut his broad forehead in half. Against an instinctive better judgment, she found herself intrigued by the ruggedly interesting face looking down at her. At some time the nose had been broken and never set properly. A jagged scar at the temple raised the end of the one eyebrow, fixing an expression of perpetual cynicism on the man's face. He wasn't particularly tall, probably a little under six feet, but he was built like a brick wall and wore his loose-fitting black tuxedo with the same negligent ease and disregard for appearance that most men afforded well-worn denim jeans. In all, he looked as though he would be far more at home in a waterfront bar than at an exclusive cocktail party.

"Well?" he prompted with a lopsided smile that matched the lopsided slant of his eyebrow, "Will I do?"

"I don't know," Cass shot back coolly, resisting an urge to respond to that smile. "What exactly is it that you *do* do?"

"I'm terrific at conjuring up a drink."

For the first time Cass noticed that he held two glasses of champagne. Automatically she accepted the one he offered her and took a sip that went straight to her head. Too late she remembered that she was drinking on an empty stomach.

"Uh, I don't suppose there's a prayer of getting near the

buffet table, is there?" she asked hesitantly. She didn't really want to encourage the man, but she needed food, and fighting her way through the crowd to the table was beyond her physical resources at the moment.

The smile became more pronounced, more slanted, with a corresponding increase of cynicism in his expression. "If you promise not to vanish into the mob, I'll be back in a minute."

Wide-shouldered and broad-chested he might be, but he was slim-hipped and surprisingly agile. As he neatly wove his way between the chattering groups, Cass finally allowed herself a smile. The man was unusual, not the type she ordinarily found at such gatherings the rare times Darin coerced her to attend.

A few minutes later he returned in triumph with a plate piled high with food. "I wasn't sure what you'd like, so I just took one of everything. There's an unoccupied window seat over there. Let's grab it."

"You're going to have to help with this," she told him, balancing the plate on her lap and popping a bite-sized sandwich into her mouth. "I can't possibly eat this much."

"I hoped you'd offer. I just got here a few minutes ago and haven't eaten all day."

They made no attempt at small talk—Cass because she was both hungry and tired; the man, she guessed, because it just wasn't his style. Their silence was neither strained nor yet easy and companionable, but when the plate was empty, he put it aside and studied her face with pleasure.

"Now you look better. Your color is coming back. When I first saw you leaning against the wall over there, I thought you were about to faint."

Now Cass did smile. "Are you always so lavish with your compliments?"

A responsive smile warmed his face. "I'm not much into idle chatter. I'd rather just say what's on my mind."

"So I've noticed," she said dryly.

His gaze became more intent, probing and appraising, noting and appreciating the black sheen of her hair, the warm olive tint of her skin, the small, straight nose above a mobile, slightly vulnerable mouth, the eyes so dark that in the subdued lighting they shone jet black.

"Will you come home with me tonight?" he asked abruptly.

Cass blinked twice, not sure she had heard him right. "I beg your pardon?"

"I asked you if you'd come home with me tonight."

"My word, you are direct, aren't you." She couldn't decide if she was amused or affronted by such an approach.

He shrugged. "I told you, I speak what's on my mind, and that's been on my mind since the first moment I saw you. No sense wasting time. . . . Well? Will you?"

Her reply was cool, succinct, and equally direct. "No."

Amusement drew creases in the corners of his eyes, and his smile revealed two rows of even white teeth. Whoever had punched his nose, she mused irrelevently, had missed his mouth.

"I was afraid you'd say that," he replied, unperturbed.

"I—I don't even know your name," she added inanely as she watched the laugh lines deepen around his eyes. Was this blunt man really as cynical as he appeared at first or was it an illusion created by the eyebrow? Whichever, she was finding him far too attractive and herself much too interested in him.

"Well, if that's the only hitch—" he said.

"Don't be silly! Of course it isn't," she snapped. "You don't just invite a strange woman to go home with you!"

"How can you say I don't when I just did?"

Before she could come up with a suitably cutting reply, a reprieve arrived in the form of a large matron with loud voice and beaming smile. She stopped in front of the window seat, her ample bosom heaving under the weight of enormous diamonds and mauve brocade.

"It's you!" she cried, closing her eyes and jutting her jaw forward theatrically. "I just had to tell you what a simply marvelous job you did on Megan's house! I'm speechless with admiration. It's divine, absolutely beyond description!"

"Thank you very much." Cass and the man beside her spoke in unison.

The woman gushed on with increasing dramatic fervor, but she had lost her audience. Cass turned to stare at the man, first in puzzlement, then in surprise, and finally in comprehension. He in turn was regarding her with new interest and speculation. When the woman finished emoting and sailed majestically away, he was the first to speak.

"Now, which one of us was she really complimenting, do you suppose?" A smile twitched at his lips. "Was it *my* renovation or *your* interior decoration that struck her, ah, speechless?"

"You're Brendan Cahill?"

"Yes. And you, I take it, are Cassandra Wells. Now why on earth did I assume that you'd be a pushy career woman and determined overachiever? Instead I find a gorgeous, vulnerable woman who looks as though a strong wind would blow her over."

Cass felt a welling of antagonism at this description. She *was* a career woman, and she might be small and tired at the moment, but no one had ever found her weak-willed. She glanced toward the fireplace and spotted the grizzled-haired man.

"And I," she said sweetly, "had you pegged as the man over there in the red and gold dinner jacket."

A husky chuckle welled up from Brendan's broad chest as he followed her glance. "Touché. I guess we're both guilty of judging each other on reputation alone. You have to admit, though, that you're young to be so successful. How old are you anyway? Twenty-six? Twenty-seven?"

"Have you no social graces at all?" Cass protested with asperity. "You don't ask a woman—" She stopped and stared at him balefully. "Never mind. I already recognize the fact that you *do*. Well, I'm twenty-nine. How old are you?"

"Thirty-six," he replied promptly, unabashed.

"You're young to be so successful, Mr. Cahill!"

"Thanks," he replied, ignoring her mockery. "And the name is Brendan. What do people call you? Cassandra seems a bit of a mouthful. Not Cassie, surely." His eyes slid consideringly up and down her chic ensemble. "You don't look like a Cassie."

Cass detested the nickname. The only people ever to use it were her brother Ben—who had called her Cassie when they were children, and then only when he'd been spoiling for a fight—and now Ben's wife Loretta, who used it with a spurious affection that thinly disguised a genuine dislike.

Cass was tempted not to answer Cahill's question at all, but even on short acquaintance she guessed that this tactless man would only persist.

"My *friends* call me Cass," she told him resignedly.

"Well, *Cass,*" he emphasized deliberately, "I understand that we're to do an interview with some design editor. What do you say we find Megan, get the interview over with as quickly as possible, and then you let me take you home."

"I thought we'd already settled that 'take me home' bit," she reminded him dryly.

His smile now was totally disarming. "I'll rephrase the statement. Let me drop you off at your house and I'll go on home—alone and uncomforted. You're pale again and looking more exhausted by the minute."

Cass found the genuine concern for her in his voice extremely undermining. What was even worse, she believed him when he said he would take her straight home. Still, the sooner she was out of his disturbing presence, the safer she would feel. Safer. What an odd word even to think. Why on earth should she consider this brusque, ill-mannered man with more than a hint of Irish brogue in his voice dangerous to her in any way? Because, she admitted to herself, although he might not have Darin's smooth, polished charm, beneath the rough exterior was a special appeal all his own. He wasn't like any other man she had ever met before. The novelty alone was dangerous.

"Thank you all the same, Mr. . . . er, Brendan, but I came with my business partner, Darin Summerhays."

For a change she had startled him. "Summerhays is your *partner?*"

"Yes. Do you know him?" she asked curiously. In spite of Brendan's presence at the party, she couldn't imagine that the two men traveled in the same circles.

"I know of him, and Megan has mentioned him a time or two, but I didn't connect him with you. Frankly, I find the thought of his working for a living a little hard to swallow."

Comments like that always upset Cass. People had no idea just how much work Darin did while she got all the credit. She had protested to him often, but he insisted that he preferred to keep a low profile. She could only assume that perpetuating the myth of idle playboy helped Darin salvage his pride. Unconsciously she searched the crowded room for him. He was now talking with a much more congenial companion than the grizzled-haired man. His sleek blond head was bent toward a stunning, curvaceous brunette.

Once again Cahill's astute gaze had followed hers. "Is that Summerhays? I would say he seems quite content to stay awhile. Shall we get on with the interview and then see how the land lies?"

Given the circumstances, Cass had no choice but to agree.

They found Megan upstairs holding court, but she excused herself to introduce them to the reporter. Half an hour later Cass and Cahill emerged from the interview. All had gone smoothly, though in listening to Brendan Cahill's answers, Cass had learned nothing more about him than Darin had already told her. As they descended the circular steps back to the lounge, she immediately looked for her partner.

"I'll tell Darin I'm ready to go now," she said coolly over her shoulder. "Don't let me keep you. It's been nice meeting you." She murmured the conventional farewell with what she hoped sounded like finality. No such luck.

"Oh, I enjoy being kept," Brendan answered blandly. "I'd enjoy giving you a ride home even more. Shall we see if Summerhays is ready to leave?"

Damn the man, Cass thought in irritation. He could see as well as she could that the situation didn't look promising. Darin had the brunette firmly in tow, his arm wrapped possessively around her waist. He would be delighted to palm Cass off on Cahill—for both personal and business reasons.

Darin's engaging smile broadened as he greeted their arrival. As introductions were made around, he slid Cass an inquisitive glance that she answered with a meaningful stare.

"We've finished the interview, Darin, and I'm ready to go as soon as you are. I have a busy day tomorrow."

Before he could answer, Brendan broke in smoothly. "I

was just leaving myself, Summerhays. If you want to stay on, I'd be delighted to run Miss Wells back into the city."

Darin must have felt the high heel of Cass's silver sandal digging into the toe of his shoe, but he chose to ignore it. "How kind of you to offer, Cahill. I'm sure Cassandra would appreciate it, and Sylvia and I thought we would take advantage of the dancing out in the sunroom." His smile grew forced as the pain in his foot became more acute, but he didn't relent. "See you tomorrow, Cass," he managed casually.

Darin ignored the daggers she threw at him. Brendan, however, intercepted them and was amused—which only increased Cass's irritation. Irately Cass hoped that Darin would limp for a week. For the first time in their business relationship she wished that her partner felt just one little twinge of jealousy about the men she went with.

She could have created a scene, of course, she considered as she waited for Brendan to bring his car around, but scenes were not her style. She forgot her partner's treachery the next moment when Brendan pulled up in front of her. His car surprised her. For some reason she expected a showy sports job. Instead, he drove a conservative black Mercedes, at least ten years old and somewhat the worse for wear.

It struck her that the car was an extension of his personality and physical appearance—dark, solid, a little battered, and basically unpretentious. But both outward frames, she suspected, were deceptive, deliberately disguising the powerful, quietly purring engines that drove them.

While Cass settled herself in the deep leather seat, Brendan noted the lines of fatigue in her face, and after a brief, "Where to?" he headed silently back toward the city.

For the first time Cass was grateful that it was Brendan and not Darin driving her home. Darin would have kept up a running commentary, expressing his opinion, with various degrees of malice, of this person or that, filling her in on all the latest gossip, and speculating on the potential commissions he proposed to follow up on in the next week.

Her gratitude didn't last long. It only took her a few miles to realize that Darin might not have been a restful companion, but then, neither was Brendan Cahill. He said nothing, but his presence in the confines of the car was both tangible and a little overwhelming. He radiated energy. Did the man never tire? She was exhausted.

"Go to sleep if you'd like," he said abruptly. Had he read her mind? The thought was very disturbing. "I won't be offended," he assured her, "and you look as though you could use it. I'll wake you when we get to your house."

Neither his silence nor his thoughtfulness was at all what Cass had expected from him. She had to face it. She had expected him to take advantage of having her to himself. She couldn't think of a man she had ever been with who had suggested she just go to sleep. To her dismay, she realized that not only was she surprised but, perversely, she was hurt. Had he become bored with her so quickly?

Several more miles passed before the silence was broken by the sound of a high-pitched tone. Brendan apparently carried the sort of a beeper doctors used. She watched from beneath her eyelashes as he picked up a telephone receiver from between the bucket seats and punched in a number.

"Cahill," he said quietly but curtly. She could hear a muffled voice on the other end of the line. Then Brendan spoke again. "All right. I'm in my car. Put him through." A pause. "What is it, Max?" Another pause. "Barksfield is stalling. I'll fly to Chicago myself and be at the office tomorrow evening. Set up an appointment with Barksfield for Tuesday morning. Threaten him with a court injunction to stop construction if he balks. Talk with the union leaders yourself. Barksfield isn't going to wriggle out of this one." Pause. "Good. I'll see you at around eight."

While he spoke, Cass had been studying his face in the light of passing cars. She had wondered at the party if the cynicism in his expression was inherent or just a trick of the scar. After listening to him on the phone—clipped, precise, and unrelenting—she knew the answer. She had seen the other side of Brendan Cahill, the hard, inflexible business-man under the casual, engaging veneer. All her feminine instincts had been right. He wasn't a man to take lightly—either personally or professionally. Darin could argue till doomsday. Neither Cass nor Cassandra's House of Interiors was going to become involved with the man.

As he hung up the phone, she quickly closed her eyes and

kept them closed, even after he turned off the expressway and they reached the stop-and-go of city traffic. She wasn't aware that Brendan had pulled up in front of her house until his arm moved around her shoulders and the soft lilt of his voice—so different from the hard tone he had used with the unknown Max—sounded in her ear.

"You're home, Cass." She opened her eyes to find Brendan's face only inches away. "I don't suppose there's any chance of your inviting me in for a drink, is there?" he asked coaxingly.

She stared warily at the hopeful, ingratiating, almost boyish expression on Brendan's face—all Irish charm now. How many women in the past had fallen for that particular engaging plea?

"Not a chance," she said flatly, pulling back.

"I didn't think so." He sighed, as though he'd just been deprived of the hope of heaven.

Cass shrugged her shoulders to indicate that she wanted the arm around her removed. "Thanks for the ride home."

The arm stayed where it was. "My pleasure."

She glanced meaningfully at the hand on her shoulder. "I have to go in now, Brendan."

The hand gave her shoulder a light caress through the thin fabric. "Will you have dinner with me tomorrow evening?"

"You're going to Chicago tomorrow," she reminded him indiscreetly. Oops! Supposedly she hadn't heard that telephone conversation.

"Damn! You're right!" The chagrin in his expression lightened to amusement. "Shame on you Cass, eavesdropping on a private conversation while I thought you were asleep." As she maintained a dignified silence, he pushed his advantage. "I'll be back Wednesday. Have dinner with me then?"

"I'm busy," she said quickly.

"All right. Thursday night."

"I'm busy Thursday too."

"Friday."

"Busy."

"Saturday."

"Busy."

Brendan's eyes narrowed. "My, you do lead a hectic social life, don't you."

Cass had to stop herself from smiling at the thought. Social life! She had had so little time or inclination for a date in so long, she had almost forgotten what it was like.

"Never mind," he drawled, putting his own interpretation on her silence. "Don't put yourself to the trouble of fumbling around for another excuse for my benefit. I get the idea." Abruptly he raised his arm to remove it from around her, but the thin chiffon overblouse moved with it.

"Wait, Brendan," she cautioned quickly. A thread from the sequin-trimmed neckline had twisted around a button on his sleeve. "You're caught."

As she leaned forward so that he could disentangle the button, her soft cheek accidentally brushed against his. She heard his sharp intake of breath before he muttered, "Do you know what? You may be right. I'm afraid I *am* caught!"

The double meaning in his words wasn't lost on her. Slowly she shifted her gaze to his face and found that there was nothing either boyish or engaging about his expression now. What she read in those hard, rugged good looks was a very adult sexual hunger, made even more potent by the glittering blue light in his eyes, the arrogant tilt of his head, and the stubborn set of his jaw.

To hell with the sequins! She had to get out of the car and away from this disturbing man. With an abrupt jerk, she broke the thread and was free.

"Thank you again for the ride," she murmured, distracted.

"Any time," he replied curtly, brushing away the gleaming sequins that clung to his sleeve.

Gingerly she edged away from him and reached for the door handle. "Don't bother to get out."

"Cass?"

She paused, unable to ignore the command in his tone, swallowed, and foolishly turned to meet his searching gaze. "Y—yes?" she stammered.

"You're a beautiful, fascinating, sexy woman, Cassandra Wells, and I'm a very determined man when I want something. You must know that right now I want you very much."

No man had ever voiced his desire for her so bluntly, so matter-of-factly, as thought what *he* wanted made it a given. At first his arrogance angered her even while she was perversely flattered. Then to her dismay she found that the deep, echoing desire in his voice had triggered an unwanted quiver of excitement in her—an insane, dangerous curiosity that urged her to sample just a taste of what he offered. This sudden, unexpected yearning sapped her will to resist when he caught her by the shoulders and pulled her back toward him.

A struggle would only provoke him, she rationalized as his mouth descended toward hers. And one didn't provoke Brendan Cahill, she was sure, without being prepared to take the consequences. Well, there would be no consequences from her encounter with the man. After that night, she never had to see him again.

He felt her quiescence and his hold on her tightened. His mouth slowly captured hers in a devastatingly gentle kiss that first tested, then lingered, and finally deepened. Gradually his lips parted hers to savor the sweetness of her mouth, and his hands moved up under the blouse to caress her bare back, taking pleasure in its smoothness. They were calloused, work-worn hands, Cass noted in a half-coherent moment. Rough but not unpleasant against her sensitive skin.

What kind of lover would he be? she wondered dizzily. The thoughtful, concerned man who had fed and taken care of her at the party, the hard-driving, determined business-man she had glimpsed during the drive, or the arrogant, indulged male who was obviously used to getting what he wanted? It took her a moment to realize the treacherous path her thoughts had traveled. This was a question she would never, *never* have answered.

A few devastating moments later, a second thought struck her. His hands might be rough, but in contrast his lips were oh, so very, very soft.

Chapter 2

CASS PICKED UP AN ENVELOPE FROM HER DELICATE LOUIS XIV desk, slit it with a letter opener—an ornate, silver trifle made at the turn of the century—and smiled as she deciphered the message, nearly illegible in the swirls and swishes of the affected handwriting. Apparently Mr. and Mrs. Parkinson were thanking her effusively for finding them the antique commode for their entry hall. Cass moved on to the second page, and a check fluttered to the floor. Her smile faded as she retrieved it and read the amount. Eight thousand dollars!

Thoughtfully she nibbled on her lower lip as her gaze drifted unseeingly to the tapestry hanging on the far wall. "Cassandra's office" was how she and her staff referred to this room, but its decor was more that of an elegant sitting room. It was here that she consulted with clients. Her real work took place at the drawing table upstairs, where Darin had found her the night before.

Ordinarily the check from the Parkinsons would never have ended up on Cass's desk. All financial matters went directly to Darin. But the letter had been hand addressed to her, and Janet, their receptionist, must have assumed that it was a personal note.

Eight thousand dollars for the antique commode? Cass questioned in disbelief. She had bought it at an auction the week before for half that. Darin must have made an error in billing . . . or had he? With a troubled frown, Cass slipped the check into the pocket of her tweed jacket and went out into the showroom in search of Darin.

The public part of Cassandra's was not large. Only a relatively small portion of the shop's income came from walk-in customers wanting to buy the unusual decorating accessories on display. The demand was great for the individually designed and hand-woven rugs, wall hangings, and floor pillows that bore the Cassandra label—but so was the price. Most often these items were created to order.

"Janet, has Darin come back from lunch?"

The girl looked up from the letter she was typing. "He came in about ten minutes ago. I think he's in his office."

"Thanks." Cass knew her voice sounded strained. She wasn't emotionally prepared to endure another confrontation with Darin. The one earlier in the day had been bad enough. He had had such hopes when he sought her out that morning.

"Don't keep me in suspense, Cass," he had begged, practically licking his lips in anticipation. "What happened with you and Cahill last night?"

"You know I never kiss and tell," she replied sweetly, still annoyed with him for foisting her off on the man.

"Come on," he pleaded, "you know I don't mean that. What did he say about the Miami condominiums?"

"They were never mentioned." The pleasure in his face was transformed ludicrously to incredulity. "In fact, except in a roundabout way, we didn't discuss business at all."

Dull, angry color flooded Darin's neck and spread upward into his ears. He had kept his temper, but only just. Cass had never seen him so angry, and it had brought a sinking feeling to the pit of her stomach. They quarreled so seldom.

"You—you mean to tell me," he sputtered in disbelief, "that after all the trouble I went to, you spent an entire evening with the man and never even *mentioned* the possibility of working with Monarch?"

"Darin, I told you from the beginning that I wasn't interested in the Monarch project. I just don't do work like that."

Nothing, not even Darin's anger, had made her budge an inch. In some ways she might be just as vulnerable as Brendan had guessed the night before, but she hadn't inherited her father's stubborn chin for nothing. With a vehement oath of frustration, Darin had turned on his heel and stalked out of the room. She hadn't seen him or talked with him since.

Now this new problem.

Slowly Cass climbed the stairs to the second floor, the check in her pocket a heavy psychological weight. At the top she turned left, away from her own work room, and continued down the hall to Darin's private kingdom. Her steps slowed as she neared his door. She detested contention. But with a shrug to relieve the tension in her shoulders, she went in.

Cass had designed Darin's office in leather, hand-blocked fabrics, thick carpet, highly polished brass, and glass. It fit his personality—smooth, sleek, and ultrasophisticated. Unlike her own office downstairs, however, his was also utilitarian. The leather-topped rosewood desk was littered with papers and ledgers, and the computer terminal resting on the custom-made table beside it clacked away as he entered a column of figures.

"Do you have a minute, Darin?" He jumped. His hands fumbled on the keys, inadvertently wiping out a line, and he swore softly under his breath. "I'm sorry," Cass said apologetically. "I didn't mean to startle you."

His perfunctory smile was uncharacteristically cool and definitely not welcoming. "I didn't hear you come in. I was working out the payroll." He frowned at the figures on a sheet next to the computer. "Could Angie really have put in twenty hours of overtime last week?"

"I'm surprised that's all it was," Cass said ruefully. "She finished up the drapes for the Tilsons' bedroom and started on the curtains for the kitchen."

Darin's frown became a definite scowl. "We can't afford so much overtime, Cass. The time-and-a-half is killing us. We would be better off hiring another full-time seamstress." He glanced briefly at her somber face and his own hardened. "I wasn't going to bother you with financial problems right now, but if you insist on taking a hard line on Monarch, I'm afraid I have to. Overhead is catching up with us. The percentage and promotion we gave Dee is hurting badly."

"You know Dee earns every penny, Darin," Cass objected. "We couldn't get along without her."

"I'm not arguing with that, Cass. I'm just telling you that we've got to increase the net profit somehow." The hard edge in his tone became harder. "We're going to have to raise prices, start taking some shortcuts on quality, or work in at least two more projects a month."

Two more projects a month! Wearily Cass sank into the chair across the desk from him. She found just the idea of more work right then totally exhausting. Her praise of Dee Newton had been from the heart. She didn't know what she would do if Dee, at first her design assistant and now a full associate in the firm, weren't so competent. Already Cass had turned more and more of the routine work over to the energetic older woman.

"I thought we were in good shape financially," Cass said weakly. "Just how serious is the trouble?"

"Immediate? We have enough cash flow to make it through the next few months' payroll without dipping into the slush fund. Long range? It could be serious if we don't make some changes—or unless you change your mind about Monarch."

Darin was certainly applying the pressure. Why did he always make her feel so guilty when she made an artistic decision he didn't like? She didn't interfere with his side of the business. Then memory of her purpose in his office that moment intruded rudely into her thoughts.

They sat uneasily in a tense, uncommunicative silence. This was definitely not a good time to question Darin about the Parkinson account, but Cass had no choice.

"You know I don't usually interfere in business matters,

Darin, but I have to ask you. Just how far would you go to solve our financial problems?"

Something in the tone of her voice narrowed his eyes as he studied her sober expression. "Are you driving at something in particular, Cass?"

Slowly she pulled the check from her pocket and tossed it on the desk. "Janet gave this to me by mistake. I—I hoped it was just an error. Even with a fifty-percent markup as a finder's fee—which is more than we've ever charged—the cost still shouldn't have been more than six thousand dollars." There was no easy way to ask the question that had to be asked. *"Was* there a mistake in the billing, Darin?"

Thoughtfully he picked up the check and turned it over in his hands. The seconds ticked away and stretched to an uncomfortable minute. "You know there was no mistake," he finally admitted bluntly, dropping the check on his desk. "I charged them eight thousand for the commode. I deliberately overvalued it."

"Darin!"

"Come on, Cass," he said in exasperation. "You know the Parkinsons as well as I do. The more money they spend, the better they like it. If you had miraculously turned up that piece in a second-hand store, paid a couple of hundred dollars for it, and offered it to them for even a thousand, they wouldn't have wanted it. This way they have the satisfaction of bragging to all their friends about how much it cost, and we gain financially. It isn't as though it isn't a good investment. In the long run, no one is hurt. Everyone is happy."

Cass wasn't happy, even though she had to admit that Darin's reasoning was sound. He was right about the Parkinsons. With a sigh, she stood and wiped a tired hand across her eyes. No, she couldn't fault Darin's logic—only the dubious business practice of overcharging a client so much. But there was nothing she could do about it now. In the future, though, she would have a lot to say before he tried it again.

"Okay, Darin. Have it your way—this time."

Cass was even more depressed when she left Darin's office than when she had gone in. Far from satisfying her, he had given her half a dozen new problems to worry about. She was already working almost to her limit. How long could she go on like that? The firm was bringing in more and more work, yet they were in financial difficulty. Why? Overhead, Darin had explained, and he would know. What should they do? Leading designers could just about name their own price, but it would be another few years before she reached that point. Could she possibly take on more work? When should profit take precedence over quality? And a question that troubled her most: At what point did professional ambition become simply greed?

Cass paused outside Darin's door. Then, instead of returning to her office, she took the narrow flight of stairs to the workrooms on the floor above. As she expected, Dee was perched on a stool at her drawing table. Windows set into the wall gave the older woman a full view of the beehive of activity in the sewing and cutting room beyond.

Dee was so absorbed in her work that Cass hesitated to disturb her. She was just turning away when Dee caught the movement out of the corner of her eye, turned, smiled warmly, and pushed her glasses up on top of her graying blond hair.

"Cass, love, come on in."

Dee Newton had run her own design house in San Francisco fifteen years before. She had given it up when she married, followed her new husband east, and started a family. Once the three children were in school, she had wanted to work again. Not that she needed the money. Her husband was now a senior partner in a prestigious New York accounting firm.

Cassandra's had been incredibly fortunate to hire her, Cass considered gratefully for probably the hundredth time that year. Besides doing more and more of the actual designing on smaller commissions, Dee supervised all the cutting and sewing in the construction room, settled personality disputes among the employees, handled the sales staff, and generally made herself indispensable. But just as important to Cass, Dee was a friend in whom she could confide.

Cass returned Dee's smile, but it was an effort. "I don't want to interrupt a burst of creative genius, Dee."

"Actually, I was just about to take a break. Come join me

in a cup of tea—red clover today." She cast a quick glance at Cass's pale face. "Though, frankly, I would say a shot of something stronger would do you more good. You look as though you're suffering from shock."

"No, no. I'm fine, thank you."

Both women recognized the patent untruth of the statement, but Dee didn't press Cass for any explanations as she brewed the tea. She knew her young friend well enough to know that she would say what she had to say in her own good time.

"Dee?" Cass finally asked, swirling the leaves in the bottom of her cup. "Did you have any regrets about giving up your business when you married?"

The question took her friend by surprise, and she shot Cass a quick, speculative glance. "That's a loaded question, love. Before I answer, I think I'd like to know if you're contemplating marriage or considering giving up the business."

"Not marriage, certainly." Cass grimaced. "When have I had any time the past year to meet a man and fall in love?"

Dee smiled knowingly. "When you meet the right man, falling in love isn't always a matter of time. I knew the minute I set eyes on Frank that he was the one and only."

"And giving up your business?"

"I would have followed him to the North Pole if that was where he wanted to go."

"But you missed your work?" Cass pressed her.

"Sure I did before the boys were born," Dee admitted, then smiled mischievously. "Then I discovered that I had a different kind of creative mission to fulfill."

She had been joking, but Cass chose to take her seriously. "A different kind of creative mission," she repeated.

"Are you looking for a potential father, Cass?" Dee drawled. "I highly recommend motherhood, but it's helpful if marriage comes first. Now, why don't you tell me what's going on in that head of yours."

"Oh, nothing really. I must be going a little looney, that's all—living, eating, breathing nothing but work. I'm so tired all the time. I've always been a happy person. Now, these past months I feel that all the . . . well, joy has gone out of life." Cass smiled wanly. "It sounds stupid and self-indulgent when I say it out loud. Half the people in the world must work at jobs they're not happy in."

It didn't sound stupid to the more experienced older woman. Dee studied her friend's face in concern. "Tell me, Cass, right now, if you could do anything you wanted—anything in this world—what would you do?"

It was a serious question, and Cass gave it serious consideration. She didn't have to consider long. "Right now I would leave New York," she announced positively. "I would love to just run away, escape from the constant pressure to produce, the unending problems of running a business, the killing pace. Sheer cowardice, right?"

A smile of compassion softened Dee's eyes. "Not cowardice," she contradicted. "Most people would call it sanity. The kind of life we lead in this business is crazy. Myself, I love the competitive rat race. But I was in it long enough before to know that it takes a peculiar sort of drive to run a company like this."

A worried frown deepened the lines in Cass's forehead. "When I started up on my own, I didn't mind the hard work at all. I was naïve enough to believe that once I was established, life would be simpler. Instead, it seems to get more and more complicated. Do you know, I can't even remember the last time I curled up on the couch and read a book or spent a day wandering through a museum or just went out into the country and sat staring at a stream. The only time I notice that a season has come and gone," she concluded wryly, "is when I change my wardrobe from cotton to wool and back again."

"If you left," Dee prompted, "where would you go?"

"Home," Cass replied without hesitation, then corrected herself unhappily. "The ranch in Utah, that is. It hasn't really been home since my father died last year, but I don't think I'll ever cut loose from my roots there."

"I didn't think you got on with your sister-in-law all that well."

"I don't," Cass admitted. "But I was only eighteen when we really had our pitched battles. Since college, each time I've gone back for a visit, we've managed to maintain an armed neutrality. I would hope I could handle her better now."

"Somehow I can't see you herding cows," Dee observed dubiously.

Cass's lips twitched at Dee's conception of what her life on the ranch was like. "I'll have you know that I was pretty good in my time," she teased.

"I'd think you'd be bored out of your mind in a week."

Cass laughed openly now. "You're every inch a city girl, Dee. I spent eighteen years on that ranch and never remember being bored a day in my life."

"Yet you left the ranch and never really went back," Dee reminded her pointedly.

Cass shrugged. "I was ambitious."

"And you're not anymore?"

The look Cass gave her friend was puzzled and a little lost. "I honestly don't know. Ambitious for what? I've been asking myself that more and more often these past few months. Do I want more money? I don't really need it to live comfortably. More work? I have so much I can't handle it now. Artistic fulfillment? I don't need to live in New York to design and weave my rugs and wall hangings. I've been weaving since I was eight years old."

"Somehow I pictured you growing up on the back of a horse," Dee admitted, "not sitting at a loom."

A nostalgic smile erased years from Cass's face. "When my mother taught me to weave, she taught me to card my own wool, spin it into yarn myself, and dye it with native berries, roots, and herbs. I was thirteen when she died. Weaving was my comfort, my escape, my expression. I wove all my adolescent anger and grief and fantasies and joys into my work. *That* was artistic fulfillment."

Cass's fervor took Dee by surprise. "You really mean that, don't you? I have to admit that I can't identify with a life like that. And if I were you, I would be out of my mind with joy that my room designs were suddenly popping up in magazines. You don't get any pleasure at all out of the professional recognition? That isn't satisfying?"

For the first time Cass's smile turned cynical. "Maybe I'd get more pleasure from the magazine spreads if I had any time to enjoy them. But satisfying? I tend to agree with Darin and just consider it terrific for business." Thoughtfully she bit her lip. "Do you know what I've discovered, Dee? I don't give a damn about being famous. All I want to be is an artist and make people happier because of my work. I know I'm good at what I do, and I don't need anyone else to tell me so. I don't need constant reassurance. But I'm also my own worst critic, and I know how much better I could be if I had more time. That's why I could happily go back to Utah and work."

"Whew! You are in a blue funk, aren't you."

"Not a *blue* funk," Cass quipped with a forced lightness. "When I talk about life on the ranch, I'm working mostly in earth tones." Reluctantly she pushed herself out of the chair. "Forgive my outburst of nostalgia, Dee. Fantasy time is over. It's back to reality. I have the Nieharts to appease in half an hour. I haven't finished two of the rooms for them."

Dee stopped her hesitantly as she reached the door. "Cass? I really hate to suggest this now. I feel a little like a circling vulture and I'm sure that what you're going through is just a temporary down, but . . ."

"But?" Cass prompted.

Dee hurried on. "Look, if you do decide after a few weeks or months that you want out, will you talk to me first? Will you consider letting me buy out your half of the partnership?"

The idea took Cass by surprise. "Are you serious?"

"In all honesty, I hadn't given it a thought until just now," Dee said ruefully, "but I'm afraid I am. You know that the money to start my own business isn't really a problem for me, but I know what it takes, and I haven't wanted to take the time and energy away from Frank and the kids to build a new company from the ground up. Taking over the design half of an established firm would be a piece of cake in comparison."

Nervously Cass bit her lip. "And I guess I've never thought of quitting the business as a realistic possibility. I haven't actually considered the practical side of it, what it would mean to Darin . . ."

Dee saw her friend's distress. "Hey, Cass. Forget I even mentioned it. It was just a crazy idea."

Cass allowed herself the luxury of turning it over in her mind. "I'm not sure right now how crazy it is," she said slowly. "I have no idea what I'm going to do, but you've given me an option and I appreciate that."

"I didn't mean to start trouble. Please, forget I said anything," Dee said.

"Your offer wasn't a serious one?" Cass asked soberly.

"Well . . . yes, it was," Dee admitted ruefully.

"Then I'm not sure I want to forget it." Cass smiled fondly at her friend's chagrin. "Cheer up, Dee. You haven't precipitated the end of the world—or even the end of Cassandra's. I just want to give it some thought."

Which Cass did, all the way back downstairs, and the thoughts were very pleasant. Idle, wish-fulfillment dreams, of course, but tantalizing just the same. Utah. The ranch where she had been born and raised, isolated on the high plateau, miles from civilization, with its good red earth, the sound of wind rustling through the aspen, the clear, pine-scented air.

"Cass?" Janet stopped her as she wandered across the showroom toward her office.

"Hmmmm?"

The receptionist noted the dreamy, far-away expression on her employer's face with a mixture of amusement and curiosity. "Are you all right, Cass?"

"What? Oh, yes, of course. Did you want something?"

Janet giggled. "Not me, but go take a look at your desk. They were delivered while you were upstairs."

"What were?"

"Have a look."

Inside the door to her office, Cass stopped short. An hour ago the desk had been clear. Now an enormous bouquet of spring flowers stood in the center, nearly obscuring the entire surface.

Janet peered over her shoulder and giggled again. "Boy, you must have made an impression on someone."

"Who sent them?" Cass asked weakly.

"I don't know. I think there's a card tucked in there somewhere."

Gingerly Cass parted the bouquet and pulled out a small envelope tucked in among the anemones. Her name was written in a barely legible black scrawl. She didn't recognize the writing, but an educated guess sent an unwelcome flutter along her nerves.

"Well? Aren't you going to open it?" Janet urged.

"Later. Uh, that's all, Janet. Thanks." Cass could do without Janet's babbling tongue spreading gossip all through the shop. As soon as the door closed behind the girl, Cass tore open the envelope and pulled out the enclosed card.

> How doth the little busy bee
> Improve each shining hour,
> And gather honey all the day
> From every opening flower.

There was no signature, but Cass didn't need a name to know who had sent the flowers. The *busy* was underlined. Brendan had added a subtle emphasis—his own ironic comment.

Each day for the next three days Cass arrived at the shop to find that another array of flowers had arrived—each with a different, pointed message. By the time the second bouquet was delivered (four dozen pink carnations), most of the staff could tell that something was in the air besides the smell of flowers. When the third bouquet arrived (six dozen yellow roses in a basket that took up one entire corner of Cass's office), the whole work force was smiling in delight at the generosity of Cass's mysterious admirer. The fourth offering brought Darin and Dee into her office to exclaim over the profusion of orchids and gardenias overflowing a sterling silver bowl.

"Come on, Cass," Darin said coaxingly. "You must have some idea who's sending these."

"I tell you the notes weren't signed," she replied stubbornly.

"Let me see them, then," he said to her in disbelief.

Reluctantly Cass handed over two of the cards, now a little tattered and worn from the constant handling they had received as she read and reread them.

Darin read aloud: "'Busy till night, pleasing herself mightily to see what a deal of business goes off a woman's

hands when she stays by it.' Is it some kind of quotation?"
he asked, perplexed. Literature had apparently not been his
long suit in college. "Weird."

"Samuel Pepys, 1667," Cass volunteered dryly. Curiosity
had driven her to have a librarian friend check out each of
the messages. "And it's misquoted. Pepys wrote it about a
man, not a woman."

"That doesn't sound very romantic to me," Dee ventured
dubiously. "What does the other one say?"

Darin frowned at the next card. "This one is even worse.
Listen: 'Dear Night! this world's defeat; The stop to busy
fools.' Not much of a compliment."

"I don't think it was meant as one," Cass retorted curtly.
"Now can we just drop the subject?"

But Darin, with his unerring nose for gossip, wouldn't be
deterred. "Where's the one that came today, Cass?"

While Darin had his head bent, examining the heavy
black scrawl, Cass threw Dee a pleading glance. To her
relief, her friend smiled in understanding.

"Oh, never mind, Darin," the older woman said, inter-
vening. "Let's leave Cass alone and get back to work. I want
you to take a look at the order that just came in for the
Robinsons. I can't believe the invoice is right. It looks to me
as though they've charged us for two bolts of fabric instead
of one."

A financial error—especially one not in Cassandra's
favor—was enough to capture Darin's undivided attention.
Cass's flowers with their oblique messages might be intrigu-
ing, but business was business.

As the door closed behind them, Cass drew the card she
had received that day from the pocket of her jacket, where
she had stuffed it unceremoniously when Dee and Darin
unexpectedly descended upon her. She frowned as she
reread the message:

> Busy, curious, thirsty fly,
> Drink with me, and drink as I.

Something was different about this one. It wasn't so much
a derogatory comment as . . . what? An invitation? She
was still puzzling over it when the buzzer on her intercom

sounded. She jumped and fumbled for the switch. Brendan's flowers, the cryptic messages, and the curiosity they were arousing were making her a nervous wreck! "Yes, Janet?" she asked curtly.

"You have a call on line two. He didn't say who he was."

Cass could hear the inquisitiveness and eagerness in the girl's voice. Premonition made her tense. "Thank you, Janet. I'll take it." She waited a minute to catch her breath, but her hand was still unsteady when she punched the button on the phone and answered brusquely: "Cassandra Wells."

"My, aren't we formal today! Brendan Cahill." A husky laugh floated across the wire. "Did you get my flowers?"

"Yes, I got them, and will you please stop sending those things? My office looks like a . . . a funeral parlor!"

"And here I thought you'd be pleased." The tone of his voice was hurt; the Irish lilt in it was pure mischief. "Did you read the cards?"

Silence.

"So, will you?" he tried again.

"Will I what?" Cass asked reluctantly, curiosity getting the better of her good sense.

"Today's invitation: 'Drink with me, and drink as I.' I could pick you up about seven."

"I told you Sunday night that I'm b-b-b . . ." Try as she might, the word just wouldn't come out. Brendan and his stupid notes had made a farce out of the excuse "busy"— which was undoubtedly what he had intended, Cass concluded ruefully.

"Don't tell me I'm about to be rejected again." He sighed plaintively. "It's very hard on my ego, you know."

To Cass he didn't sound humbled in the least. "I'm not rejecting you, Brendan. I'm simply trying to make it clear—"

"Good. Then I'll see you at seven."

"Brendan, will you listen to me?!"

"Tonight I promise you my absolute, undivided attention."

Cass should have been angry. Instead she found herself fighting an impulse to laugh. The man was incorrigible. He had such a brazen way of trying to wear her down. In defense she conjured up the vision of his face as she had seen it in the gleam of on-coming headlights—hard, determined, unyielding. The memory was sobering enough to stifle any amusement.

"Well?" he said into the silence on the line.

"Look, Brendan, I cannot go out with you tonight or tomorrow night or the night after that or the night after that—"

"Why?" he interrupted unapologetically. "Are you married, engaged, involved?"

For a moment Cass was tempted to take the easy way out and tell him yes, she was married and had four kids. But besides the conviction that he wouldn't believe her for a minute, she found that she couldn't bring herself to utter an outright lie. She compromised with a partial truth.

"No, I'm not involved with anyone—unless you put my clients in that category. I have the preliminaries on two apartments to present tomorrow, the renderings for a beach house on Long Island to finish before Sunday, a six-room addition to a house in Connecticut to have ready by Tuesday morning, and consultations with half a dozen other assorted clients to fit in sometime between. The idea of taking an evening off tonight is ludicrous when I'll probably get no food and little sleep the entire weekend. Now, does that answer your question?"

A long silence followed this tirade. For a minute she thought Brendan had hung up. Then, "Cass?" he said at last.

"Yes?" she answered warily.

"Cass, hasn't anyone told you that you're working too hard? No wonder you looked ready to faint the other night. I'm a workaholic myself, but at least I have the good sense to know that I have to give myself a break now and then."

She was taken aback. Not only had Brendan believed her explanation, but she could hear the concern in his voice. Inexplicably it brought a rush of tears to her eyes. She brushed them impatiently away with the back of her hand.

"Cass? Are you still there?"

"Yes, I'm still here."

"I've upset you and I'm sorry."

"I'm—I'm not upset."

"Damn! I've gone and done it again. Look, Cass, I won't hound you any more. No more flowers, no more notes. Okay?"

"Thank you, Brendan. I would appreciate that." She thought she meant the words. Why, then, did she have this empty feeling in the pit of her stomach? "The flowers were lovely," she added lamely. "Really. I'm sorry I was so rude."

"Not rude exactly—just blunt. I tend toward bluntness myself," he said lightly, "in case you haven't noticed."

Silence. She had no answer to that one.

"Well," he said at last. "I guess I'd better let you get back to the sweatshop."

"Good-bye, Brendan." The feeling of emptiness spread through her entire body.

"Cass?"

"Yes?"

"Take care of yourself."

The next few days passed just as Cass had predicted. As Brendan had promised, no more flowers arrived. Her life continued at its usual frenetic pace, but all too often, in brief moments of peace between the storm of work and meetings, Cass found her thoughts drifting to the unusual, unpredictable Brendan Cahill.

The image of Brendan the businessman—the one that had troubled her the most—was blurring. Instead she visualized him as he must have looked when they spoke on the phone. Foolishly, she dwelt on the charm of his rugged face, his unique, perceptive blue eyes, and the words of caution he had offered in his deep, lilting voice. Never had the memory of any man been so disturbing to her. For the sake of her peace of mind, it was a good thing she wouldn't be seeing him again.

"Cass!"

The irritation in Darin's voice indicated that this wasn't the first time he had tried to get her attention. She turned away from the window in her workroom to find him standing in the doorway, hands on his hips, tapping his foot impatiently.

"You wanted something, Darin?"

"I would like to talk to you in my office, please. Now, if you don't mind! I don't know what's gotten into you lately," she heard him mutter as he turned on his heel and stalked off down the hall.

With a sigh, Cass followed. She had a pretty good idea what Darin wanted to talk about and would have preferred to postpone the discussion—permanently. Apparently he wasn't going to give her any choice.

"All right, Darin. What is it?" Cass asked, collapsing into a chair and propping her feet up on a table.

"I would hazard a guess that you already know! I just had a very unpleasant call from Walter Benjamin."

Walter Benjamin—the grizzled-haired man from Megan Cooke's party. Darin paced back and forth behind his desk, his blond hair ruffled, his tie slightly askew, his eyes dark with anger, and his hands balled into tense fists.

"Oh, for heaven's sake, sit down, Darin." Cass sighed impatiently. "I've had a hard enough day as it is without you stalking about like a wounded lion."

"I *feel* wounded, Cass," Darin bit out. "And you're the one who shot me down, without even paying me the common courtesy of telling me what you were going to do." He sat, albeit stiffly, on the edge of his chair, waiting for an explanation.

"I didn't offend him deliberately, Darin. In fact, I thought I handled him very tactfully."

"Then why did he complain—quite justifiably—that after meeting with them this morning, you suggested that he and his wife try another decorating house. Isn't it true?"

She shrugged. "If that's what Benjamin said, it must be."

"I just don't believe you did it! I was counting on the Benjamin account, and you knew it. Tell me, Cass, why you just casually threw a twenty-thousand-dollar commission out the window! I'd be simply fascinated to hear."

Cass kept her temper in the face of Darin's deliberate provocation. He knew she hated his sarcasm. "There was no way I could work with the Benjamins, Darin. If I had done their apartment the way they wanted it, it would have turned out looking like a French bordello—flocked wallpaper, crushed red velvet, fringed lamp shades, and nude statues spouting champagne. You ought to be pleased to hear," she concluded dryly, "that I restrained myself from telling them that their taste was atrocious. I think I was damned diplomatic under the circumstances. I pleaded a lack of time to do it justice."

"Which Walter and Faye didn't find an acceptable reason for refusing to work with them. You never considered a compromise, I suppose?" he asked in disgust.

"Darin, there was no hope for a compromise! They knew just what they wanted. I think they must have just seen some old Mae West movie or something," Cass added as a sardonic aside. "Nothing I could have suggested to them would have made them change their minds."

Brendan digested this, and after a long silence Cass heard his noncommittal grunt. He leaned back in his swivel chair, extended his legs in front of him, and focused his gaze on a point above Cass's head. His anger was gone now, but not his tension. It troubled her to see him so upset.

"Darin?" His eyes moved down to her face, but he said nothing as she pushed herself out of her chair and moved around the desk to his side. "Darin. I'm sorry, but you have to know I wouldn't turn down a commission without very good reason. I would have been ashamed to have had Cassandra's name connected with the kind of thing they wanted. And it surely wouldn't have done our reputation any good."

"You didn't like the Benjamins from the first moment you met them," he observed coldly.

"No, I didn't," she admitted, "but that didn't enter into the decision. I don't turn away a client because of a personality conflict. This was a matter of professional integrity. A lot of very obnoxious people," she added wryly, "have excellent taste. The Benjamins just don't happen to be among them."

For the first time a smile twitched at Darin's lips and amusement wiped the coldness from his eyes. "You're right, of course, Cass. That awful dinner jacket Walter had on the other night! I should have guessed they would give you a hard time. Now it's my turn to apologize."

Cass squeezed his shoulder affectionately. "No apology necessary. I just want you to have faith in my judgment. I will never turn down a client because of a personality difference—at least one that doesn't affect the integrity of my work. Trust me. Any decision I make will be a strictly professional one. I promise!"

Two hours later, Cass would have gladly given up her precious Waterford crystal vase to have been able to take back that promise. She was bent over her drawing board when Janet tapped tentatively on the door. "Cass?"

"Mmmm?" Cass replied without looking up.

"You have a client downstairs. Darin is with him now and would like you to join them as soon as possible."

"Right," Cass said absently, finishing up a window treatment with a few bold, broad strokes of her charcoal.

Her mind was still on the possible choices of fabric for the drapes when she strolled into her office, unaware of the shock awaiting her. Both men rose as she entered. She caught only a glimpse of Darin's smug, satisfied smile before the second man turned to face her—Brendan Cahill.

"Hello, Cass. Nice to see you again."

"Brendan," she acknowledged warily, cryptically.

"We've just been talking through the financial arrangements, Cass," Darin explained.

She choked. "For what?"

"Brendan wants Cassandra's to redecorate his apartment. I told him he was in luck," he added, enormously pleased with the situation. "That fortunately for him, a slot in the schedule opened up just this morning and you had time to take on a new client."

Cass weakly took her place behind her desk, her mind reeling from this unexpected turn of events. She silently cursed herself for not keeping the Benjamin account, red velvet and all. Whether Darin knew it or not, she concluded bitterly, he had certainly gotten back at her for the debacle she had made of it. If he had deliberately devised a punishment for her, he couldn't have come up with a worse one. It was sitting right there in front of her—and smiling ironically at her chagrin.

She risked a second glance at Brendan from under her eyelashes and knew immediately that it was a mistake. One good look at the man and Darin might as well have not been

in the room. The power of Brendan's rugged, untamed
presence in her dainty, elegant little office was incongruous
and all the more overwhelming because of it.

Their glances met and held. Cass hadn't remembered how
thick Brendan's eyelashes were or how they curled, nearly
obscuring his upper lid. She hadn't noticed before that the
little flecks of black in the iris of his eyes gave them that
deep blue color. Their intensity, however, came from an
intangible quality within him that was almost mesmerizing.
In fact, she found it impossible to look away, even when
Brendan's gaze became more searching, when his eyebrow
rose into a more pronounced, cynical slant, and when his
smile slowly faded. Tension reverberated back and forth
across the room as Cass fought to shake off the strange hold
he had over her. To her relief, Brendan himself ended the
moment.

"Well, Cass?"

"Why are you here, Brendan?" she asked bluntly.

He shot Darin a quick glance, then shrugged and replied
smoothly, "Your work at Megan's impressed me. And after
meeting you last week, I knew you were the decorator for
me."

This last comment was open to interpretation, and Cass
saw that Darin read into it all the things she would have
much preferred to keep to herself. His glance lighted on one
of the bouquets of flowers on her desk, and she could
practically see the wheels of his mind spin into motion,
putting two and two together, figuring the possibilities,
multiplying the potential, and calculating the dividends. At
last he stood, smiled meaningfully at Cass, and shook hands
with Brendan.

"Nice seeing you again, Mr. Cahill. I'll get back to work
now and leave you two to, ah . . . work out whatever
arrangements suit you best."

A tense silence followed his exit. This time, Cass had the
good sense not to look at Brendan as she waited for him to
take the lead. This was his party, not hers.

"So, Cass," he asked at last, "how do we start?"

"Start what?" she asked caustically. She had a pretty
good idea of where he expected to finish up—in her bed.
She quickly suppressed a traitorous part of her that was

wondering if she would really mind. Of course she would mind. The man was bulldozing her—an apt description, she thought mirthlessly, given his line of work. "Start what?" she repeated when he didn't reply. "Your apartment?"

His smile told her too much. "I guess that's up to you."

"I thought I had made myself clear last week!"

"Oh, you did, I assure you," he said easily. "You made it very clear that you were too busy to have time for anyone but your clients. I realized then that if I wanted to see you, I had better become one of them—a client, that is. So, here I am."

Chapter 3

CASS MET BRENDAN ON THE FRONT STEPS OF HER BUILDING that night at seven. At his suggestion she had reluctantly agreed that it would save time if they were to have dinner at his apartment, look it over, and begin preliminary talks.

"Hi, Cass," he said as he came around the car to open the door for her.

"Good evening, Brendan," she said more formally, holding out her hand in a conventional greeting.

She thought she had herself well under control, but unfortunately, she wasn't prepared for her unexpected reaction to his touch. Little shock waves of sensual awareness jolted through her as Brendan's fingers slowly closed around hers. His calloused thumb began making small circles on the back of her hand. To her dismay she found that his physical impact on her was something beyond her control, which made it even more deeply, dangerously disturbing. She had been moved by him when he had kissed her and confused and angry with him that afternoon, but for the first time she was frightened of his power over her.

Whether Brendan felt her involuntary shiver or read the sudden apprehension in her expression, she didn't know. Whichever, he slowly released her hand and frowned down into her eyes. "Are you all right, Cass? You're pale."

"I'm fine. Just hungry, I guess." She forced a cool smile. "Shall we go?"

Cass hadn't formed any precise notion of what Brendan's apartment would be like, but she wasn't prepared to find it at the top of a twenty-six-story business building in midtown Manhattan. Her first thought when he turned into the underground parking garage was that he had changed his mind about eating at his home and was taking her instead to one of the restaurants in the area. When he led her to a bank of elevators set into the concrete-block wall, her second thought was that he needed to pick up something at his office first. Her second guess was wrong but still closer to the truth.

A metal plate over the door of the elevator he selected read "Monarch Enterprises." The inside panel had only five buttons—"G" for the garage and numbers for floors twenty-three through twenty-six. When the door had closed on them, Brendan inserted a key into a lock, pushed the button for the top floor, and the car moved upward.

Curiosity coupled with hunger got the better of her and she asked tentatively, "Er . . . we're going to your office?"

"If you'd like to see it," he said casually.

Cass was beginning to get the right idea even before the elevator stopped and the doors slid back to reveal, not the corridor of a thriving business enterprise, but a private foyer. Beyond the arch in front of them was what appeared to be a living room, but Cass couldn't be sure.

The room was a huge, undivided oblong, entirely carpeted with durable, neutral brown-and-tan-flecked carpeting. The walls were painted an institutional beige, and drawn across three sets of windows were innocuous drapes of plain brown antique satin. The furnishings, arranged in small groupings about the room, were all solid, functional pieces, constructed of heavy wood with nylon upholstery. To top it all off, the dropped ceiling was made up of acoustical tiling, interspersed occasionally with sections of translucent plastic that concealed the overhead lighting source. Only a fireplace against one wall made Cass question whether she had entered someone's home or had inadvertently stumbled into a dentist's waiting room.

No, not a waiting room, she decided, incredulity mixing with a growing dismay. It couldn't be. There wasn't a magazine in sight. In fact, there wasn't a single personal, human touch to give the place definition. Even the ashtrays, the bric-a-brac adorning the tables, and the various lamps scattered about looked as though they had been chosen indiscriminately from a catalogue. The room had all the coziness of a lounge in an airline terminal. If this was indeed where Brendan lived, he really did need her help.

"Well, here we are," he announced—in this case not unnecessarily. Cass needed verbal confirmation.

"Home?" she inquired uncertainly.

"Yes. My apartment."

His apartment, not his home. Cass wondered if he recognized the fact that this qualified response told her a great deal—actually too much.

Brendan checked his watch. "Dinner won't be delivered for another half hour. I apologize for ordering without consulting you first, but making arrangements in advance saves a lot of time, and I don't know about you, but I'm starved. Can I fix you a drink while we wait?"

"Yes, please. Rum and coke if you have it."

Cass needed a drink at that moment. The prospect of having to transform this apartment from a sterile void into a warm, welcoming home was staggering. It was going to be a monumental task—especially since she was convinced now that Brendan didn't care a whit.

While Cass began a professional appraisal of the situation, Brendan retreated to an adjoining room, presumably the kitchen. He returned a few minutes later with two drinks in hand—her rum and coke and whiskey on the rocks for himself.

"Shall we drink to an interesting relationship?" he asked her now, at his most charming, and indicated that she join him on a tweed couch facing the fireplace.

"To an interesting *business* relationship," Cass amended, barely touching the rim of her glass to his.

Brendan smiled and took a sip. "You don't give in easily, do you?" His glance slid assessingly over her slim figure, perched primly on what, to her surprise, proved to be a very comfortable sofa.

Once Brendan had taken his disturbing presence out of her office that afternoon, Cass considered her situation. There was only one course of action open to her—keep her promise to Darin, do her job as quickly as possible, and get Brendan out of her life once and for all.

She had chosen her outfit for the evening with great deliberation. Nothing about the dark, tailored, pinstriped suit hinted of a social occasion. The leather purse on the floor beside her was large and utilitarian. Side pockets had been designed to hold a measuring tape, notebook, and sketch pad. She had parted her black hair in the middle and brushed it into a sleek, severe pageboy that just curved against her jawline. The black pumps she wore were low-heeled and serviceable. Only a black, red, and white scarf tied loosely around her neck and tucked into the low neckline softened the total effect.

She had taken great pains to project a strictly business image, and apparently Brendan had received the message. Rather than being put off, however, to her chagrin Cass saw that he was merely amused by her efforts.

Brendan himself had changed out of the gray suit, white shirt, and conservative tie he had worn earlier and into casual navy blue cords, soft leather loafers, and what looked to be a hand-knit, ivory fisherman's sweater. His dark hair, styled short and full in front and longer in back, curled down onto the sweater's turtleneck. The image he projected as he lounged back in the corner of the couch had nothing to do with business, and the message he was sending her with his penetrating blue eyes was enough to make every feminine instinct she possessed quiver with sensual tension. The man was a menace.

Cass blinked several times to try to reduce Brendan's potent effect on her from "very sexy man" to "just another client," and she forced her attention onto business.

"Have you lived here long, Brendan?" she asked, beginning her usual preliminary probing.

"Quite a while. Nearly six years."

"Six years?" Cass repeated faintly. He had lived in this place for six years and none of his own dynamic personality had rubbed off on it? She found it almost inconceivable. Any person living a normal life invariably accumulated bits and pieces of personal clutter that added atmosphere to a room—photographs, memorabilia, books, records. Either Brendan kept his personal self well out of sight, or he didn't ordinarily bring his private life home.

"Yes. Six, nearly seven," Brendan was saying. "When Monarch bought the top four floors of the building, I had this part converted into an apartment." He indicated a door to the left of the entryway. "My office is just the other side of that wall. There's another entrance, of course, from the floors below, for my secretary's use and as an access from the other offices. When I'm in New York, I really spend most of my time at my desk in there."

Surprise, surprise! Cass thought wryly. This room was enough to drive anyone to a more congenial spot. None of what she was really thinking, however, showed on her face as she asked, "You travel a good deal, then?"

He shrugged. "A few days here, a few days there. A week at a time in one place or another. It adds up."

"To what?" She had spoken unthinkingly, really questioning his more general life concerns, but she was just as glad that Brendan chose to answer it literally.

"Oh, probably five or six months out of the year on the road."

Her eyes narrowed. "You've lived in this apartment happily for over six years, are away from the city a good share of the time, and now you're suddenly moved by a burning desire to redecorate?"

His smile was slow and suggestive. "Let's say that you . . . uh, inspired me."

"How flattering," she snapped.

"I never flatter," he countered. "On principle. I just call it like I see it, and as I told you today, I liked what I saw."

"Megan Cooke's house, you mean?" she suggested dryly.

His smile broadened. "That too."

"All right! All right, then," Cass interjected quickly before he could add something outrageous. "Let's get down to business, shall we?" Deliberately she pulled her notebook and a pen from her purse. "Do you entertain much up here when you're in town?"

"Nothing that need concern you, Cass. I may play the field, but it's one woman at a time."

"I was speaking of entertaining business associates," she informed him coldly, with what patience she could dredge up under the circumstances.

He sighed in disappointment. "And here I thought we were getting somewhere at last."

"We are. At least *I* am. Cassandra's," she recited, with what she hoped was a restrained detachment, "prides itself on the fact that we don't just decorate houses. We strive to create a compatible, workable, harmonious environment for a client. This, of course, can't be done as a theoretical exercise. Therefore, I need specific information from you with which to work."

"Very impressive," he observed solemnly. "What information?"

"Oh, what colors, fabrics, and furniture styles you prefer. Things like that."

"And that's it?"

"Of course, in order to design a room properly, I also have to know the various functions you want each room to serve."

Brenden was unchastened by her formality. "I can't wait until we get to the bedroom," he murmured provocatively.

Cass groaned inwardly but refused to take the bait. She didn't have the courage at that point, though, to tell him that ordinarily during the course of her preliminary talks with her clients she would have amassed personal, even intimate, details about their life-styles. She shuddered to think of what comments he could come up with, given that information.

Damn both men! she swore for the tenth time that day. Her partner was undoubtedly at that moment cherishing visions of bigger, more impressive commissions yet to come from Monarch. She didn't dare linger on what she suspected was going on in Brendan's head. To her relief, a buzzer broke into these unproductive thoughts.

"That must be dinner," Brendan said, pushing himself off the couch.

Cass watched, intrigued despite herself, as he crossed to a panel set into the wall near the elevator doors, opened it, and flipped a switch. A television monitor lit up. The camera was inside the elevator she and Brendan had used. She could see a middle-aged man in a red and gold uniform standing beside a laden trolley. Brendan pushed a button and the elevator rose with its passenger.

"That's some security system," she commented.

Brendan shrugged. "Both the blessing and the curse of ensuring privacy. Anyone can reach the three lower floors, but this floor takes a special key or this button."

They watched in silence during the half minute it took the elevator to reach them. Then the doors opened automatically and man and food emerged.

"Good evening, Mr. Cahill," the waiter greeted him deferentially, rolling the trolley across the room to a table on the far side near a window.

"'Evening, John."

Not only did Brendan know the man, Cass noted, but the routine was obviously familiar. Without waiting for instructions, the waiter whipped out a white linen table cloth, napkins, dinner service for two, wine and water glasses, candles in crystal holders, and even a silver vase holding a single red rose.

"Would you like me to stay and serve, sir?" the man asked when the table was finally set to his satisfaction.

"No, thanks. If you'd just open the wine and set the food on the side table, we'll serve ourselves. You can clean up tomorrow."

"Very good, sir."

To his credit, the waiter kept his face tactfully averted from Cass and on his work—or else he was well paid to be discreet, Cass considered morosely as he completed the requested services and quickly withdrew.

The meal on the warmers underneath the silver covers was good and substantial but not elaborate—filet mignon, potato puffs, glazed carrots, and dinner rolls, with a spinach salad on the side, apple pie for dessert, and a pot of coffee. The wine Brendan had chosen was a good French Burgundy, but again nothing either spectacular or extravagant. If Cass had given the question any consideration before, she would have guessed that Brendan Cahill was a basic meat-and-potatoes man.

He kept an impersonal, desultory conversation going while they ate, saying nothing to bait her. In fact, his major concern seemed to be that Cass eat a good meal. If she hadn't been so wary, she would have found his concern and consideration touching. But after her reaction to his handshake, she knew that letting Brendan touch her—in any way—was dangerous.

After they had finished their coffee and pie, Cass doggedly turned the conversation back to the purpose of her visit.

"Could I see the rest of the apartment now, Brendan?"

"You wouldn't like to rest and have a liqueur first?"

"No, thanks. It's getting late, and I have to leave soon."

Brendan sent her a look she didn't care to try and interpret. If he had imagined plans for later on, he was going to be disappointed.

The apartment consisted of the living room, adjoining kitchen, three bedrooms, and two bathrooms, but all the rooms were large, undoubtedly designated at one time as office space, Cass was sure. Little attempt had been made either to disguise their original function or create the illusion of a home. The kitchen would have done credit to a school lunch program, she concluded wryly. It contained every appliance imaginable, the larger ones all in spotless white enamel, and the oversized double sink was made of stainless steel. Very institutional. Two of the bedrooms, guest rooms presumably, were connected by a bathroom that had probably been converted from a supply room. These bedrooms were innocuously decorated in dull colors, with the same functional, nondescript furniture that characterized the rest of the apartment.

The only room that had any personality at all was what obviously served as Brendan's own bedroom. It was the one room that showed any signs of being lived in, but precious few signs at that. A lamp, clock radio, telephone, address book, notepad, pen, and a couple of novels cluttered the nightstand beside the oversized water bed that took up most of the center of the room. One wall was covered by a combination unit comprising a bookcase, stereo system, and television. Facing it from the opposite corner was a leather recliner and reading light. Through an open doorway Cass could see a large room, partitioned off to serve as bathroom, dressing room, and walk-in closet.

Up to that point Brendan had followed silently behind Cass while she made her tour of inspection. She had discouraged conversation by scribbling busily in her notebook and making rough sketches of each room.

"Well?" he asked at last, as she flipped her notebook closed, stuffed it into the side pocket of her purse, and gave his bedroom one last look.

"This is senseless, Brendan," she replied tartly.

"This referring to what, exactly."

"Redecorating! You don't give a damn about having this place redone. You're perfectly happy with it the way it is. You don't even *live* here! This apartment is just a . . . a stopping-off place, a glorified executive lounge with facilities for an occasional guest or the annual Christmas party!"

He didn't deny the accusation, merely shrugged negligently. "If I'm willing to pay for you to turn it into a Cassandra showcase, why should you care?"

"Because I don't like to waste my time," she said through clenched teeth, "and I wouldn't think that you do either!"

"I certainly don't intend to waste any time." The words spoken in context were appropriate. It was the connotation, the glint in his eye, and the determined set of his jaw that left too much room for speculation.

"Do you have any idea what this . . . this whim of yours is going to cost you?" she asked crossly. "The whole place needs major structural changes and there's hardly a stick of furniture worth salvaging. You can probably take a tax write-off by donating the lot to charity, but we're still talking in the neighborhood of a couple of hundred thousand dollars!"

"Summerhays made it very clear that you don't come cheap—your design house, that is," he added innocently as the spark of antagonism in her eyes flared to a conflagration. "But then, nothing worthwhile ever does."

"You must be out of your mind," Cass muttered in exasperation.

"Absolutely in control of my senses," he assured her solemnly, emphasizing his point by dwelling with obvious pleasure on the perfection of her small, straight nose and full, sensual lower lip, caught now between her teeth. "In fact—" Abruptly he stopped and frowned. "Do you know, I haven't seen you smile once this entire evening."

This sudden, unexpected observation took Cass by surprise, and she reacted by blurting out the truth. "I haven't had a lot to smile about lately."

"And it's all my fault?" he asked in consternation.

For a minute she was tempted to tell him yes, but in all honesty she couldn't. Slowly she shook her head. "No. It's not entirely your fault, Brendan, though you haven't helped the situation any. I've—I've had a lot on my mind."

"Business or personal problems?"

She didn't care for his probing, but she felt compelled to answer. "That's the worst part," she admitted wearily. "I've reached the point where I can't tell one from the other."

"Poor baby."

His tone made her bristle. "I'm not asking for sympathy, Brendan. I'm simply stating facts."

"No, Cass," he said thoughtfully. "You're not the type to ask for sympathy. I like that."

Before she realized what he was doing, he had his hands on her shoulders. At the first touch she stiffened, but she didn't protest as he pulled her toward him to lie against his broad chest, her head cradled in his large hand, her cheek nestled against his shoulder.

At first he just held her tense body in a silent, gentle embrace. Then, "Relax, Cass," he murmured soothingly. "You feel as though you're strung on wires."

Gradually, against her will, her muscles began to unknot. The tight band of pressure around her head began to ease. Tension drained from her shoulders and back. Strangely, she felt comforted by the warmth, strength, and illusion of physical protection from her emotional problems that Brendan's body seemed to offer her.

She was so tired. She was so tired of battling the business world—Darin and his increasing demands on her, pressure from all sides, lack of time, rising prices, dwindling capital, difficult clients, her own conflicting needs and desires, and her even more confused inclinations. Held like this in Brendan's arms, the outside world seemed far away and not nearly so unmanageable. In relief Cass gave herself to this moment of respite, reassured by the fact that there was nothing demanding in the hands that roamed gently up and down her back, nothing but understanding and fellow-feeling in the lips that pressed tenderly against the top of her head.

"There. That's better," Brendan murmured when she was completely pliant in his arms. "Tell me, Cass. What can I do for you?"

"You can stay out of my life, Brendan." She sighed unhappily into his shoulder.

He pulled back far enough to look down into her face. For several moments he assessed what he saw there, and Cass found it impossible to look away from those probing blue eyes, eyes that saw far too much.

"I don't think I can do that, Cass," he said simply. "It's been a long time since I've wanted a woman as much as I want you." He announced this with the same devastating bluntness that had caught Cass unprepared before. "And I think that you want me too. I can see it in your eyes."

"No, Brendan," she objected unconvincingly.

"Yes, Cass."

"Please. I just want you to leave me alone!" she pleaded, not at all sure she was speaking the truth. Brendan was quick to pick up the doubt he heard in her voice.

"Is that so? Show me."

He had already penetrated her guard once, but in truth, Cass had no desire to stop him when he tightened his hold around her, put a hand under her chin, and lifted her face to his. This kiss was different from the ones he had given her previously. His lips were hot and seeking. He kissed her as though he couldn't get enough, and his mouth awoke an answering hunger in her that had been dormant for much too long to be easily assuaged. He had her drowning in the sensations he created, betraying far too clearly the physical effect he had on her.

To his credit, he didn't take advantage of her weakness. Slowly he released her, supporting her weight until the world had stopped spinning around her.

"Now," he said, holding her lightly by the shoulders and

smiling down into her bemused face. "Would you care to reassess the situation?"

"I—I suppose it would be useless to tell you I didn't, ah . . . enjoy that, wouldn't it?"

"Utterly useless."

"Will you believe me, though," she continued solemnly, "when I tell you I didn't *want* it to happen?"

His lips tightened at the haunted expression in her eyes. "I just might—if you tell me why."

She moved her shoulders and twisted out of his grasp. "My life is in enough of a mess right now without your complicating it."

"You're the first woman that's ever referred to me as a complication," he said curtly. "Should I take that as a compliment?"

Cass was too emotionally drained and physically exhausted to continue on with this battle of words. Fatigue overcame her discretion. "Take it any way you please, Brendan. I don't give a damn!"

She should have known better than to antagonize him. He took a step forward. She retreated. Another step. Another fast retreat. The back of her knees hit the edge of the water bed. Her arms flailed for a moment before she lost her balance and tumbled backwards, her skirt sliding upward to leave her knees and thighs bare. Brendan not only let her fall, he followed her down onto the bed.

"I choose to take it this way," he muttered just before his lips took hers with a devastating mastery that instantly annihilated any resistance she would have offered. "Do you still want me to leave you alone?" he asked against her mouth.

Beneath them the water moved, rocking their bodies together, igniting fires in Cass wherever they touched. He was right. At that moment she wanted him as much as he wanted her.

"No," she cried. "I don't want you to leave me alone."

Brendan's quest became more seeking as Cass's lips parted to welcome him. While his tongue sought out the moist warmth of her mouth, his fingers wandered from the nape of her neck, around to her smooth throat, and down into the deep V of her jacket. One by one he loosened the buttons and parted the lapels; then he slipped his hand beneath the lace of her bra to cup the fullness of her breast. The warm flesh swelled against his palm at the first touch, and his fingers toyed with the hard bud of her nipple. As his knee insinuated itself between her legs, she could feel his need for her rising. She moaned with a need and desire of her own and unconsciously arched her back to press herself closer against him. Both the bed and his body responded to the provocative movement.

This was a precarious moment for Cass, and Brendan made a tactical error. "Now tell me you don't give a damn," he murmured into her ear. "Now tell me that I'm nothing to you but a complication."

Nothing but a complication! His words intruded harshly into her euphoric state, a world of sensual pleasure where nothing mattered but the present moment. With a jolt Brendan had brought her back to unwelcome reality. Her body was telling her one thing, but now her mind was telling her another. It would be the easiest thing in the world to give in to her desires, to welcome the relief and oblivion Brendan offered her—the easiest thing and the biggest mistake she could make.

"No, Brendan! Please don't!" she whispered breathlessly.

"Don't what?" He nibbled gently on the lobe of her ear.

"Please, let me go!"

"You don't mean that." His lips followed a path down the taut cord in her neck towards her bare breast.

Anxiously her head flailed from side to side. "I do!"

Conviction gave her strength, and she pushed against Brendan's chest. The bed rocked violently. Her breathing became heavy, and reluctantly he raised himself to look down into her agitated face.

"Cass? What's the matter?"

She had to find the words to stop him, even though she was only half coherent, her thoughts still in turmoil from the overwhelming effects of her sensual arousal. "You're an escape—only an escape!"

The lines in his forehead deepened in puzzlement as he shifted his weight from her on to one elbow. "A what?"

"An escape," she gasped, her breathing still ragged. Her

heart was pounding as though she had narrowly avoided danger. A fight-or-flight reaction, she thought wildly, well justified under the circumstances.

"An escape from what?" he insisted, but he offered no objection when she moved to sit up.

Cass was sick at heart, disgusted by her own emotional weakness and envious of Brendan's strength. "I don't want to talk about it!"

"You don't think you owe me *some* explanation?" he asked in disbelief. "One minute you're as warm and willing as any woman I've ever known, and the next you act as though I'm attacking you!"

"I'm sorry!"

"I'm not asking for an apology, Cass. I'm asking for an explanation. What did I say? What did I do wrong?"

"You—you didn't do anything wrong, Brendan," she confessed, driven. "The problem isn't you, it's—it's *me!* I tried to explain before but you wouldn't listen!"

"Well, I'm listening now." The ghost of a smile relaxed the tension in his face and eased the strain between them. "And I have to tell you, Cass, that you have one hell of a way of getting a man's attention."

Nervously Cass chewed on her lip. "I said I was sorry."

"Never mind," he soothed her. "Go on. Explain."

"I—I knew that night at Megan's that you could make me want you if you put your mind to it," she admitted reluctantly. "I was ripe for an affair, and deep down I knew it. That's why I refused to go out with you. I didn't dare allow myself to become emotionally involved—and I could, much too easily, but for all the wrong reasons." She searched his face hopefully. "Now do you understand?"

"Frankly, no."

Helplessly she shook her head. "I told you, my life is in a mess right now. My work is getting to me. I'm exhausted, confused, and I don't know what I want to do with my life any more. Don't you see? An affair with you would be a great temporary escape. I could run away from my real problems, concentrate on you, but in the long run that wouldn't really solve anything. It would only confuse the issues and complicate things even more. I would end up hating you. It wouldn't be fair to either of us."

Brendan had listened carefully to all she said but was obviously unconvinced. "I like the concentrate-on-me bit best," he drawled, "and I'm willing to take the chance if you are, Cass."

"Well, I'm not!"

He reached out toward her. "Let me—"

"No!" With a twist of her body she moved away from him to the side of the bed. Her fingers were shaking as she rebuttoned her jacket and ran a smoothing hand over her hair. "I—I already know how persuasive you can be."

Brendan frowned as he caught the determined set of her jaw. "I think you've been reading too much pop psychology, Cass. And I think it's a bunch of . . . well, it's stupid."

"It's not stupid, Brendan. At least, not the way I see it. I've reached the point where I can't run away from my problems any longer. I have to make some decisions soon— and without any interference from you!"

She took a deep breath. He wasn't going to like what she was about to say. If she lost one of the biggest accounts Cassandra's had ever had, Darin would kill her—and she didn't give a damn. Her promise to him didn't include sleeping with her client.

"I told you I was ripe for an affair," she continued bluntly, "and that's the truth. But in the state I'm in now, it could have been with you or anyone. You just happened along at the right moment and were more persistent than the ordinary man. I was certain the first night we met that we were totally wrong for each other. Now that I know you better," she finished ruthlessly, "I'm even more convinced that any relationship between us would be a disaster. We have nothing in common."

As she spoke, a slow-burning anger darkened Brendan's eyes, and when he spoke his voice was laced with sarcasm. *"Nothing* in common? Do you want me to demonstrate again?"

"I admit to a . . . a physical compatibility."

"Generous of you," he snapped.

"Sexual attraction isn't enough!"

"Have you heard me asking for any more?"

"No, I haven't, and that's the point, Brendan. We have nothing else in common."

"Concoct any excuses you please if it makes you happy, Cass, but in the end it all comes back to the fact that you want me and I want you. *That's* the point."

The haunted expression had come back into her eyes. "Ten years, five, even one year ago, Brendan, I believed that wanting something, then working for it and getting it, was what life was all about. I don't believe that anymore. I'm discovering the hard way that getting what you think you want can be the worst thing that can happen to you—especially when it comes too quickly. It's a very subtle, destructive trap."

His mouth thinned in displeasure as he took her by the shoulders and turned her to face him. "I suppose that somewhere in that complicated mind of yours, that makes sense to you, but it sure as hell doesn't make any sense to me."

"Then maybe this will," she cried, shaking off his hold. "I want you to stay out of my life!"

His eyebrow rose into the familiar slant that now held both cynicism and disillusionment. "How can I believe that, Cass, when it's pretty obvious that you have no idea what it is you do want? You've already admitted that your life is in a mess, that you're not happy with what you have now. So you see, I can't leave you alone until you know for certain if what you want includes me or not."

Chapter 4

THE SUN WAS RISING ON THE NEXT DAY WHEN CASS FINALLY fell across her bed to grab what sleep she could.

She had worked all night—partly from choice and partly because her intimacy with Brendan had made sleep impossible. She was plagued by the memory of his kiss, his touch, and the feel of his body moving against hers. Even worse, she was haunted by the knowledge that she had come so close to welcoming his lovemaking. After he had dropped her off at her home, she had salved her conscience with hard, fast work—the only way out of the mess she was in.

Just before nine the phone beside Cass's bed rang. Still half asleep, she reached for the receiver, dropped it once, and had to fumble around on the floor for it.

"Hello," she finally mumbled. The voice on the other end brought her fully awake. "Ben! Are you in New York? . . . Where? . . . Is Loretta with you? . . . Of course. Do you want to come up here or shall I meet you someplace? . . . Great. Give me half an hour."

In a little less than the alotted time, Cass entered the lobby of the St. Moritz and found her brother Ben and his wife Loretta waiting. They made a striking couple, Cass noted as they rose to meet her, a trace of cynicism tainting her appreciation. Loretta had always been extremely conscious of the fact that her tall, handsome, dark-haired husband made an excellent foil for her pale blond, willowy beauty. And she played her feminine wiles like a virtuoso, dressing in flowing pastels, smiling demurely up into Ben's rugged face, and clinging to his arm as though her survival depended on his support.

Ben ate it up. Cass despised the manipulative tactics.

Cass had also discovered long ago—most often to her frustration and sorrow—that both Loretta's looks and manner were dangerously deceptive. They hid a selfish, mercenary disposition and a will of iron. Life on an isolated ranch, ten years of marriage, and two children had done nothing to soften her, as far as Cass could tell.

"Ben, Loretta. This is certainly a surprise."

Ben caught her awkwardly in a brotherly hug. "Good to see you, Cass."

Loretta, ever mindful of her immaculate grooming, pressed a powdered and perfumed cheek lightly against Cass's, then slid a hard, appraising glance over her sister-in-law.

"Cassie, darling!" she said in feigned concern. "You look simply dreadful! What have you been doing to yourself?"

As tactful as always, Cass thought ironically. She had combed her hair and dabbed on a little makeup before leaving home, but it didn't conceal the pallor of her face or the lines of fatigue. And Ben hadn't given her time to change. She still wore the pinstripe suit from the night before, only now it was creased and pulled out of shape, as though she had slept in it—which she had. Next to Loretta's perfection she looked like a New York bag lady, but she wasn't about to give her sister-in-law the satisfaction of disconcerting her. She dredged up a sweet smile for the older woman's benefit.

"So thoughtful of you to worry about me, Loretta, but don't. I've just been working for my living—as usual. And neither of us is getting any younger."

Age was something Loretta didn't care to think about,

and she was four years older than Cass—thirty-three, the same age as Ben.

Ben felt Loretta stiffen and quickly intervened. "Let's go into the restaurant and have some breakfast."

"When did you get into town?" Cass asked after they had ordered.

"Yesterday evening," Ben replied, a touch of irritation in his voice. "We tried your apartment and got the answering service. I didn't want to just leave a message."

Cass sat back while the waiter put coffee in front of her, and then she slowly stirred in the sugar and cream. She didn't like the feeling she was getting about this sudden trip of theirs. Something more was brewing than Loretta's cup of tea.

"How long can you stay?" she asked probing lightly.

"We'll probably catch a flight back early tomorrow, as a matter of fact," Ben said uncomfortably. "This was just a quick trip. Loretta wanted to do a little shopping, take in a show or two—but we didn't want to go without seeing you, of course."

"Of course," Cass murmured noncommittally. Ben was avoiding her eyes—which wasn't a good sign. This was no little holiday jaunt, not with Loretta looking coiled to spring. "Did you want to see me about something in particular, Ben?" she asked, wanting to get all the cards out on the table.

"Well . . . uh, yes, as a matter of fact."

"Go on," Loretta prompted him impatiently.

"I thought I would tell you in person that the will has gone through probate. You remember Dad's lawyer, Mr. Bennett? Well, he called last week to say that the title to the ranch is clear now. I—I just wanted to make sure that you understood the terms of the will."

Cass listened to him stumbling over his words and the premonition of trouble became stronger. "I thought I did," she said carefully.

"Well, you understand, then," Ben continued, "that the way Dad set it up, you and I own the ranch—the land, livestock, and buildings—jointly. Not a certain portion of the property for you and another for me."

Cass frowned. What was he driving at? "Yes, I understand. We hold all the capital jointly—fifty-fifty, but we divide the profit from the ranch seventy-thirty. That's always seemed fair to me, since you have a family to support and do all the actual running of the ranch." She glanced at him sharply and asked bluntly, "Do you have a problem with that? Do you want a bigger share of the profit?"

"Oh, no! That's not the problem," he said quickly.

"Then what is it, Ben?" She was growing impatient with his hemming and hawing. "Something's bothering you."

Her brother looked to his wife for support, and Loretta gave him an encouraging nod. "Well, we've—*I've* been thinking about it ever since Dad died . . ."

"Thinking about what?"

Even though she had been expecting something unpleasant, it still came as a shock when Ben blurted out: "We . . . I want to sell the ranch."

Loretta picked up the argument before Cass could reply. "Cassie, darling, living here in New York, you can't have any idea what it's like for Ben and me to have nothing to look forward to but years and years of slaving away on the ranch, wasting our youth, with no prospects for the future, no hope of living a—a more *civilized* life." She tried out one of her wistful smiles. "You've been away so long, I'm sure you've forgotten how brutal the winters can be, how hard the work is, and what it's like to have calloused hands and dirt under your nails."

During the pause while the waiter served the food, Cass looked from her own ink-stained fingers to Loretta's soft, white, well-manicured hands, daintily holding her teacup. Their father, Jake Wells, had never begrudged the money for plenty of hired hands to do the bulk of the work, both in the house and out on the ranch. Loretta had never lifted a finger to help out in all the years Cass had known her. Cass would have laughed out loud if the situation weren't so serious.

"You honestly want to sell Wells' Springs, Ben?" Cass asked solemnly, ignoring Loretta's pathetic plea.

"It's been hard with Dad gone," he admitted, looking a little lost. "I've—I've never had to make decisions before."

"But surely Will—"

"Will is only the foreman," Loretta interrupted quickly. "The burden of running the ranch naturally falls on Ben."

She smiled up into her husband's face with such a display of sympathetic concern that if years of experience hadn't taught Cass better, she would have believed that her sister-in-law really cared about something besides her own selfish interests.

"My poor baby," Loretta cooed, "just isn't cut out for that kind of work, is he, Ben?"

Loretta ought to write a book called *Fifty Ways to Undermine a Man's Ego and Make Him Love It,* Cass thought in disgust. Ben must have sensed what she was thinking.

"It's for the kids too," he added defensively. "They would be much better off going to a regular school."

"And Ben won't hear of sending them to boarding school the way other ranchers do," Loretta interrupted with a sigh that barely disguised her impatience. Cass was happy to see that at least Ben had won one battle. "It's been bad enough these past three years with Jacob and those dreadful correspondence courses, but now with Julie starting this fall, Ben and I would be too busy to have a moment to ourselves."

Which translated, Cass thought cynically, into the fact that Loretta was sick and tired of having to teach the children at home and wanted them out of her hair. Cass pushed her food aside untouched and turned to her brother.

"Ben, ranching is all you've ever known. Your college degree is in animal husbandry. If you sold out, where would you go? What would you do?"

Ben ran a nervous hand across his forehead and, as usual, let Loretta speak for him.

"My father would be delighted to give Ben an excellent position in his insurance firm in Salt Lake," she said enthusiastically.

Ben apparently didn't share her enthusiasm. He winced. And Cass knew that the notion of an outdoor man like himself chained to a desk wasn't any more palatable to him than it was to her. Before she could comment on the fact, Loretta checked her watch and laid her hand over Ben's.

"Darling, we have to leave in a minute if I'm going to make my fitting at Bergdorf's. Let's get the paperwork over with, shall we?"

"Paperwork?" Cass asked suspiciously.

"Just a formality," Loretta assured her innocently.

Cass kept her face impassive as her brother drew a folded sheet of paper out of his inside pocket.

"Uh, your signature on this will have to be witnessed to make it legal, Cass, but the hotel has a notary public."

"And just what am I signing?" She asked the question mildly, though her jaw was tight with suppressed emotion.

"Er, your power of attorney, allowing me to act in your behalf on property we hold jointly."

Cass was too angry for a moment to speak. When she finally found her voice, she was amazed at how cool and detached she managed to sound.

"Which legalese boils down to fact that I would be giving you permission to sell the ranch and the right to sign my name. Correct?"

Her seemingly calm acceptance fooled him. "Yes," Ben said in relief. "That's right."

"And do you already have a buyer?"

"Well, no," he admitted. "But I couldn't just put it on the market without telling you."

Not *asking* her or *discussing* it with her, but *telling* her, Cass thought irately. Had they really thought that she would sign away her inheritance so meekly, so unquestioningly? If that was the case, they had badly underestimated her. Neatly she removed the folded paper from Ben's limp hold.

"If there's no buyer, then there's no hurry, is there?" she stated flatly, sticking the paper in her purse. "And since you'll be leaving so soon, I'll take this with me and look it over at my leisure." Her voice became hard. "I don't think it would be wise to put the ranch on the market just yet, Ben—not without my permission. If a buyer should happen to turn up on the doorstep, of course, let me know and we can discuss the matter again."

Her lack of immediate agreement and cooperation took them by surprise. Ben's jaw dropped. Loretta looked as though she would have enjoyed slapping her. Both were at a loss for words. Cass wasn't. It was her turn to check her watch.

"I have to be getting to work, and I wouldn't want to keep you from your appointment," she said sweetly, pushing back her chair, rising to her feet, and throwing a bill on the table for her share of the check. "I probably won't see you before you leave, so have a good trip back. Give my love to the kids and Aggie and Will. And keep in touch. Let me know how everything's going."

Cass didn't look back as she wended her way through the tables. She could imagine the expression on their faces vividly enough. Outside the hotel she caught a taxi and directed the driver downtown to Cassandra's. Leaning back wearily in the seat, she pulled the power of attorney from her bag and read the blanks that Ben and Loretta had so thoughtfully filled in for her. They had, in effect, tried to strip her of any say whatsoever in the sale of the ranch.

Without an ounce of compunction, Cass folded the offensive paper twice and tore it into shreds.

When Cass pushed open the front door of Cassandra's a short while later, she found Dee, Darin, and Janet huddled around the front desk in conference. She paused in the doorway to catch her breath, hitched her bag higher on her shoulder, and wondered what had them all in such a stir.

"You've tried her apartment, Janet?" Darin was asking.

"Every ten minutes since that Mr. Cahill started calling."

Darin frowned. "Well, did he tell you what he wanted?"

"He wanted to talk to Cass."

"I understand that," he said impatiently. "But why?"

The girl was a competent typist and highly decorative receptionist, but she wasn't given to independent thinking—which ordinarily suited Darin's purposes just fine. Not this morning.

"I don't know why," Janet said plaintively. "He wouldn't leave a message."

"Well, let *me* talk to him the next time he calls."

"This isn't like Cass at all," Dee was mumbling through their exchange. "We were supposed to have met with the sewing shop crew at ten. I checked her calendar to see if there was some conflict, but she doesn't have anything else scheduled for today."

Just as Cass was about to speak and obviously put their minds at rest, the phone rang. "Cassandra's House of Interiors . . . Just a moment, please." Janet held out the receiver and whispered, "Darin, it's Brendan Cahill again."

He answered the call with a forced joviality. "Cahill? This is Darin Summerhays. Cass had an early appointment with a client," he improvised glibly, "and apparently it's taking her longer than she expected. Is there anything I can do for you? . . . Of course . . . No, no problem. I'm sure seven will be just fine . . . I'll tell her as soon as she comes in. Good to talk to you again."

"I'm in, Darin," Cass said as he hung up, "so why don't you tell me now."

Darin, Dee, and Janet swung around to find Cass standing just behind them.

"Cass! Where the hell have you been?" Darin's brusqueness didn't hide his very real concern. "We've been looking all over for you."

Cass ran a weary hand over her forehead, aware that her colleagues were watching the play of emotions on her face with a mixture of puzzlement and anxiety.

"Sorry, folks. My brother Ben and his wife called this morning." Quickly and succinctly she explained the gist of the conversation with her family. "You can understand," she finished wryly, "why I didn't think to call in. I'm sorry about the meeting, Dee. We'll make it this afternoon."

"We'll do nothing of the kind," her friend said with her usual good sense. "You look dead on your feet. You're going to go home and go to bed. There's nothing here that can't wait until tomorrow."

For once Darin was in full agreement. One look at her and he ordered with the ruthless candor of long acquaintance: "Go home and get some rest this afternoon, Cass. You look absolutely terrible."

Cass grimaced but couldn't argue with his assessment. She felt terrible. Still, she couldn't afford to give up an entire day. She had too much to do.

"Flattery will get you nowhere, Darin," she drawled. "I

feel fine"—a lie that fooled no one—"and I have work to do. All I need right now is a cup of coffee. I'll make an early night of it tonight."

"Ah . . ." Darin began, not quite able to meet her eye. "I'm afraid not."

"Not which, Darin?" she asked suspiciously. "Work, coffee, or an early night?"

"I'm afraid it's the early night that's the problem." His glance slid to the phone, and Cass's followed.

"Brendan Cahill," she stated resignedly. She might be tired, but she wasn't dense. "What did he want?"

"He's been trying to reach you all morning. He had the peculiar notion that you were avoiding him." Darin noted the sudden ebb and flow of color in Cass's cheeks with a notion of his own—one he didn't like at all. "Were you?"

"I told you where I was," Cass reminded him crossly.

"Uh, right. Anyway, Cahill is taking you to dinner again tonight. He'll pick you up at your apartment at seven."

"I gather that you took the liberty of accepting for me?" Cass asked curtly.

"You know I would never interfere in your personal life, baby," he said dryly, "but Cahill happens to be a client. I was just doing what you asked of me and trusting your good judgment. I don't imagine I have to remind you," he added pointedly, "of a certain promise you made me yesterday concerning clients and your professional detachment."

Ben, Brendan, and Darin. Of the three men involved in her life at the moment, she wasn't sure which one of them angered her most. Unfortunately for Darin, he happened to be the only one within striking distance.

"No, you don't have to remind me! What else did Brendan say?" she snapped.

He frowned at her tone and searched her face with a mixture of suspicion and displeasure. "Only how pleased he was to be working with you. What else would he say?"

"Not a damn thing!"

"That's good, because I told him you would call as soon as you came in."

Cass couldn't think of a suitable reply that would express her annoyance but wouldn't make the situation worse, so she resorted to silence, pivoted on her heel, and started up the steps to the sanctuary of her workroom.

"Cass?" Darin stopped her halfway with a hand on her shoulder, not at all pleased with her attitude.

"Yes?" she answered without turning around.

"You will call Cahill, won't you?"

Cass faced him now, deadly serious. "Don't push me on this, Darin. Don't push me into something we could *both* regret. You have to let me handle it my own way."

Whatever threat her words implied was too oblique for Darin, but his expression became equally serious and the grip on her shoulder unconsciously tightened.

"I don't have a clue to what's going on between you and Cahill, Cass, and frankly, I don't give a damn about how you choose to handle him outside the business relationship. But I'm asking you as your partner and your friend. Please, don't blow this commission because of some personal pique. We need it too badly."

Chapter 5

BRENDAN ARRIVED AT CASS'S DOOR RIGHT ON THE DOT OF
seven.

Earlier, she had compromised on the matter of returning
Brendan's call by confirming the appointment with his
secretary without asking to speak to the man himself. Then
she had taken the first part of Darin and Dee's advice and
had gone home. After a couple of hours bent over the
drawing table in her bedroom, she took the second part of
the advice—to get some rest.

To her surprise, she had actually slept. In fact, she had
overslept, which was why she wasn't quite ready when the
doorbell rang. The night before, she had been waiting
downstairs when Brendan arrived to pick her up. That
night, she pushed the door release and asked him to come
up.

"I assumed that we were going to eat at your apartment
and didn't dress up," Cass said a little defiantly after she had
opened the door and saw the suit and tie he wore.

That night she had changed tactics and was wearing a
pair of faded jeans, a tailored blouse, and a navy

corduroy blazer that had seen better days. Her hair was hanging loose, but before they left, she intended to pull it back with a barrette at the nape of her neck. She had no intention of giving Brendan any unfounded encouragement by dressing up for him.

"Actually, I made reservations at a restaurant," he drawled. "A small detail I would have made clear if you'd returned my call."

"I did return it," she protested lamely.

"Leaving a message with my secretary doesn't count."

Cass resorted to a noncommittal shrug. "So, do you want to wait while I change?"

To her chagrin the blue glance that slid over her was warm with appreciation. "Don't bother. You manage to give even a pair of old jeans class. We'll go someplace where it doesn't make any difference what you wear."

"Whatever you say." She opened the door wider and stood back. "Come on in and sit down. I'll be ready in a minute. I'd offer you something to drink," she added unhospitably, "but all I have is cooking sherry."

Brendan wasn't really listening. The decor of Cass's apartment had captured his attention. "Good lord!" he murmured, almost reverently.

Cass paused on her way to the bedroom. "Is something the matter?"

"Not a thing. It's just not what I expected—your apartment, I mean." Carefully he picked up a black carved Santa Clara pottery bowl from a table. He turned it over and around in his hands before setting it gently back in its place. "I wouldn't have believed it," he said, shaking his head.

"Wouldn't have believed *what?*" she asked in annoyance. She couldn't imagine he was talking about the bowl.

He shot her a quick, puzzled smile. "I wouldn't have believed what you can learn about a person from being in her house for two minutes."

Brendan's observation startled her. Not that he was telling her something she didn't already know—she based her decorating technique on that concept—but having seen the way he lived, Cass wouldn't have expected him to be in the least sensitive to his surroundings. His perception came as an unwelcome surprise, especially since it was applied to her own home. The thought troubled her, and she looked around, trying to see the room objectively through Brendan's eyes.

What she saw was a fairly large living room—once a bedroom in the days when the old four-story brownstone townhouse had belonged to a single-family—with high ceilings, the original wooden moldings, and French doors that opened onto a small balcony that overlooked a tiny enclosed garden.

The structural features, however, obviously didn't interest him nearly as much as what she had done with the space. The room wasn't expensively furnished. She had more love, taste, and imagination than money to put into the decor. The furniture was an eclectic mixture of old and new. The objects and art work that decorated the floor, walls, shelves, and tables represented a variety of cultures, styles, and periods. The hand-woven items were mostly Cass's own work. One entire corner was filled with plants. Another was taken up by Cass's loom and baskets filled with yarn and the fur, leather, feathers, and scraps of fabric that she designed into her patterns. The result was that she had created not a decorator's showcase but a home—a home with the indelible stamp of her personality. The general impression, as far as Cass saw, was one of ordinary, comfortable clutter and familiar, semiordered chaos.

What, she wondered curiously, sliding a glance in Brendan's direction, did it tell him about her? And did he really care? She would have liked to have asked, but prudence kept her silent. In fact, prudence was telling her to get him out of there. Even in a business suit, he looked as though he could be very much at home in this room. The idea was unsettling enough to urge her to forget her hair and go as she was.

"I'm ready when you are," she announced abruptly, grabbing her handbag and portfolio from a table.

"I don't mind waiting," Brendan assured her blandly.

Impatiently Cass switched off the stained-glass chandelier overhead. "Let's go."

Brendan's choice of restaurant was a place called Willie's,

located in a half-basement on West Forty-sixth Street. From the outside it looked like a dive, and the inside wasn't all that much better. A bar with wooden stools took up the center portion of the long, narrow room. Booths with worn leather seats and heavy oak tables lined the two walls. No matter how unpromising it looked, though, Cass didn't make the mistake of assuming that Brendan was going to punish her by feeding her an inferior meal. She had lived in New York long enough to know that the best food turned up in the most unlikely places. And knowing Brendan's hearty appetite, her guess was that this was one of them. She was right.

An hour later she sighed with contentment, pushed aside her plate—sloppy with the remains of the best barbecued spareribs she'd ever eaten—and wiped her greasy fingers on the paper napkin. Her inclination was to linger over coffee and savor the memory of the meal, but her purpose that night wasn't to spend a pleasurable evening in Brendan Cahill's company. She had work to do.

Cass was removing the last spatterings of the barbecue sauce from her face with the moist cloth provided when she caught Brendan watching her with amusement. "What's so funny?" she asked suspiciously.

His smile broadened into an irreverent grin. "I was just thinking. I had originally made reservations for dinner tonight at an exclusive little restaurant across town. This morning I wouldn't have dreamed of bringing you to a place like this. I couldn't have pictured the sophisticated Cassandra Wells digging with gusto into a pile of home fries and eating messy ribs with her fingers."

Carefully Cass arranged the washcloth on the table, refusing to respond to the humor in Brendan's eyes. "So, what changed your mind?"

"Your apartment," he said smugly. "You're a fraud, Cass. You aren't the fastidious, citified person you pretend to be. At heart you're a down-home country girl. I bet you even ate cotton candy at state fairs and still listen to Waylon Jennings while you work." He noted her betraying flush with satisfaction. "Where did you come from, Cass?"

"You're so smart," she snapped. "You tell me."

His reply came with a speed and certainty that startled her. "The West. New Mexico, Arizona, Colorado. Am I right?"

"Close," she admitted grudgingly. "Southern Utah. How did you guess?"

"The Indian dolls, sand paintings, rugs, and pottery were a giveaway. And the collage of photographs you have on your wall—the mountains, the ranch house, the horses and barns. I bet you even came by those Levis honestly—no city chic." He studied her face with even greater interest. "And the picture of the teenager on horseback with the braid down her back. You, right? I would love to see you on a horse."

"Tough luck," she drawled. "In New York, I tend to take taxis."

"I've never seen ranches anywhere but in Texas. Is that ranch still there?"

She would have liked to have stopped his inquisition then, but the time wasn't quite right yet. Brendan was playing right into her hands. Her turn would come. "Yes."

"And the two men I saw in the pictures? Old boyfriends?"

Cass gritted her teeth. "One was my father, the other is my brother."

"Oh. Does it have a name—the ranch, I mean?"

"Wells' Springs," she replied tersely, discouraging now.

Brendan wasn't deterred. "What is it like?" he asked curiously. "I've been to Utah only once, to look over a ski resort. You know, one of those places above Salt Lake City? But I don't think of mountains in connection with southern Utah. More like sagebrush and desert."

Cass hadn't expected to become so upset by his question, but her conversation with Ben that morning had shaken her more than she realized. She couldn't believe her brother would really consider selling the ranch. Her mouth tightened against a sudden wave of nostalgia for her home. The subject of Wells' Springs was much too touchy just then to discuss with Brendan, even in this impersonal way.

"If I'd known you were so interested," she said tartly, "I'd have brought along a couple of picture books so that you could have a look for yourself."

"I'd rather hear about it from you."

"Sorry, I'm not a travel agent."

"Then I'll just have to have another look at your apartment. So informative."

That was the lead-in Cass had been waiting for. "I'm so pleased that you understand how much you can tell from seeing a person's home. That's going to make my job a lot easier."

Brendan didn't care for her little satisfied smile. "What exactly does that mean?"

"Just what I told you last night: that I can't design a room without knowing a good deal about my client. I'm sure you'll want to hear what *your* apartment told me about *you*."

He shrugged. "You didn't need to see my apartment. You could have found out anything you wanted to know in *Who's Who in Business and—*"

"Oh, I'm not talking about statistics or cold facts about your rise to power with Monarch Enterprises," she interrupted. "You didn't hire Cassandra's to redo your offices. You hired us to redecorate your home. Therefore, what I was interested in was the *personal* you."

He watched in puzzlement as she delved into the portfolio and pulled out a sheaf of papers. "What are those?" he asked.

"These are the renderings for the redesign of your apartment, Brendan. I've finished everything but the bathroom that connects with the master bedroom. I'll need to have a good look at it first."

To her relief, he didn't mention the incident on the bed that had interrupted their tour of inspection the night before. But Cass herself had to stifle the sudden surge of blood through her veins at the thought of those moments she had spent in his arms. It would be a long time before she could remember the experience without feeling torn apart by contradictory emotions—pleasure, desire, guilt, regret.

She peeked at him from under her lashes and saw that, fortunately, his attention at the moment was focused not on her but on the papers she held in her hand. Better still, he was frowning, and the knowledge that she had caught *him* off guard for a change calmed her.

"Those can't be the renderings, Cass," he objected. "You haven't had time to finish the whole place so soon."

"You inspired me," Cass returned dryly, mimicking his own response of the evening before.

Brendan was patently displeased by this turn of events, and Cass wasn't surprised. Once she knew that he didn't give a hoot about what his apartment looked like, it hadn't taken much perception on her part to figure out that his plan was to stretch out these preliminary meetings with her for days, if not weeks. He hadn't counted, however, on Cass's determination to finish the job with the greatest possible speed.

Cass stifled a victorious smile. She couldn't imagine that many people were able to beat the inimitable Brendan Cahill at his own game. But she had. The scowl on his face made the wear and tear on her nerves and the loss of a night's sleep well worth the effort, the victory all that much sweeter. What was more, she thought in satisfaction, she knew that even under such pressure she had turned out some of the best designs of her career.

"Let me see them," Brendan demanded in disbelief.

Cass deliberately moved the drawings out of his reach. He would see them, all right, but first she had to make sure he didn't give her an argument about her concept.

"Not just yet, Brendan. First I have to tell you what there was about your apartment that helped me reach certain design decisions."

He paused a moment, shrugged, and then bent his head to light a cigarette with his gold lighter. When he finished, he leaned his head against the back of the leather booth and gazed at her from under his thick lashes.

"All right, Cass. Let's have it."

Cass was prepared to enjoy the next few minutes. She'd had a lot of time in the early hours of the morning to consider carefully what she would say to him on this occasion. She hadn't liked being questioned by him earlier about her own apartment, but she had let him do so, because now he would have a hard time objecting to the validity of her own assessment.

"I told you last night," she began, "that I could tell you don't really care what your place looks like as long as it serves its purpose. It isn't *home* to you in the way that most people use the word. It's merely a place you inhabit now and then as the occasion demands. You care about the apartment about as much as you would a hotel room. The furnishings throughout are functional but totally nondescript and uninteresting, the atmosphere is sterile, and the entire place lacks any vestige of your own personality."

"So?" he asked as she stopped for a breath, his eyes still hooded.

"*So,* here's what all that tells me about you."

Casually he knocked the ashes off the end of his cigarette. "Carry on. I'm fascinated to hear."

"It tells me that you're a man who doesn't want to be tied down—either to one place or to one person. It tells me that you don't want to be encumbered by anything that might possibly resurrect any memories—either good or bad. Which means you don't dwell on the past but live entirely in the present and for the future." She studied him thoughtfully for a moment. "I would guess that this has a lot to do with the nature of your business, but that to a lesser extent it's the result of a bad marriage or an unhappy relationship with a woman. Not a recent one, though—something that happened so long ago that the wounds are well scarred over. Currently, I have no doubt that you have more than your share of affairs," she continued dryly, "but no woman has ever lived in that apartment with you for very long. If one ever has, you've managed to obliterate any traces." It was her turn to lean back in the booth, searching his face for signs that she had broken through his complacency. "Well?" she asked impatiently when she found none. "How am I doing?"

"Not bad. Not bad at all. I would be happier, though," he suggested flippantly, "if you would add that I'm good with children and kind to animals."

"Unfortunately, I didn't find any sign of either," Cass muttered crossly. "They might have had a humanizing effect on the place."

Brendan stubbed out his cigarette. A smile slowly curved his lips until it broadened into a grin and a flash of white teeth. A deep chuckle welled up out of the depths of his broad chest.

To Cass's dismay she saw that not only had she failed to disconcert him, she had succeeded in amusing him. Even worse, what she read in the lines of his rugged, expressive face wasn't the anger or chagrin she had expected but—of all things—admiration! It couldn't be directed at her! She peered through his dark lashes, and the glinting blue eyes confirmed the worst. It was!

His unexpected reaction, the warmth in his eyes, the teasing twist of his smile—they were having the strangest effect on her. Her heart began to pound and her breath caught in her throat.

"Oh, Cass, Cass, me love," Brendan crooned, his Irish lilt exaggerated for her benefit, "was there ever a woman like ye?"

"You—you aren't angry?" she asked weakly.

"How could I be angry when that was as accurate and perceptive an analysis as I could imagine? What's more," he added sardonically, "I don't know a single person who would have had the nerve to tell me all that to my face."

"I only told you what I saw," she said defensively.

"What you saw—and guessed, of course."

"You just admitted that I was right," she countered.

"Do you hear me denying any of it?"

"Well . . . no."

His smile turned wry. "The early marriage, for example. That was a very astute deduction. Only I don't admit to any scars, and it wasn't so much a bad marriage, really, as a mistake—the marrying-your-childhood-sweetheart-right-out-of-high-school kind. Jill realized it before I did and ran off with the drummer in a rock band."

"And were you . . . bitter?" Cass couldn't resist asking.

To her surprise, Brendan laughed at the idea. "Bitter? Hardly a day goes by that I don't give thanks for her up and leaving." He smiled in amusement at the disbelief on Cass's face. "I mean it. I'm not sure that I'd be where I am today if it hadn't been for Jill's . . . ah, defection. Oh, I was ambitious enough, even at twenty, but I didn't have any clear idea where I was heading."

"So? What did her leaving have to do with your ambitions?"

"I have to go back to *before* she left me."

He spoke with cool detachment, as though he were telling someone else's story. Cass found it chilling.

"When we were first married we took out a mortgage on an old run-down house in Baltimore, where I had a job with a housing contractor. Weekdays I built houses for him and weekends and holidays I spent my time renovating our own house. I didn't recognize the symptoms but, but I was already well on my way to becoming a workaholic—which makes Jill's boredom with me and the tedious life I had her mired in very understandable." His lips twisted in a smile that mocked himself. "Under the circumstances, I'm sure you can imagine the attraction of a free-and-easy-going musician."

Of course, he had been little more than a boy then, but looking now at the man Brendan had become and feeling the strength and charisma of his personality, Cass found it almost impossible to believe that a wife of his could have found *any* man more attractive. These traitorous thoughts, however, she wisely kept to herself.

"Am I boring you?" he asked when he noted that her attention had wandered.

"No, of course not. Go on. What happened?"

"Well, with my wife gone, I took a good look at the ten-room house I had spent my time renovating and wondered what I was going to do with it, rattling around in a big old place like that all by myself. So I decided to get rid of it. Much to my surprise . . . Did I mention I was very naïve at twenty?"

"I can't believe you were naïve at seven," Cass commented, half under her breath.

"Well, I was. About business, anyway," he amended in response to her skeptical sniff. "No one was more surprised than I was when the house sold for four times what I had originally paid for it."

"So surprised," she observed dryly, beginning to understand where these revelations were leading, "that you decided to buy another old run-down house and try again— just to see if the first time had been sheer luck, of course."

"Well, no."

"You *didn't* buy another one?"

He grinned. "Not just one. Three. I told you, I was

ambitious, and with Jill out of the picture, I had no responsibility to anyone but myself. So I quit my job, worked on my houses full time, and within a year sold all three at enough profit to start my own contracting business."

"A shame you didn't drive poor old Jill off even sooner," Cass suggested caustically. His casual attitude toward his neglected wife and broken marriage had irrationally annoyed her, and the tension between them began to build.

"Now, why didn't *I* think of that?" he asked, shaking his head in mock chagrin. "I guess it was just as I said. I was too naïve."

Cass's annoyance began to turn to anger. "Just think, if you hadn't had a wife tying you down, you could have made your first million at twenty instead of having to wait until you were nearly twenty-three."

"You're absolutely right," he agreed with seeming regret. "I can hardly bear to think of all those wasted years."

His flippancy infuriated her. "You've explained so much, Brendan," she bit out. "No wonder you look upon people and places as disposable as . . . as paper towels! That's how you made your fortune."

"My *first* fortune," he corrected her, unmoved by her sarcasm.

"Temporary relationships and short-term housing—dump either when it's served its purpose. Do you realize how callous you sound?"

"Success in business doesn't help a person win votes in popularity contests," he drawled. "And I'm only callous about some people and some property."

Before she realized his intention, he had leaned across the narrow table, picked up her hand, and pressed his mouth against the rapid pulse in her wrist. As his tongue traced the pounding blue vein upward, her heart caught in her throat, her breathing stopped, and a shock of tingling excitement surged along her nerves. Anger drained out, replaced by a painful, forbidden pleasure.

"I've never been callous where you're concerned, Cass," Brendan murmured against the soft, vulnerable skin of her inner arm. "Let me make love to you and I'll show you just how sensitive I can be."

At the moment Cass was in no position—either mental or physical—to argue with him. Quickly she pulled her arm away before he felt the betraying quiver of response that ran through her. She could have saved herself the bother. One look at his face told her that he knew exactly what he was doing to her. She bit her lip to stop its trembling.

"Do you know what I think of you, Brendan?" she asked when she had regained some measure of control.

"No," he said wryly, "but I'll bet you're about to tell me."

"You're right! I think you're utterly ruthless and completely unscrupulous when it comes to getting what you want."

"Ah, ruthless I'll admit to, Cass, but never unscrupulous." His gaze lingered on her slender neck, watched the rising color there, and he smiled lazily. "And making snap decisions is the secret of my success. When I decide I want something, I go for it. Like I wanted you. Remember?"

The color flooded into her cheeks. She remembered all too well her initial reaction to him and cursed herself for not getting rid of him the minute she laid eyes on him. But how was she to know that he was going to disrupt her entire life?

"Don't you *ever* consider other people's feelings before you barge ahead like a . . . a steamroller?" she asked tartly.

"It depends on whose feelings we're talking about," he answered mildly. "I believe I understand yours better than you do yourself."

"Oh, you're impossible! You're graceless, insensitive, outspoken to a fault . . ."

"Which boils down to the fact that I've been nothing but honest with you. I never lie to a woman, Cass. Is it my fault that you can't handle the truth?"

"You're arrogant, self-centered, overbearing, ill-mannered . . ."

"You learned all this from one look at my apartment?" he teased.

". . . and you're driving me crazy!" she concluded in frustration, dropping her head into her hands. "Why, oh, why, can't you just leave me alone?"

The very real desperation in her voice sobered him. "You really meant it, then."

"Meant what?" she asked wearily.

"What you said last night, that becoming involved with me would be a . . . complication?"

"Yes, I meant it!"

He couldn't doubt the sincerity of her reply. "But you also told me," he continued slowly, "that I would be a terrific escape."

"A *temporary* escape," she corrected him bitterly.

"I have to admit," he said slowly, "that I've never thought of myself as means of escape before—unless someone has financial problems they want me to solve, of course." He paused to study her expressive face, and his own grew more thoughtful. "Are you sure that even a temporary escape wouldn't help you get through whatever's eating at you now?" he asked softly.

The offer he was making certainly wasn't subtle, but it was tempting nevertheless—mainly because she could hear the compassion and genuine concern in his voice, as though he cared about her as a person, which she didn't know was true or not. What a strange, unpredictable man he was. She would never figure him out.

"Not—not the kind of escape you're offering me," she said, more uncertainly than she would have liked. "I told you, it wouldn't solve my problems."

"What problems?" he asked coaxingly. "You've already told me that it isn't another man."

For one insane moment, Cass was tempted to tell him. After all, Brendan was a businessman himself. Her intuition, however, told her that he wouldn't understand what the pressures of her work were doing to her. He was a man who thrived on pressure.

"Well, Cass? What is it?"

"You wouldn't understand," she said flatly.

His mouth thinned into a line of displeasure. "So where does that leave us?"

"That's up to you, Brendan," she said soberly. "Now that you know how I feel, do you want to call it quits and forget about redecorating your apartment?"

"Do you?" he asked harshly.

"I can't!" she blurted out.

His eyes narrowed. "What do you mean, you can't?"

She hesitated and then told him the truth. "I—I promised Darin that I wouldn't refuse to work with a client because of any personal reasons," she said bluntly. "Which means that unless *you* change your mind, we go ahead with the redecoration."

"And like it or not, you're stuck with me?"

"As a *client*—yes," she admitted.

"But that isn't how you see me, is it, Cass?" he asked softly.

"I—I don't have to answer that."

Their glances met and held until they nearly became a tangible link between them. Cass felt the stirrings of an unfamiliar emotion in her chest—as though she wanted to laugh and cry at the same time. What was worse, in her heart, Cass knew that she didn't want her relationship with Brendan to end like this. Escape or not, he had suddenly become essential to her happiness.

What she was feeling must have shown on her face for Brendan to see. A peculiar, unsettling expression came and went in his eyes, too fast for Cass to put a name to. "Never mind, sweetheart," he said gently. "I already know the answer."

"So what do you say, Brendan?" she asked uneasily. "Do we pack it all in?"

The familiar, cynical smile slanted his mouth and brow. "You know better than that, Cass. I haven't arrived where I am by betting my time and money only on a sure thing. I'll take my chances with you."

"Some chance," she challenged him, "when you're not even giving me even odds. I've already told you why I can't just walk away from the whole thing."

"You're right, Cass," he agreed thoughtfully. "We'll even things out. I promise that while you work, I won't take any unfair advantage of the situation—no harassment, no pestering, no . . . undue persuasion."

She studied his face suspiciously, wondering if she could trust him to keep his word, wondering—traitorously—if she really wanted him to. He read the doubt in her face but, fortunately, not the whole cause for it.

"I told you," he said solemnly, "I never lie to a woman about my relationship with her—especially one I admire and respect."

Her heart leaped at his words and she believed him. She had assaulted his character earlier in the most scathing terms, but never once, not even in the heat of the moment, had she ever considered accusing him of deceit, hypocrisy, or dishonesty.

"What happens if you lose?" she asked curiously.

"If I do, I guess I'll just have to learn to cope with disappointment, won't I?" His rugged face broke into a grin, and a particularly warm light brightened his eyes. "You might even think that that would be good for my soul."

His grin was infectious, and for the first time in their relationship, an answering smile of uncomplicated amusement curved her lips. "Do you know, this is silly, Brendan. Anyone listening to us would think we were discussing a chess match!"

Brendan watched the smile transform Cass's entire expression. The change he saw in her was not just startling, it was breathtaking. A rush of color glowed under the tan in his cheeks, beads of perspiration formed on his forehead, and his hands shook slightly as he lit another cigarette.

"They'd be wrong, wouldn't they?" he murmured. "This is definitely no game—at least not one I've ever played before."

Cass frowned at the enigmatic words and the sudden strain in his voice. "Is something wrong?"

"I hope not. Now, let's get to work, shall we?"

Puzzled by his quick change of mood, she reached for the stack of renderings on the seat beside her and spread them out on the table. "Here we go, then."

"You can say that again," he muttered.

Chapter 6

"DAMMIT, DEE," CASS MUTTERED IN DISGUST, HAVING TO restrain herself from throwing the bolt of drapery fabric across the room. "This just isn't what I ordered. The texture is different, and look at the purple cast in the green when the light hits a fold. This would be simply ghastly with the yellow walls. How much work have you done with it already?"

"We have four panels finished," Dee told her reluctantly.

"I guess we'll find a use for them somewhere." Cass sighed. "But the rest of the bolt goes back and we hold up on the job until we get the right material."

"This company manufactures in California. It'll put us three or four weeks behind schedule."

"It can't be helped."

Cass ran a weary hand across her eyes. What an absolutely dreadful morning. It seemed like two months instead of two weeks since she had last seen Brendan. The day after he had approved her renderings, he left for the midwest, hopping from one city to the other. She would never have believed it, but she missed him terribly. He was supposed to have returned the previous night, and she had half expected him to call. . . .

". . . painters haven't started yet," Dee was saying. "If you changed the walls to a—"

"I don't have the time to change the color palette of the entire room just to match the drapes," Cass interrupted sharply. She saw the surprise and hurt on her friend's face and apologized. "I'm sorry, Dee. I didn't mean to snap. But I simply cannot use purple. It's the one color Mason Trent absolutely detests."

"So what do you want to do?" Dee asked carefully.

"Give the manufacturer a call, will you, please? With any luck they may have the right fabric in stock and could send it out express. Let me know as soon as you find out anything. I'll be in my workroom."

"Cass?" Darin stood lying in wait for her at the bottom of the stairs. "Would you come into my office a minute, please?"

"What is it now, Darin?" she asked resignedly, following him down the hall. She recognized that plaintive tone of voice and could have done without it just then.

"The new seamstress," Darin said tersely after he had slammed the door behind them.

Cass noted his irritation with bewilderment. Hiring help for the sewing room was Dee's responsibility, and another seamstress had been Darin's suggestion in the first place. "What's wrong with her? She's had years of experience, and Dee's absolutely delighted with her work . . ."

"That's the problem," he cut her off. "Do you have any idea how much we're *paying* for those years of experience?"

Cass saw the light. The demon money was rearing its ugly head again. How much longer was she going to be able to endure the increasingly frequent arguments with Darin over their financial problems? How many mornings like this was she going to be able to live through? She was suddenly assailed by an overwhelming impulse to end it all then, that moment, to state flatly: "I've had it, Darin. I'm quitting, selling out, going back to Utah." She even got as far as opening her mouth, but the words wouldn't come. Her mouth snapped shut on a troubling thought. How much did

Brendan have to do with her reluctance to leave New York just then?

"Surely Dee could have found someone cheaper," Darin continued to grumble.

"Darin," Cass said with what little patience she had left, "you can't just pick some girl off the street, pay her minimum wage, and train her overnight to tailor drapes and slipcovers. Dee found us a woman who is not only competent but fast. We'll save money in the long run."

"That remains to be seen," he continued pessimistically. "And I also want to speak to you about Janet. She came in this morning asking for a raise."

Cass had had enough. She checked her watch and made a move for the door. She had to escape, no matter how much it would inflame Darin.

"I'm sorry, Darin, but I can't talk about it now. Brendan is just back from St. Louis, and I have to meet him in his apartment. The construction work is finished and the painters start this afternoon."

Well, most of it was true anyway, she told herself to appease her conscience as she grabbed her purse from her office and gave Janet the number where she could be reached in an emergency—but only in an emergency, she warned the girl grimly, like death, fire, or an outbreak of bubonic plague.

Ten minutes later Cass left the taxi at the front of Brendan's building, took the elevator to Monarch Enterprises, and walked up the broad, carpeted steps from the twenty-fifth floor to his private office above.

"Good morning, Edith," Cass politely greeted the secretary as she entered the foyer. The middle-aged, gray-haired dragon who guarded the entrance to Brendan's inner sanctum raised her cold, fishy gaze from the typewriter and turned it in Cass's direction.

"*Now* what do you want?"

Over the past two weeks, as Cass checked the progress of the workmen, she had talked with Brendan's secretary now and then. In that time she had discovered that Edith's public manner—the grim mouth, stony face, and acerbic tongue—were indeed the outward manifestations of the inner person —a grim soul, stony heart, and acerbic disposition.

How Brendan put up with her Cass didn't know, but she supposed that the woman must have some stellar qualities undetectable on short acquaintance—efficiency, loyalty, discretion. It had been in a shrewder moment that Cass had decided that Edith's greatest asset to Brendan lay in the fact that she had all the emotions of a block of marble and was unlikely ever to pose a threat in terms of human problems.

"Is Mr. Cahill back?" Cass inquired sweetly.

"He's next door," the secretary snapped, turning back to her typewriter. "Impossible to get anything done with all that pounding and sawing going on last week," she muttered. "Workmen coming and going. If Mr. Cahill had been here . . ."

Gratefully Cass left her to her muttering and slipped through the double glass doors to Brendan's apartment. Inside, she closed her eyes for just a moment and breathed deeply to still the sudden fluttering of her heart. When she opened them again, she looked around and found Brendan bending over the two steps leading to the dining area, his coat and tie off and his sleeves rolled up as he examined the carpentry work the painters were to attack that afternoon.

"Well? Does it pass inspection?" Cass asked.

Brendan spun around, a smile banishing the fatigue and frown of concentration. "Cass!"

"I—I just thought I'd stop in and see how things were going," she said breathlessly.

"The carpenters left a few minutes ago . . ." he began, then stopped abruptly. "Good lord! You look as if you've been dragged through a wringer."

Cass grimaced wryly. "Thanks a lot. Just what I needed to hear."

He might find something lacking in her appearance, but his eyes were still warm with appreciation. "I warned you that I offer the unvarnished truth."

"I'm even prepared to endure that for a few moments peace right now," she told him ruefully.

"Ahhhh," he said, enlightened. "Escape."

"Well, sanctuary, anyway." Cass sighed as she collapsed onto a metal folding chair. At the moment she would have preferred the comfort of one of the apartment's original couches, but refugees couldn't afford to be choosy, and the room had been stripped bare before the construction began.

"Being hounded, are you?" Brendan teased. "Clients? Creditors? Process servers? IRS? Feds?"

Cass smiled, as he had undoubtedly intended she should. "Nothing quite so spectacular. I must confess that it was being *niggled* to death that brought me crawling cravenly to your doorstep."

He bowed elegantly and pulled up a chair beside her. "I assure you, my humble doorstep is honored. And I'm delighted to see you," he added softly, capturing her small hand between his broad palms.

Brendan hadn't intended his touch to arouse her, but it did. It was as though Cass could feel his enormous energy flowing from his hands to hers, and the feeling was both pleasurable and sustaining. Her fingers tightened responsively on his until she realized what she was doing and doubted the wisdom of leaving her hand where it was any longer.

"Brendan . . ."

With a quick squeeze he loosened his hold and dispelled what could have become a tense moment. He was more sensitive to her shift in moods, Cass realized, than she would ever have imagined.

"So what's been niggling at you?" he asked.

She would have loved to confide in him seriously, but she had no conviction that his interest in her extended to faulty wiring, broken air conditioners, seamstresses out with the flu, Mason Trent's purple drapes, and Darin's dire predictions of falling profits.

She stood abruptly, took a restless turn around the room, and distilled a terrible morning into a truthful, if flippant, "Nothing and everything. Just your average, mundane Monday morning business disasters. I don't mean to bother you with my problems. They're stupid, really."

She didn't realize that he was standing behind her until he took her by the shoulders and turned her to face him. He smiled down into her eyes.

"I've been in business a lot longer than you, Cass. Do you think I haven't learned that an accumulation of little disasters is a whole lot harder to cope with than one big catastrophe? A big one starts the adrenaline pumping until the problem is solved. Little ones just wear away at you like water dripping on stone."

She liked his analogy, even if it didn't solve all those little disasters. "I haven't been much of a rock lately," she told him ruefully, "and it seems as though *I'm* the one who's always getting wet."

"And here I would have sworn from experience that you were three-fourths granite," he said, only half teasing this time.

"More like clay, ready to crumble at the first touch."

Hers was a more unfortunate analogy, she realized. Brendan's hold on her shoulders tightened slightly, as though he were putting it to the test. "Definitely not clay," he murmured before slackening his hold. "You'll do."

"Do what?" she asked stupidly as his thumbs began defining little circles on her collar bones.

There was a pause before he replied, "Survive."

Cass's intuition told her that this was not what he had wanted to say, but prudence kept her from pushing him. There was already an added warmth in his eyes, a deeper note in his voice, a caressing quality to his moving hands on her shoulders. Altogether, this assault on her senses was having a dangerous effect on Cass. Her breathing was becoming more erratic by the moment, a slow flush bloomed in her cheeks, and her thoughts were growing increasingly incoherent as she searched for a response—any response.

"And—and here I haven't even asked you about your trip," she managed. "Was it successful?"

"Very."

"That's good."

"Mmmm."

His attention was riveted on Cass's face. Her frazzled air had been dispelled, and her eyes on his were more dazed now than glazed. The lines in her forehead had vanished, the set to her jaw had loosened, and the tightness around her mouth had eased, leaving her lips soft, slightly trembling, and vulnerable. Brendan drew a ragged breath.

"I missed you while I was away," he murmured.

"I thought you might call last night when you got in. Just to see how the work was going, of course."

"Of course."

"You didn't call."

"I intended to, but by the time I got into town, it was too late." His gaze became more intense, until all she could see was the deep blue of his eyes. "Do you know, Cass, I can't count the times I picked up the phone the past week to call you."

"Why—why didn't you?" she breathed.

"I didn't want you to think that I was pestering you."

"I wouldn't have."

"I couldn't know that, could I?"

"No."

"Should I have called?"

"I would have liked that."

"Did you miss me?"

"Sometimes."

Their words were simple and direct. What their eyes were saying to each other was much more complicated and enigmatic. After a moment of this silent communication, Brendan asked softly, "Would you construe a welcome-home kiss as harassment?"

"No," she confessed.

All this time Brendan had kept his hands on Cass's shoulders. Now he moved them to her waist and around to her back, to draw her near. As her breasts touched his chest, his muscles tensed, his arms tightened, and he pulled her hard against him. Cass waited nervously, even expectantly, for his kiss, while Brendan took a moment to appreciate the sight she presented—the taut line of her neck as she tilted her head up to his, her half-lowered eyelids, her slightly parted lips. The blue of his eyes deepened as her soft breath fanned his cheeks. The delay had brought a rush of color to her face, adding to her beauty. He couldn't wait any longer.

His arms held her with conviction, but his lips sought hers far more tentatively, as though he feared that the new, fragile affinity between them might shatter at the touch. He kissed her gently, tenderly, first at each corner of her mouth and then full on her soft lips. It was all over in a moment.

He had not attempted to arouse her or ask for anything in return. In fact, he had given her little time to respond to the kiss at all.

"You see," he said, raising his head. "No undue persuasion."

His voice was husky, and Cass could have sworn that his hand trembled slightly as he pushed a lock of her hair behind one ear.

"No undue persuasion," she repeated, struggling to overcome her own trembling weakness. She had never known that such a gentle kiss could create such havoc.

A lopsided smile tugged briefly at his lips as he said teasingly, "I must be tired. I didn't get much sleep last night."

A vivid image appeared in Cass's wayward mind—Brendan lying asleep, sprawled across the waterbed down the hall. Did he sleep in the nude? She drew a sudden breath at the idea, and as Brendan continued to hold her lightly in his arms, she found to her dismay that her own imaginings and his soft, tentative embrace had left her feeling anxious, dissatisfied, even deprived. She badly wanted more—a deeper, lingering kiss. She wanted to give as well as take.

The impulse was too strong for Cass to resist. Her fingers slipped from his broad back to the strong column of his neck and upward to entwine themselves in his thick, dark hair. Brendan felt the tug downward and understood the unspoken message. For the moment of a heartbeat he hesitated. Then his lips claimed hers again, and there was nothing tentative, gentle, or tender in this kiss. It was filled with a pent-up hunger, as though he had been starving for her touch. She could feel his solid body quivering against hers as his tongue sought and found the moist warmth of her mouth. Her own body answered. Her tongue dueled with his, and she pressed herself harder and harder against him, exalting in the feel and taste of his passion.

"Cass, Cass . . ." He groaned into her open mouth. "What are you trying to do to me?"

His words brought her to her senses. With a sudden movement, she jerked her head away and pressed her face into the curve of his neck. For several minutes he held her like that, stiffly, not speaking, not moving.

As their pulses slowed and their breathing returned to normal, Brendan's taut embrace gradually relaxed and Cass slipped out of his arms. She had to move away from him before she did something insane—such as begging him to make love to her. She felt like a fool—or worse, a tease. She was the one who had demanded professional detachment from him, and yet she was the one who had nearly precipitated a crisis.

Brendan waited, silent and tense, while she wandered around the room, forcing her attention on the work in progress, concentrating on the construction from a safe distance. When she finally turned back to him, an impersonal smile was planted on her mouth.

"Well?" she asked brightly, as though the moment of shared intimacy had never happened. "How do you think things are coming along?"

"Much, much faster than I had expected," he murmured, as much to himself as to her.

Cass didn't make the mistake of thinking he was commenting on the redecoration. She tried again. "But you're satisfied?"

Another unfortunate choice of words. Brendan stared at her in disbelief. "You've got to be kidding!"

"I'm—I'm sorry," she muttered in embarrassment.

"In this case," he said curtly, "I'll accept the apology. I think I had one coming."

The tension in his voice did nothing to still the chaos inside her. Cass hurried to retrieve some sense of normality by retreating behind the safe wall of her business purpose there. She would speak her piece and get out of the apartment and away from Brendan—fast.

"Well," she summed up crisply, "I would say that everything is right on schedule. The construction is completed, the painters should be here soon, and the tile people are scheduled for the first of next week. I'll be back to check on progress then." She glanced at her watch and made her move toward the door without looking back at him. "My goodness! It's much later than I thought. Nearly noon. I'd better let you get back to work."

"Cass?" Brendan stopped her as she had her hand on the doorknob.

"Yes?" she asked without turning around. As she felt him approach from behind, she fought the mad impulse to seek the protection of the dragon Edith on the other side of the door.

"Have lunch with me."

Her first impulse was to refuse. But she hesitated, and the hesitation was her undoing. Inclination battled with self-preservation, and inclination won the upper hand. She salved her conscience by giving him neither a yes or a no. "I don't have much time."

He neatly overcame that objection. "There's a little French restaurant just down the street. They keep a table for me, so we won't have to wait."

She turned slowly to face him, and the smile that accompanied his words melted away any further resistance. "All right," she found herself saying.

Once they were settled at their table, she was glad she had come. The tension between them had slowly dissipated until they were back on a casual footing.

As usual, Brendan took his food seriously, and as before, he set out to make the experience of eating the meal as pleasant and restful as possible, entertaining her with stories of some of the more interesting characters he had met up with in his travels. By the time Cass finished the hors d'oeuvres and her first glass of wine, she was relaxed and thoroughly enjoying his company. By the time she finished the veal Oscar and her second glass of wine, she had nearly convinced herself that there was no reason to be worried about the kisses she and Brendan had exchanged. She had undoubtedly read far more into their encounter than had really been there.

"What are you up to this afternoon?" Brendan asked as, by mutual agreement, they lingered over their coffee.

"Working for you, as a matter of fact."

"Am I a tyrant?" he asked innocently.

She smiled. "Oh, you have your moments, but today isn't one of them. You're sending me on a couple of very pleasant errands. I'm going out to spend some more of your money."

"Considering the size of the first bill I got from Summerhays," he observed dryly, "I expect whatever it is you're buying to be solid gold and encrusted with diamonds."

"Not quite that," she drawled, "but wait until you see the living room. I found an artist who does the most marvelous work with mosaic tiling."

"I can't wait to see what that's going to cost me!"

"I did warn you," she reminded him unsympathetically, "that redecorating that place wasn't going to be cheap, especially when there was hardly a stick of furniture worth keeping. What did you do with all that ghastly living-room stuff anyway?"

"Gave it to a home for the elderly, and I'll have you know they were delighted to get it."

"Poor dears." She sighed. "I would have thought their lives would have been dreary enough without adding those awful things."

Brendan grimaced. "You are merciless, aren't you?"

Cass gave him a mischievous smile and paraphrased ironically, "I never lie about my reaction to furniture, Brendan—especially to a man I often admire and sometimes even respect."

She had intended it as a joke, but Brendan seemed to take her words seriously. Suddenly he was staring at her in the oddest way. The vein near the scar at his temple was pulsing, his jaw was set and tense, and his big hands gripped his coffee mug so hard that his knuckles were white. His silent regard began to unnerve her.

"Did I offend you?" she asked uncomfortably in the mounting tension. "If I did, I'm sorry. I was only joking."

"Were you?"

She didn't know what to say, but then, Brendan didn't seem to expect an answer. He had transferred his gaze to the coffee in the bottom of his cup. The air between them became painfully charged. Cass stared helplessly at the top of his head until he finally looked up at her, the genuinely cynical smile she had come to both dislike and mistrust fixed firmly in place.

"Shall we go?" he asked with chilly politeness, the companionship they had shared over lunch swept away by those words as though it had never existed. Without waiting for an answer, he peeled several bills off a roll, tossed them negligently on the table, and stood to pull back her chair. "I have to get back to the office, and I know you have work to do."

"Right," Cass replied stiffly.

She rose and preceded him out into the small foyer, filled now with people waiting for tables. As Cass worked her way through the crowd to the door, she could feel Brendan close behind her, his breath fanning the top of her head. Once outside, he caught her by the shoulders and turned her to face him. His eyes, a deep, dangerous blue-black, whipped once over her face before he pulled her tightly against his chest and pressed a hard, punishing kiss against her parted lips.

"What was that for?" she asked shakily when he finally raised his head.

"You figure it out," he said coldly and cryptically. "Let me know when you come up with the answer." He pushed her away from him as though her touch was repulsive and drove the final icicle into her heart with an indifferent, "See you around, Cass."

No smile accompanied his words. Not even a wave of the hand. He simply turned on his heel and strode off down the street toward his office without a backward glance, leaving Cass standing on the sidewalk watching his retreating figure, as stunned as she was affronted and deeply hurt.

The next few days were grimmer than any Cass remembered in her working life. Dee had succumbed to the flu that had infected half the staff, and nothing seemed to be getting done in her absence. The air conditioning kept going on the blink, Darin took on two more clients without consulting her, and a water pipe burst in the storage room, ruining several bolts of fabric.

But with all these calamities at hand, one thought obsessed her. She had not heard another word from Brendan.

What was he trying to do to her? she wondered a dozen times a day. Had he written her off as a lost cause? Was he punishing her in his own devious way? If so, for what? She had gone over their conversation in the restaurant syllable by syllable and couldn't find an explanation.

She finally reached the conclusion that speculation was useless. There *was* no logical explanation. In fact, nothing *about* Brendan was logical.

In the short time she had known him, she had seen so many conflicting facets of his personality: Brendan hard and unyielding; gentle, tender, and concerned; teasing, amusing, and witty; cynical and ironic. Brendan passionate and sensitive one minute, then brusque and totally unfeeling the next. She was at a point where she could no longer judge whether what she had seen at any given moment was genuine or whether he had simply donned a different persona to suit whatever the particular situation, mood, or companion demanded. She would never, she concluded, penetrate the complexities of his mind.

But that didn't stop her from jumping every time the phone rang, half praying, half dreading the thought that it might be Brendan. It never was. Twice she picked up the phone to call him herself. Twice she hung up, her hand shaking. He had told her to call him when she had the answer. She didn't.

Withdrawal was her only defense against the chaos, frustration, and emotional turmoil that enveloped her. She performed her duties like an automaton, avoiding Darin whenever possible, delaying creative judgments, and putting off all but essential purchases. She was in no psychological condition to make decisions that could turn into financial or artistic disasters.

By Friday, Cass decided to pack it in early. It seemed likely that Dee would be back the first of the week and, with any luck at all, work would return to normal—though at the moment Cass wasn't quite sure just what normal was.

"Uh, Cass?" Janet stopped her as she crossed the showroom. "Are you leaving? I still have this stack of calls for you to return."

"Just leave them on my desk. I'll deal with them Monday."

"Mrs. Everett is expecting you to call this afternoon before her husband gets home," Janet persisted.

Cass headed for the front door. "She'll just have to stall him." At the moment she didn't give a hoot about the Everetts' quarrel over their bedroom wallpaper.

"Darin wanted to see you before you left," Janet called after her urgently. The receptionist was becoming more and more agitated by Cass's irresponsible behavior. She didn't cope well in a crisis.

"If he asks for me again, tell him I've gone," Cass ordered curtly. She wasn't about to endure another argument with Darin. "Tell him I'll see him Monday." The words trailed after her out of the shop, and the door closed on whatever new objection Janet might have raised.

At home, Cass threw herself across the bed, exhausted, but sleep eluded her. Food might have helped, but the frozen dinner she had tossed into the microwave oven did nothing to stir her flagging appetite. At last she opted for a long, hot bath. That was better. Some of her taut muscles began to relax. In fact, she was nearly dozing off when she heard the telephone ring.

Her eyes flew open. Could it be Brendan?

She leapt out of the bathtub and grabbed for her short toweling robe, sickened with self-disgust by the way her heart jumped into her throat. She picked up the receiver on the third ring.

"Hello?" she answered breathlessly.

"Cass? . . . Ben." She swallowed her disappointment, and for a moment found it impossible to respond. "Are you there, Cass?" her brother asked anxiously.

"Yes, I'm here."

"How are you?"

"Fine, thanks," she answered automatically. "And you?"

"Just fine."

Cass let the conversation lie there, making it clear the responsibility to continue was Ben's. He hadn't called her five times in all her years in New York, and only then when he had had something specific to say. She didn't trust his purpose this time.

"Ah, Cass, I've had an offer for the ranch."

Cass remained silent. This was what she had half expected, and she couldn't think of any news she wanted to hear less at that particular moment in time.

"Did you hear me?" Ben persisted.

"Yes, I heard you."

"Well?"

"Well, what?" she asked dryly.

"Well, you said if I had an offer, you'd discuss it."

"I also advised you not to put the ranch on the market," Cass reminded him coldly.

"I didn't," Ben protested indignantly. "Loretta just happened to mention to a friend of hers from Salt Lake that we were thinking of selling. She and her husband are interested in buying if the price is right."

Hot color began to seep into Cass's cheeks. "Just *happened* to mention it, did she?" she asked in disbelief.

"All right," he admitted defensively. "So Loretta's been doing a little asking around. You can't blame her for that."

"I not only can, I do! And I'm in no mood to have this discussion now, Ben. At the moment, no price is right. Loretta can just pass that on to her friend!"

"But, Cass . . ."

She slammed the receiver down on his protest and sat on the edge of the bed, hugging her arms around her and staring numbly into space, feeling as though her whole world was falling apart. The ring of the doorbell jarred her back to reality. Blindly she stumbled into the living room. If Darin had dared to bring their business troubles here to her home . . .

"Yes?" she snapped into the speaker.

"Cass?"

Her whole body went limp. "Brendan?" she asked weakly, though there was no mistaking that deep, lilting voice.

"May I come up?"

With a nerveless hand she pushed the buzzer, and she was still leaning against the wall when his knock sounded on the door beside her. Quickly she retied the belt of her robe, ran her fingers through her disordered hair, and opened the door to him.

Brendan took one look at her pale, strained, tired face and frowned. "Are you all right, Cass?"

"Yes, yes, of course," she said, making an effort to pull herself together. "It's just been a hell of a week at work."

His frown deepened. "I tried to call first," he said curtly, "but the line was busy."

The sharpness in his tone shook her, and she answered at random, twisting her hands in front of her. "I—I was talking to my brother Ben, in Utah. He's had an offer for the ranch—Wells' Springs—and wants to sell it. But I own half of it and I love the ranch. I don't want to let it go. Ben's furious with me—" Abruptly she stopped as she saw an unexpected concern flash across Brendan's face. "I'm—I'm sorry. Here I am, babbling on about matters that can't possibly interest you." With an effort, she forced the ghost of a smile to her lips. "Well, what brings you here?"

"You," he replied tersely, not liking the overbrightness of her eyes, the nervous twitch at the side of her mouth, or the tight lines in her forehead. He hesitated a moment as she simply stared at him. Then, "May I come in?" he asked more gently.

For the first time Cass realized that she had left him standing in the hallway. A flush rose in her cheeks. "Oh, oh! Yes, of course. Come in."

She stood back so that he could enter and closed the door behind him. When she turned back abruptly, with an uncharacteristically jerky movement, she hit hard against his solid frame. The sudden impact of her body against his took her breath away, and before she had a chance to catch it again, his arms had tightened around her and his mouth was on hers in a hungry, searching kiss.

"You didn't call," he said at last, his voice deep and husky.

"I—I didn't have any answers," she replied weakly.

"No? Well maybe this will help."

Once again his mouth sought hers, and once again he caught her off guard, at a time when her resistance to him was at its lowest ebb. She had neither the strength nor the inclination to fight the powerful rush of feeling that coursed through her. Her need for him at the moment was too great. Her arms wound around his neck. Her fingers tangled themselves in his thick, dark curls. Her back arched to press her breasts harder against his broad chest. She returned kiss for kiss with a growing passion that made her whole body tremble with desire.

"Cass, Cass," he moaned as she stroked the back of his neck and nibbled gently at the lobe of his ear. "Do you know what you're doing to me?"

"I hope so!" she breathed, almost a quiet prayer, and stopped his mouth with her lips.

His hold tightened convulsively. Then one arm moved beneath her knees and he swept her into his arms, cradling her against his chest. A half dozen long strides took him across the living room to the open door of the bedroom. It was dark within, except for the light of the moon and the streetlamp that filtered through the thin curtains. Two more strides took him across to the bed, where he laid her gently on the pillow. Her arms around his neck never slackened and he stretched his sturdy frame out beside her, still locked in her embrace.

After only a moment's hesitation, he deftly untied the belt of her robe and parted the front opening. Unerringly his hand found the soft mound of her breast and caressed it until it firmed to fill his large palm. When his mouth moved from her lips to capture the taut bud between his teeth, his wayward hand slipped downward, to stroke the silken flesh of her waist, her stomach, her hip.

Time stood still for Cass until Brendan's knowledgeable fingers became gradually more and more seeking. When he touched the soft, sensitive skin of her inner thigh, a strangled sob suddenly welled up from deep in Cass's throat. Her body tensed and her hands curled into fists on his back. The pitiful sound and the abrupt movement took Brendan by surprise. He paused, raising his head to look down into her face. The light was dim and her eyes were tightly closed, but he could still see the tears streaming down her cheeks.

"Are you all right, Cass?" he asked, his voice husky with a mixture of passion and concern.

"Yes, yes!" she cried, tossing her head back and forth on the pillow.

He pulled farther away and read the tortured indecision in every line of her body.

"Are you sure, Cass?" he insisted. "Are you sure this is what you want?"

"Sure?" she whispered brokenly. "I'm not sure of anything anymore! You've turned my world upside down and inside out, Brendan." A soft, mournful laugh floated from between her lips, but she reached for him achingly to caress his back through the fine chambray of his shirt and stared at him with dazed eyes. "I tried, Brendan. I really tried. And I've fought and I've fought. I've fought Darin and Ben and you, but I can't fight any longer."

The words were nearly incoherent, but the meaning was clear. For a moment Brendan stiffened; first anger, then compassion played across his face in rapid succession. Finally, gently, with infinite care, he pulled out of her embrace and closed the gaping lapels of her robe over her nude body.

"What are you doing?" she asked in despair, fighting the hands that were retying the belt.

"Shhh, sweetheart. Just lie still."

"No, no!" she cried. "Please! Don't leave me."

"I'm not going anywhere," he crooned. "Not for a while, anyway," he added under his breath.

"I need you!"

"Hush, Cass. It's all right. I know what you need."

With that, he gathered her into his arms and held her hard against him, cuddling her, stroking her hair, raining kisses on her wet cheek, letting the warmth and strength of his body do their work. Gradually, he felt her taut form begin to relax until finally she was calm. Slowly she leaned back to look into his face, her own all eyes.

"I made a fool of myself, didn't I?" she asked, sick at heart and mortified.

"You ought to know better than that," he chided, only mildly reproving.

A puzzled frown furrowed her brow. "But—but you stopped."

He laid his hand against her cheek and wiped away a lingering tear with his thumb. "Yes, I stopped—selfishly."

"S—selfishly?" she repeated.

"Mmmmm." Gently he put her away from him. "You see, I remembered what you told me that first night in my apartment, that if we made love, it would be nothing but a temporary escape for you. And that's all it would have been tonight."

"I—I would have been satisfied with that," she said uncertainly, not really sure she believed it herself.

"Perhaps," he agreed, not arguing the point. "But *I* wouldn't have been. I discovered—to my chagrin," he added, the cynicism back in his voice, "that I had no desire to be a convenient diversion for you, a respite from business problems and family quarrels. When—if—we make love, it has to be for our own pleasure, not just as a means of escape."

His words had the sobering effect on her that Brendan had intended. "It—it wasn't just that . . ." Cass began hesitantly.

"Wasn't it?" His voice was grim now, his expression shuttered.

She couldn't give him an honest answer, because she honestly didn't know herself. All she knew was that the moment of desire had passed. And she wasn't sure whether she thanked or hated Brendan for his perception and control.

Abruptly she moved and sat cross-legged on the bed, tightening the belt of her robe. "So what happens now?" she asked solemnly.

He sat on the edge of the bed, his back to her, and shrugged. "Nothing. We just leave things as they are." He reached down for the shoes he had kicked off earlier. "As a matter of fact, I'm going to make it easy for us. I'm leaving town tomorrow on business."

"For how long?"

Again he shrugged. "When do you think the apartment is going to be finished?"

"At the rate the work is coming along, I'd say no longer than a month," she answered bleakly.

He thought that over, then turned to her and nodded. "That sounds about right."

"For what?"

His face softened, and the tension between them was banished by the warmth of his smile. "I didn't answer you the other day when you asked how I liked the redecoration, Cass, but I'll answer you now. I think you're doing a brilliant job. The whole place is going to be stunning when you're finished."

She blinked uncertainly at this abrupt shift in subject and mood, but she couldn't help but warm to his praise. "I'm so glad you like it, Brendan. Do you know," she admitted humbly, "of all the designs I've ever done, I don't think I've ever been happier with my work."

He studied her face through his thick lashes. "Does that mean it's the sort of place you'd choose to live in yourself?" he asked. "I'd consider that the best confirmation."

"Oh, yes," she said with more enthusiasm than she realized.

"Good!" he said in satisfaction. "Then I don't want you to spare any expense. Since I'll be away, I want you to buy anything you want, anything that appeals to you. You have my blessing to add any furniture, paintings, or accessories you like. You don't need my approval. Just send the bills."

Cass blinked. No client had ever given her a carte blanche quite like that before. "Are—are you sure you know what you're saying? You don't want to choose things like lamps and paintings for yourself?"

"I have absolute confidence in your taste," he assured her. With that he stood and tucked his shirt back into his waistband. "I'd better be off now and let you get some rest."

Cass was left to follow him through the living room to the door. "Will—will I hear from you while you're gone?" she couldn't help asking.

"Perhaps," he answered vaguely, "but you can always reach me through Edith if a problem crops up."

What a strange end to a strange evening, Cass concluded as she watched Brendan shrug into the sports coat he had dropped onto a chair. When he turned back to her, his face was impassive, but his eyes held a lingering warmth as they studied her feature by feature. Then, gently, he took her by the shoulders, molded them for a moment with his big hands, pulled her closer, and pressed a farewell kiss against her soft mouth. Slowly he released her, his gaze holding hers.

"Until we meet again. Think of me while I'm away, Cass."

Chapter 7

"NINE WILL BE FINE, EDITH. THANK YOU FOR CALLING."

Cass replaced the phone on the hook, swiveled on her stool, and stared thoughtfully out the window of her workroom. She jumped as an amused voice spoke from the doorway.

"Who was that?" Dee asked. "You look as though you'd just been given a dose of castor oil."

"I don't think they give kids castor oil any more," Cass returned dryly. "And Brendan's secretary is more like a glass of sour milk."

"So that was the infamous Edith again, was it?" Her friend sniffed. "And just where is the elusive Mr. Cahill this time? In the past four weeks he's managed to hit Miami, New Orleans, Dallas, Phoenix, Los Angeles, and Seattle." She ticked each city off on her fingers. "I thought next he might move on to Canada and I would have to start using my toes to keep count."

"So why bother?" Cass tossed off, trying unsuccessfully to conceal her distress. "You can't blame the man for wanting to stay out of the way while his apartment is all torn up."

"You finished with it the day before yesterday," Dee reminded her, angry on her friend's behalf.

Dee had watched Cass become increasingly pale and wan over the past month as the days passed and Brendan didn't return. Even his communication with Cass had been restricted to messages delivered through his secretary. Cass had lost so much weight she looked like a wraith haunting the shop—the ghost of Cassandra's, Janet had labeled her in one of the girl's more flippant, insensitive moments.

"So what did the devoted dragon have to say this time?" Dee asked lightly, trying to dispel the atmosphere of gloom.

"Brendan is in Denver," Cass replied slowly. "He's coming back to New York this evening. He wants me to meet him at his office at nine."

"He wants you to meet him *tonight?*" Dee stared at her blankly. "I don't get it. He waltzes out of your life for a month with scarcely a word to you, and then thinks he can just waltz right back in again, as though nothing has happened?"

Cass's face—if possible—turned a shade whiter. "Nothing *has* happened, Dee," she said flatly. "He's a client, remember? And it isn't as though he just skipped town without a word. He told me he was going to be gone while we finished up the work and warned me that he would be out of touch. If I counted on anything else, the fault was mine. So, now he's coming back, and I assume he wants me to go over the apartment with him tonight to explain the changes I've made and show him where everything is. There's nothing unreasonable in that."

"Huh," Dee snorted.

Cass gave up the futile rationalization. Dee had a way of reducing a situation to its basics. Cass's shoulders slumped and she twisted her hands in her lap anxiously.

"All right, all right, Dee," she said flatly. "But what do you expect me to do, rant and rave, curse the day I ever met him?"

"That would be a start," her friend said gently. "Better than keeping it all bottled up inside."

"Oh, I haven't kept it bottled up. I've taken it out on my loom. Wait until you see the work I've finished."

"You could have talked to me," Dee suggested.

"You couldn't have told me anything I haven't already told myself. And maybe I didn't want to admit, even to you, what a fool I've been," Cass replied bitterly. "I'm plenty old enough and experienced enough to know better than to become involved with a man like Brendan Cahill. I knew from the beginning that no woman could ever count for much with him. He makes a great start," she concluded cynically, "but he lacks staying power."

Neither Cass's cynicism nor her belated words of wisdom made any impression on her friend. "Boy, you really fell for that guy, didn't you?" she observed fatalistically.

Cass waved the observation away with an impatient hand. "Don't be absurd, Dee. How could I possibly love a man I don't really know and certainly don't understand? All right." She sighed as her friend gave her a wry grimace. "I admit to a . . . a *physical* attraction. But since he's been gone, I can see him with some perspective. Brendan's a ruthless, power-hungry, insensitive, boorish bachelor, on the make and much too used to getting his own way."

"And that's all?" Dee asked, unconvinced.

"Well . . . maybe not all." The memory of his gentleness toward her during their last evening together rose to haunt her. "He has his better moments. At least, I think he does. Either that," she added dryly, "or he puts on one hell of a good act."

"So, are you going to meet him tonight?"

Cass shrugged philosophically. "Do I have a choice? This is business, if you'll recall, and I have to see him sometime. If I don't go tonight, I wouldn't accomplish anything but postponing the inevitable."

"Want me to come along?"

For a cowardly minute Cass was sorely tempted, but she declined the company. "No, thanks, Dee. I think I'd lose what little self-respect I have left if I couldn't deal with Brendan by myself."

Just before she left her apartment to keep the appointment that evening, Cass was wishing she had taken Dee up on her offer—if only to provide a distraction from herself, she thought morosely. Her stomach was churning, her hands were trembling, and her mouth felt as though it were filled with sawdust.

Dee was right, of course. Cass was in love with Brendan, had really known it that night with him in her apartment. She could never have offered herself as she had done to a man she didn't love. Her numbing fear now was that Brendan would take one look at her and recognize the depth of her feeling for him. A feeling, she concluded miserably, that he obviously didn't share. Why else would he leave her for an entire month without a single word? Well, she refused to give him the satisfaction of knowing what a fool she was.

She studied her appearance in the mirror and wrinkled her nose in disgust. The long sleeves, full skirt, and high neckline of her summer dress helped to hide her thinness, but her high cheekbones were much too prominent and her face was still too pale. Impatiently she applied more blusher, a deeper shade of lipstick, and cover-up to erase the dark circles under her eyes. The result was no miracle, but at least she looked more like her normal self—hopefully normal enough to fool Brendan. With a sigh of resignation, she went outside to catch a cab.

Edith had specifically instructed Cass to use the main entrance to the office building. The guard at the front desk would have her name. She was to take the elevator to the twenty-fifth-floor offices of Monarch. The door in front of the elevator, the secretary informed her, would be unlocked. From there Cass was to go upstairs to Brendan's office, where he would meet her.

Everything went just as ordained.

Cass's high heels clicked on the marble tile in the lobby downstairs. The plush carpeting upstairs, however, muted the sound. She was ten minutes early, but Brendan was there waiting, standing by Edith's desk with his back to Cass as she pushed open the door.

He hadn't heard her enter, and Cass took the opportunity to study him for one precious moment. He wore a dark business suit that looked as though he had traveled in it all day. But even the slightly rumpled jacket couldn't conceal the breadth of his shoulders or the muscles in his solid back. All she could see was the back of his head, but the four weeks had seemed so excruciatingly long to her that she almost expected to find streaks of gray in his thick, dark hair. When she had to fight an almost overwhelming impulse to move up behind him, put her arms around his waist, and run her fingers through that hair, Cass knew she couldn't afford to linger there in the doorway any longer. With an effort she summoned up her composure, controlled her features, and moved farther into the room.

"Hello, Brendan," she said quietly and formally. "I'm sorry if I've kept you waiting."

Brendan spun around and the letter opener he was holding fell to the carpet with a muffled thud. "Cass!"

For a breathless moment his gaze all but devoured her, taking in every detail of her appearance, from her sleek black hair, to her impassive face, down the length of her slender body, to her slim legs below.

"You took me by surprise," he muttered, turning away from her to bend down and retrieve the opener from the floor.

When he straightened and faced her again, his hooded eyelids hid any expression, and Cass couldn't tell whether the flush in his cheeks was from the bending, from the surprise of her sudden arrival, or from just seeing her again. She averted her face and focused unseeingly on the blown-up photograph of a Monarch Hotel on the far wall.

"Did you have a good trip?" she asked uneasily, grasping for something to say.

"No," he said bluntly.

"I'm sorry."

Silence.

"Uh . . ." she tried again, "what was wrong?"

"Everything."

Another silence.

Cass tried lightness. "Well, that's comprehensive."

"I can see the past few weeks have been good to you, Cass. You look your same, beautiful self."

Was there bitterness in his voice? Her glance flew to his face and stayed there, unsure of what she was seeing. "I—I've been working hard."

"As usual?"

"Yes, as usual."

He winced, and it was as though a mask he was wearing cracked, crumbled into pieces, and fell away. Behind it was a vulnerability she had never seen before. His rugged face was twisted, his mouth tight with suppressed emotion, and from his eyes shot sparks of . . . could it possibly be pain?

"I thought, I hoped . . ." he began.

His words trailed off into an even worse silence, one that Cass couldn't endure. There were more terrible things, she decided, than making a fool of oneself—such a thing as perhaps letting love slip through one's fingers out of misplaced pride.

"I don't know what it is you thought or hoped, Brendan," she told him slowly and solemnly. "All I know is that for the past four weeks, I've missed you so much I didn't think I could bear it."

Brendan swallowed and said nothing but, as though a light had gone on inside him, an inner glow banished all the tension and pain from his face. Fortunately, Cass recognized the reason for his silence. This normally blunt, direct man she loved so much was having difficulty putting his feelings into words. Fortunately also for her overwrought nerves, he was a man of action.

One moment he was halfway across the room from her. The next, she was being drawn into his convulsive embrace. He wasted no time finding her lips. Before she could draw a breath, she was drowning in the wave of mutual longing that flooded over them. He didn't raise his head until they had both satisfied their initial hunger. By then, he had found the words.

"Oh, Cass," he whispered huskily, "I love you so much!"

"I want to believe that so desperately, Brendan," she said shakily, "but I don't understand why you didn't call, why you didn't write."

He left one kiss on the pulse in her neck, then laid a large palm against her cheek. Any lingering fear that his desire for her had dulled quickly fled. The truth was written in every softened line of his rugged face.

"For the first time in my life," he explained, humbly for him, "I was afraid of feeling too much for a woman. The first night I met you, I knew that you could disrupt my whole life. Day by day you became more and more important to me."

"But the other day, after lunch, you—you just *left* me. You said to find the answer and I never did."

"Don't you understand? I was hurt. I had fallen in love with you, and do you remember what you said to me? You called me a man you *often* admired and *sometimes* even respected. How do you suppose that made me feel?"

"I—I was only joking," she objected lamely. At the time there was more truth in her words than she had intended— and Brendan knew it. "I had no idea I was anything . . . anything *special* to you."

"Surely you knew how much you meant to me that night in your apartment. Why else would I have left you alone? Why else wouldn't I have taken what you offered?"

"I didn't know why," Cass whispered, shaken by the passion in his voice. She couldn't help thinking of all the needless agony she had endured during the past four weeks.

"But now you understand, don't you?" he asked urgently. "You were so tense, so distraught and unsure. You were in no condition to make a decision of any kind. I knew then that it was too soon—perhaps for both of us."

Cass couldn't deny the truth of what he said, at least about her own condition. She loved him, but she hadn't been ready then to acknowledge it. "Is that why you went away—to give us both time to think things over?"

"Partly." He smoothed her hair back from her cheek, leaving his fingers to caress the softness of her earlobe. "But partly, too, I know my own limits of endurance. I couldn't have gone on seeing you without making love to you. I wanted you so much, I ached for you." He smiled ruefully. "You'll never know what it cost me to leave you alone that night. I admit that I went away and left you alone hoping that you'd miss me. I even hoped that you might wonder if perhaps you didn't care for me more than you realized."

"Well, it worked," she said, smiling openly, unrestrainedly, for the first time in weeks. "I love you, Brendan."

He swallowed an obstruction in his throat. "I can hardly believe it, Cass. When I first saw you tonight, looking so distant and cool, I thought I had made a terrible mistake. I thought that I had lost you completely."

Cass knew a very satisfactory way to dispel any doubts he might have. She, too, could be a woman of action. Her arms tightened around him, and she let her kiss speak for her.

Brendan was shaking when he finally held her away. "If we keep this up, the only part of the apartment we're likely to see tonight is the bedroom."

"Don't you think I did a good job on it?" she asked innocently. "You notice that I kept the water bed."

"I haven't been in the apartment yet. I wanted to see it the first time with you. That's why I asked you to meet me here in the office."

The smile he gave her was enough to melt the coldest heart, and hers had thawed with his first kiss. Now it nearly set her on fire.

"Come on." He held out his hand to her, and together they crossed to the connecting door.

"Close your eyes while I turn on the lights," she said. She wanted to watch the expression on his face when he saw the living room for the first time. "All right. You can look."

"My God!" Brendan breathed.

The initial impact of the room was indeed dramatic, even stunning. No one would have recognized it as the same place Cass had stepped into six weeks before.

She had designed it all in black and white, with glass, mirror, and chrome. The walls were entirely black, covered with a nubby linen, the same fabric and texture as the white drapes at the windows. The dropped acoustical panels had been removed and the plaster ceiling painted black. Small spotlights ran on chrome tracks around the edges.

A broad platform at the far end of the room narrowed and curved around each side to break up the space. A room divider of chrome tubing separated the raised dining area from the living room below. All carpeting had been removed, replaced in the sunken living room by great swirls of inlaid black and white marble.

The furnishings were very simple, with clean lines and smooth textures—ebony, leather, glass, and chrome. The only color was in the accessories—the paintings, the brightly colored throw pillows on the black leather sofas, and the enormous potted plants that stood between the windows and near the grand piano, nestled in the lower curve of the platform.

"Look above the fireplace," Cass directed shyly.

Obediently Brendan turned. Over the black marble mantel hung an enormous wall hanging—the Cassandra decorating signature. She had created it especially for him. The design was a black and gray eagle, soaring on a field of stark white, woven out of coarse wool and adorned with hooked shag yarn, leather strips, and feathers.

She explained it simply. "That's the way I see you."

"I don't know what to say," he murmured, deeply moved.

Cass smiled. "You don't have to say anything."

An answering smile lit his face. "No, I don't, do I? I'll show you."

By the time he slackened his hold and raised his head, Cass was breathless, trembling, and radiantly happy.

"Good heavens," she panted, her eyes shining. "You're—you're the most appreciative client I've ever had. It's your good taste, of course."

"Do I detect an ambiguity in those words?" he asked provocatively.

"Maybe," she admitted mischievously.

"If my taste is good," he said, pursuing the matter, "what does that say about my timing?"

His words implied an invitation that she was perfectly willing to accept, but she delayed the delicious moment. "I would say . . ."

"Yes?" he prompted.

Cass pressed herself against him until he could feel every warm, responsive curve of her body. She laced her fingers behind his neck and caressed the nape with her thumbs. Her lips parted, the color deepened in her cheeks, and when she replied, her voice was a deep, soft, sensuous purr.

"Now I have a quote for you, Brendan—slightly adapted. I thought of it so often while I worked on the wall hanging."

"What's that?" he asked huskily.

"'Doth the eagle mount up at thy command and build his nest on high?'"

She felt his body respond to the question even before he

swept her up in his arms and murmured against her impatient lips: "Stay with me tonight, my love, and I promise we'll find the answer together."

Cass stretched luxuriously, settled herself comfortably on Brendan's shoulder, and pressed her face into his neck. The water bed rocked in counterpoint with each movement.

"Darin is probably on the verge of apoplexy by now," she observed with a regretable lack of concern. "I was supposed to have met with a new client half an hour ago."

Brendan caressed her soft breast and placed a kiss on the top of her head. "Are you sorry you stayed a little longer?"

Her fingers twined themselves around the curly hair on his chest and she gave an admonishing tug. "You know better than to ask that." Somewhere in the distance a phone rang. "How about you?" she murmured. "Are you sure the Dragon Lady won't come in search of you?"

He peered at her with one eye. "Who?"

"Edith. Your dragon."

"A very appropriate description," he agreed. "Her fiery breath has made even the most persistent salesmen turn tail and run."

Cass grimaced. "I know the feeling. She doesn't approve of me either, you know."

"Edith disapproves of the entire human race on principle." He grinned. "Men in particular."

Cass's eyebrows rose in surprise. "Do you mean she treats you just as badly as she does everyone else?"

"Worse. One day she informed me that she found snakes far more trustworthy than any person she had ever met. On the whole," he drawled, "I agreed, but I still declined the honor of having her pet boa constrictor grace our outer office. She's never forgiven me."

"Why do you keep her on?"

He shrugged. "Rotten disposition aside, she has her virtues. She never complains if I'm away from the office for weeks on end. In fact," he observed wryly, "I think she prefers to rule her kingdom unhampered by my presence. And you can count on her absolute discretion—though I can't promise she'll take the news that you're moving into my apartment with good grace."

Cass was startled by this matter-of-fact statement. "Am—am I moving in?"

His arms tightened around her. "Just as soon as you can arrange it," he said huskily. "Like by tonight?"

"Tonight?" He was moving so fast she couldn't take it all in.

"Let me know what time this afternoon, and I'll send movers over to help you pack."

He held her as though he would never let her go, and his voice grew thick and deep with a desire that an entire night together hadn't quenched.

"Cass, from the first moment you showed me your sketches for the apartment, I've hardly been able to think of anything else but having you here. I know that the sort of home you live in means a lot to you, and I wanted you to be happy. That's why I wanted this place to be everything you dreamed it could be, why I wanted you to fill it with all the things you would like to have around you."

It took a minute for the words to sink in, but when they did, Cass was stunned by the revelation. "You mean—you mean," she faltered, "that from the beginning, you intended that I design the apartment for *myself?*"

"Of course." He pressed a long, lingering kiss on her parted lips. His words were husky with emotion as he murmured, "Say you'll live with me, Cass."

Live with him, not *marry* him. Such a difference between the two, and that particular choice of words was not a mistake Brendan would make. His intentions were clear. His body was warm against hers, but a cold chill was creeping into her heart. Cass didn't know why she should be so startled and deeply troubled by his proposition, but she was.

For once, Brendan was insensitive to her mood. "You've already guessed that no woman has ever lived with me since I was divorced. I've never asked anyone before," he told her solemnly, "and frankly, I never thought I would. But that was before I met you." He buried his face in her hair, breathing in the fragrance there. "We can make it work, Cass."

Make *what* work? she wondered bleakly. What kind of life did he envision for them?

Brendan pulled back and looked down into her face, puzzled by her lack of response. "What do you say, Cass?"

"I—I don't know what to say," she hedged. "Maybe I'm not as convinced as you are that living together would work out."

"I promise you, sweetheart, it would. I've spent most of the past month thinking it through."

She wished with a bitter sweetness that he had given *her* the same advantage.

His hands began a gentle caress on her tense shoulder. "You already know that I wasn't exactly devastated when my wife left me," he explained, "but the brief excursion into matrimony taught me a life lesson. When a person is wedded to his—or her—work, marriage is an impossible situation, especially if children are involved." He smiled cynically. "I never could understand how some men can cope with polygamy. I would become schizophrenic."

The chill in Cass's heart had turned it into a cold, numb lump, and she didn't know whether to laugh or cry at this last ridiculous observation of his. Brendan murmured an objection but didn't try to stop her when she pulled out of his arms and rose up on one elbow to look down into his face.

"But living together would be different?"

"For us," he said with conviction, "it's the ideal arrangement because we're so much alike."

"Alike in what way, Brendan?" Somehow Cass managed to keep the disbelief and growing despair out of her voice.

He shrugged. "We each have our own profession and we're both workaholics. We both understand the time commitment each other's work demands. I know that often you have to put in eighteen and twenty hours at the shop. You know that I have to do a lot of traveling. Neither of us would begrudge the time the other spent away." Desire burned in his eyes. "We'd have all the pleasure of being together when we could and yet all the advantages of living our separate lives when it came to work. What could be better?"

Cass could have named a dozen "whats" right then, but they obviously weren't viable alternatives for the ambitious, self-centered Brendan Cahill. Now she knew just what sort of life he envisioned for them—and it sounded like a living nightmare to her!

She was shaking from emotional overload as she threw back the down comforter and reached for her clothes. They still lay in a pile where Brendan had let them drop when he undressed her the night before. He had undressed her, she thought bleakly, a lifetime ago, in a different incarnation. To her, he would never again be the perfect lover, the man she longed for and expected to spend the rest of her life with. And she would never again be the same person as that naïve, radiantly happy, emotionally satisfied woman who had slept with him.

Brendan watched her dress with quick jerky movements, a puzzled frown putting the lines back in his softened face. "What are you doing?"

"Getting dressed."

"I can see that. But what's the hurry?"

"I have to go now."

He threw aside the comforter and reached for his robe on the other side of the bed. He was tying the cord just as she was slipping into her shoes.

"Well, when should I expect you back?" he asked, joining her as she searched in her purse for a brush.

"You shouldn't," she said bluntly, giving up the search and heading blindly for the door.

He caught her by the shoulder and spun her around. "What are you trying to tell me, Cass?"

"Not trying. I *am* telling you. I won't live with you, Brendan."

"What?"

"You heard me."

He searched her face and was bewildered by what he saw. Cass's face had no makeup on now to help conceal the lines of despair around her eyes, the pallor of her cheeks, and the unhappy curve of her mobile mouth. Unconsciously his fingers bit into her shoulders.

"You *do* love me, don't you, Cass?"

Helplessly, wordlessly, she nodded her head. She couldn't deny him that—though at the moment, for the life of her she didn't know why she cared about him so much.

"Then what's wrong? You know, don't you, that I'll do everything I can to make you happy."

Make her happy! In her unstable emotional state, she nearly laughed aloud at the idea. Brendan obviously didn't have a clue as to what that would take—outside of the bedroom, that is, she concluded bitterly.

"You do believe that I love you, don't you?" he persisted.

Cass didn't answer this. From the moment he had asked her to live with him, she had begun to doubt that Brendan knew what love—the kind of love she wanted and needed—was all about. Everything he had said since had only turned that doubt into conviction.

"Cass?"

A new, growing anger was quickly bringing feeling back into her numb heart, replacing despair with outrage. Her voice was low and tight with suppressed emotion as she twisted out of Brendan's hold and started down the hall to the living room. "Good-bye, Brendan."

"Cass?" He hurried to catch up with her.

"Stay away from me!"

He reached out his hand to her imploringly. "Please, tell me what's wrong!"

She swung around so quickly he nearly bumped into her. "I'll tell you what's wrong, you selfish . . ."

"Cass!" he exclaimed, stunned. "What did I say?"

"You really don't know, do you?" she said bitterly. "You have no idea how *unfeeling* your proposition is. I'm beginning to think that maybe old Edith and I have more in common than I thought. No self-respecting snake would make his . . . his *mate* such a cold-blooded offer."

"What the hell are you talking about?" He ran a frustrated hand across the back of his neck. "What does our living together have to do with snakes?"

"I'll be delighted to explain!" She paced the living room that she had planned for him with such imagination and pride—and the memory choked her. "So I can move in here with you, can I, and just go on merrily about my work? Of course, my job might very well be driving me crazy, but you wouldn't be interested in that. Your commitment to our relationship wouldn't extend beyond the bedroom door, and you wouldn't care what kind of a mess my professional life was in as long as it didn't interfere with *your* work and *our* sex life."

"Cass!" he objected, but she ignored the interruption.

"Though I imagine if I were depressed enough, you would be magnanimous and try and help me forget my troubles—at least temporarily—with a night or two of passionate lovemaking. Providing, of course, that you were in town and available when I needed you," she added caustically. "Well, that may be your idea of a workable relationship, but it isn't mine. I'm conceited enough to believe that I have more to offer a man than my body, but that wouldn't be of any interest to you. You're too self-sufficient to need a lover for anything more than a necessary physical release. Well, I'm not. What's more, I'm even selfish enough to want a man around that I can turn to for comfort and understanding and advice when I'm in trouble. I want to *share* a man's life, not just . . . just *hang around* as a convenient adjunct to it."

His face had whitened at her words. "You really believe that was what I was saying?"

"You've given me no reason not to!" She shivered, though the room was warm, and hugged her arms around herself. "All that concern for my welfare," she said brokenly, reaction setting in. "Was I working too hard? Was I getting enough rest? Was I eating well? I had my doubts from the beginning, but mistakenly I came to believe that maybe, just maybe, you cared about me—as a person! All you really cared about was whether or not I had enough time and energy left over for you!"

She turned unseeingly toward the door, her eyes filled with tears of anger and despair.

"Please, Cass," he begged, following. "We have to talk. Perhaps—perhaps I put it badly."

"You told me once that you never lie to a woman about your relationship with her." She spoke through the lump in her throat, her back to him. "I believed you then and I believe it now. You meant exactly what you said. And I've heard more than enough to know that living with you would be the biggest disaster I could bring on myself."

"You didn't mean it, then—when you said you love me?"

Slowly she pivoted to face him and her mouth twisted

with a cynicism that rivaled his own. "Oh, I meant it, Brendan. Fool that I am!"

"Cass, please," he said softly, pleadingly. "I love you. Come to me. We can work this out."

Cass shrank away from his hand on her shoulder and groped for the doorknob. It appalled her to realize that as angry, hurt, and disillusioned as she was with him, one touch of his lips on hers could very well destroy any vestige of good sense and self-respect she had left. She couldn't make the mistake of underestimating his powers of persuasion.

He made no physical move to stop her as she left, but his words followed her through the office. "Please, Cass, you can't leave like this."

She stopped at the door to the corridor—oblivious to Edith's fishy stare—and turned to where he stood at the entrance to the apartment. Cass had reached a decision and hadn't known it herself until the words came out.

"I not only can leave, but I am—getting out of here, out of New York, and out of your life."

You know the thrill of escaping to a world of Love and Romance as it is experienced by real men and real women...

Escape again...with 4 FREE novels and

get more great Silhouette Intimate Moments novels —for a 15-day FREE examination— delivered to your door every month!

*S*ilhouette Intimate Moments offers you romance for women...not girls. It has been created especially for the woman who wants a more intense, passionate reading experience. Every book in this exciting series promises you romantic fantasy...dynamic, contemporary characters...involving stories...intense sensuality...and stirring passion.

Silhouette Intimate Moments may not be for everyone, but if you're the kind of woman who wants more romance in her life, they will take you to a world of *real* passion, *total* involvement, and *complete* fulfillment. Now, every month you can thrill to the kind of romance that will take your breath away.

FREE BOOKS

Start today by taking advantage of this special offer—the 4 newest Silhouette Intimate Moments romances (a $10.00 Value) *absolutely FREE,* along with a Cameo Tote Bag. Just fill out and mail the attached postage paid order card.

AT-HOME PREVIEWS FREE DELIVERY

After you receive your 4 free books and Tote Bag, every month you'll have the chance to preview 4 more Silhouette Intimate Moments novels —*before they're available in stores!* When you decide to keep them, you'll pay just $9.00, (a $10.00 Value), *with never an additional charge of any kind and with no risk!* You can cancel your subscription at any time simply by dropping us a note. In any case, the first 4 books, and Tote Bag are yours to keep.

EXTRA BONUS

When you take advantage of this offer, we'll also send you the Silhouette Books Newsletter free with each shipment. Every informative issue features news on upcoming titles, interviews with your favorite authors, and even their favorite recipes.

Get a Free Tote Bag, too!

EVERY BOOK YOU RECEIVE WILL BE A BRAND-NEW FULL-LENGTH NOVEL!

Escape with 4 Silhouette Intimate Moments novels (a $10.00 Value) and get a FREE Tote Bag, too!

Chapter 8

"You don't know what you're saying, Cass." Darin's face was white with shock. "You can't leave like this!"

Cass winced. Unconsciously he had echoed the last thing Brendan had said to her that morning. If she had needed any further reassurance that she had made the right decision, Darin's words confirmed it. Just the thought of Brendan was almost too painful to endure.

"I'm sorry, Darin," she said regretfully, "but my mind's made up. I just left Dee, and she's more than eager to buy out my share of the partnership. Under our original agreement, you have first option, of course—"

"You know I can't run this place without a designer," he snapped.

"And I'm giving you one. Nearly all our clients know Dee. She's worked with a good share of them. There shouldn't be any problem at all."

"No problem?" he asked bitterly. "You *are* Cassandra's. With you gone, there's nothing left."

"You know that's not true," she protested. "Dee has wonderful credentials, connections that neither you nor I have, and a professional reputation on the West Coast that you can play up. And she told me this morning that once she's a full partner, she and her husband are willing to invest their own money in whatever expansion you think the place needs. Financially, Cassandra's will be better off than it would if I stayed on."

He dismissed her comments with an angry wave of his hand. "You confided your plans to Dee without telling me? Why?"

Cass ran a weary hand over her eyes. "I was only thinking of you, Darin. I *had* to talk to Dee first. I couldn't just pull the rug out from under you by suddenly announcing that I was leaving, not without offering you an alternative to solve the problem. And frankly, if you want to know the truth, I was hoping to avoid exactly the argument we're having now."

"You must know that it's come as a shock. We've worked so well together, Cass," he pleaded.

"You'll work just as well with Dee, probably better," she promised him. "Dee is much more of a social being than I am and will turn up at all those tedious parties I so assiduously avoid. What's more, she has a far better head than I do for figures," she consoled him. "She keeps track of every penny she spends. That ought to make you happy."

Darin looked neither happy nor consoled. Anxiously he chewed on his lower lip and drummed his fingers on the desk. "I suppose if you want to go," he said morosely, "there's nothing I can do to stop you. When does the sale go through?"

"You know that Dee's husband is an accountant. She called him this morning, and he said that the audit of the books and the actual paperwork could take a couple of months. Unless you object, though, I can sign an option to sell, take my share, and leave when I want."

"And when would that be?" he asked coldly. "Are you going to pack up and move out this afternoon?"

"You know I wouldn't leave you in the lurch like that, Darin," she objected. "But I would like to go in another week or ten days. By then, I'll have finished up everything I'm working on now." Reluctantly she added, "If you think you need me longer, though, you know I'll stay and do anything I can to help make the transition as smooth as possible."

A knock on the door of Darin's office interrupted them. "Come in!" he called impatiently.

Hesitantly Janet stuck her head in. "Cass, it's that Mr. Cahill on the phone again."

"I told you," Cass said coldly, "that I am not in to Mr. Cahill—now or ever."

Janet giggled uneasily. "He said to tell you that if you won't talk to him on the phone, he'll come over and tear the place apart until he finds you."

"Inform Mr. Cahill that it wouldn't do a lick of good. Tell him that I'm leaving immediately for . . . for Boston on a buying trip and won't be back until next week."

"If you say so," Janet said doubtfully, "but I don't think he'll believe it."

"Just do as I tell you." Cass sighed.

As Darin listened to this exchange, his eyes narrowed and his mouth tightened into a thin line. "Now I get it," he said tersely as Janet closed the door behind her. "You had a fight with Cahill. That's why you're suddenly up and running away."

"I am not running away!"

"Oh, no? Then what do you call it?" he asked cynically.

"All right," she admitted. "Brendan did . . . precipitate the decision. But I've been considering quitting for a couple of months now." She pleaded with her friend and partner for understanding. "Please, Darin. I don't want to hurt you, but if I didn't leave now, it would only be a matter of time before the business began to fall apart anyway. I just can't take the pressure. You know that I'm constantly behind schedule, hurrying to catch up, and it's starting to affect the quality of my work. I just can't be creative to order day in and day out, month in and month out. I have to get away from here before I burn out completely and you have to haul me away."

For the first time Darin's attitude softened. "No one knows better than I do how hard you've been working, Cass. Maybe that's why I just can't trust this hasty decision. Take some time to reconsider."

"I don't need more time, Darin," she said firmly.

"But what on earth would you do with yourself if you quit the business?" he asked in frustration. "Have you given any thought to that?"

"As a matter of fact, I have. I'm going back to Utah, to the ranch, and weave—at my own speed. I even talked to a distributor this morning who will be delighted to market whatever I produce with the Cassandra label on it." She grimaced ironically. "I'll never get rich that way, but I'll make enough to live on."

Darin's frown returned. "Go back to Utah? I thought you told me Ben intended to sell the ranch now that your father's gone."

"You mean *Loretta* intends that Ben sell it," Cass corrected him acidly. "But he won't. Not if I have anything to say about it. There have been Wells on that land for over a hundred years. I have to believe that Ben wouldn't really let the ranch go out of the family, not if I put up a fight. It's so beautiful, Darin, and unspoiled." Her eyes were suddenly misty with an inner vision. "Civilization hasn't reached there yet. It's like stepping back in time. If you could see it, you would know how I feel about it, understand why I want to get away from the city."

Helplessly Darin shook his head. "Oh, Cass. For four years you're the one who has been telling me—every time I bitched about the family going broke—that you can never go back to the way things were. And you were right. Haven't you considered the fact that maybe you've been romanticizing what living there was like? You've been away over ten years. Everything changes, whether we like it or not."

"I don't want to hear it, Darin," Cass cried. He had put into words her own nagging doubts.

"I'm just trying to keep you from making a mistake you'll regret for the rest of your life, Cass," he said gently. "You're throwing over your whole career for what? A whim? A temporary aberration? What happens if you sign the option and leave, only to find that this haven you expect doesn't exist anywhere but in your memories? What then? It would be too late to turn back."

"But I just can't stay in New York any longer," she said brokenly. "I have to get away."

"All right, I can understand that," he said soothingly to her. "And if it's any comfort, I can see now that a good share of your problems are my fault. You warned me, but I was too insensitive to listen. I went ahead and stupidly pushed you into this mess with Cahill. I'm sorry about that," he apologized with real chagrin.

She accepted his apology with self-deprecation. "You couldn't know that I would make a fool of myself over him."

For the first time he noted the dark circles under her eyes and the haunted expression in her face. "You're in love with him," he announced flatly. She shrugged. "But you quarreled?" he asked, probing. Another shrug. She didn't want to discuss Brendan with Darin or anyone—not then when the wounds were still so fresh. "All right, Cass. I won't push you anymore," he said with understanding. "But as your friend, I'm telling you, you can't throw your career away because of a man."

"I *told* you, Darin, it's *more* than that."

"Okay, okay," he agreed hastily. "I believe you. But don't burn your bridges behind you, Cass. Take a vacation —two, three weeks, even a month. I even think that going back to the ranch would be a good idea. Try out the life-style again. Forget your work. Forget Cahill. I can practically promise you that after awhile, after you've had a chance to rest and recuperate, you'll discover that the city has gotten into your blood and you can't go back to the way things were, that you won't even want to. *Here* is where you belong now."

Cass didn't want to believe him, but he had watered her own seeds of doubt. Her problems with Brendan aside, *was* she giving up a successful career for a whim? "If you could only see the ranch for yourself, Darin—" she began desperately.

"If that's an invitation," he said thoughtfully, "I accept."

"Wh—what?"

"If you're determined to go to Utah, let me come with you—a constant reminder of the civilized life you want to leave behind you," he tossed off flippantly.

"You're not serious!" She was as much amused as dismayed at the thought of Darin trying to cope with ranch life.

"Indeed I am." A beguiling smile broke over his face.

"Will you let me come if I promise that I won't nag you, that I won't say a word to try and persuade you to come back?"

"Then why would you want to go with me?" she asked, not sure she trusted him to keep quiet.

It was his turn to shrug. "You need a break. Well, so do I, and I've never been a fan of the wide open spaces. Who knows? I might just succumb to the lure of the mountains. You might convince me that staying there is the wisest move you could make."

Cass considered his suggestion thoughtfully. It was really a very good idea. Darin had been a wonderful friend and a tireless business partner. She didn't want to leave him with hard feelings.

"No nagging?" she asked.

"Not a murmur," he promised. "Not a single, solitary word. And you know, Cass, with both of us gone, it'll be a good chance to see how Dee handles the business by herself. I won't ask her to bother with any of the financial details, of course, but she'll have to deal with the clients, wholesalers, salespeople, and staff. It'll give me a chance to see what kind of a problem-solver she is."

Cass could have hugged him. He was some kind of problem-solver himself. "Thank you, Darin."

"So?" he said brusquely. "When do we leave? Can you finish up what you need to in the next week?"

"If it kills me!" Cass exclaimed with passion.

He smiled. "Let's not get carried away, but I'll have Janet make our plane reservations for a week from today. And why don't you let me talk things over with Dee later on this afternoon? Now, my pet—to work!"

Cass wouldn't have felt such relief if she could have heard what went on behind Darin's closed door a few moments after she left. He pulled out an index card from his file, reached for the phone, and punched in a number, absently chewing on a pencil as he waited for an answer.

"Monarch Enterprises," a nasal voice intoned.

"Yes. This is Darin Summerhays calling. I'd like to speak to Brendan Cahill. . . ."

"My God! Be careful, Cass!"

Darin's face was the same gray shade as the aspen trees

that grew in clusters on the mountainside. Expertly Cass tooled the car around a sharp curve in the dirt road heading toward a narrow wooden bridge.

"If you really want a heart attack," she suggested casually, keeping her own eyes glued to the road, "look down."

He made the mistake of taking her suggestion. Green now blended with the gray and white in his face. Below the primitive, unrailed bridge was a narrow gorge—not fifteen feet wide where they crossed, but more than a hundred feet straight down. He quickly closed his eyes until the insubstantial bump of rough-hewn wood gave way to the solid bump of rutted dirt.

"That was Rattlesnake Gulch," Cass informed him blithely, following another turn and starting up the steep incline on the other side.

"How much longer to Wells' Springs?" Darin asked faintly.

"Only another twenty minutes. Relax. Enjoy the scenery."

"You expect me to relax," he grumbled, "when I feel as though every bone in my body had been shaken loose?"

Cass smiled sympathetically. Darin prized his creature comforts and had had a long, hard day. After a week's planning and preparation, he and Cass had finally flown from New York to Salt Lake City early that morning. From there they had chartered a twin-engine plane to the small town of Escalante—elevation 5,258 feet—and picked up a rental car to drive the remaining distance to the ranch. He had held up fairly well, she admitted, until the roads had begun to deteriorate. The blacktopped highway became a graded road, and the graded road soon dwindled into a hard-packed dirt track.

She had tried to keep Darin entertained at first by pointing out local landmarks and answering questions—"Clint Eastwood made that movie on the Arizona border in Paria Canyon. . . . No, John Ford shot most of his westerns in Monument Valley, in the four corners area. . . . Up to the north the pass is called Hell's Backbone. . . ." But Darin's interest had waned with each passing mile, as civilization became only a fond memory.

"You told me that the ranch was only about thirty miles

from Escalante," he complained as they hit one particularly rough patch. "You didn't happen to mention that the thirty miles were straight up."

"That's the way you get to the top of the mountains," Cass explained reasonably. "Though geologically speaking, this isn't really a mountain."

"You couldn't prove it by me," Darin muttered, darting a nervous look out the window at the sheer two-hundred foot drop-off on his side.

"This is the Aquarius Plateau," Cass continued, undaunted by his lack of enthusiasm. "It was carved out by billions of years of erosion. At its highest points, it's over ten thousand feet. The ranch is at about eighty-five hundred feet."

"How on earth did you and Ben get to school?"

"We didn't. We did home study. Twice a year we would go into Escalante to take the tests." She frowned. The kids' education was one of the arguments Ben had used for wanting to sell Wells' Springs.

Cass was still brooding about this when they reached the top rim of the plateau. From there the road curved around a large outcropping of rock and dropped down toward a lush green valley. She stopped the car and leaned her arms on the steering wheel, her eyes filled with pride and love.

"There it is, Darin—Wells' Springs Ranch. The rail fence marks the northern boundary. The house is just over that hill, on the other side of that grove of trees."

"Then let's get going," he said impatiently.

Cass, however, wasn't to be hurried. She started slowly forward, savoring the moment of arrival. She hadn't been home in nine months, not since she had come for her father's funeral.

Even Darin, she thought, should be able to appreciate the approach to the ranch house. The grass-lined lane cut through a meadow, across a small brook, and into the poplar, pine, and cottonwood trees. When they emerged from the woods, the sprawling ranch house was in sight. Nothing to be ashamed of there either. The center portion of the one-story house was the original log structure, built by her great-grandfather. Her father and his father before him had each added a stone wing until now the house was shaped like a giant U. The circular lane in front spoked off in several directions, around either side of the house and down to the corrals, barns, and various outbuildings.

Cass pulled up beside an old, battered half-ton pickup and frowned. She recognized the truck, the well-used Jeep parked beside it, and even the newer sedan, but she didn't recognize the heavy four-wheel-drive wagon on the other side. Did Ben and Loretta have company?

Before she had time to give the question any more consideration, the door of the house flew open and two small bodies hurled themselves across the porch and down the steps. Her nephew and niece barely gave her time to get out of the car before clinging to her with their strong, suntanned arms.

"Aunt Cass, Aunt Cass, we've been watching for you for hours and hours!" eight-year-old Jacob cried.

"I made a prethent for you," five-year-old Julie lisped shyly, peeking around Cass to stare wide-eyed at Darin.

Cass returned their hugs, kissed each well-scrubbed face, and noted that Loretta had dressed them up in their company best. She rather missed the torn and faded overalls.

"Who's that?" the boy asked bluntly, pointing at Darin, who was now climbing stiffly out of the car.

"Julie, Jacob, I want you to say hello to a friend of mine, Mr. Summerhays."

"Is he going to stay with us too? Like the other man?" Jacob asked expectantly. "We've never had so much company."

"What other man?" Cass asked, smiling at the children's enthusiasm. She remembered the excitement of rare but welcome visitors to the ranch.

Julie answered for them both. "Him," she said, pointing toward the three adults standing on the porch of the house.

Ben and Loretta had come out to greet the new arrivals, but Cass scarcely noticed them. In the center of the trio stood a man a good three inches shorter than her brother and not nearly so classically handsome, but he captured her entire attention. She blinked to make the apparition vanish, but the man was no figment of a fevered imagination. It was Brendan Cahill in the flesh.

A surge of conflicting emotions kept her immobilized—shock, delight, despair, and then, uppermost, anger. How dare he follow her out here? She supposed she had the babbling Janet to thank for his appearance. Brendan would have had no compunction about coaxing Cass's whereabouts from the girl. She'd been a fool not to threaten Janet with violence if she so much as breathed a word.

She closed her eyes and wished him a thousand miles away. Her fervent prayer the past week had been that she would never have to see Brendan Cahill again. Total separation was her only hope for a quick recovery from her stupid, adolescent infatuation. She refused now to call what she had felt for him love. He had simply been the wrong man at the right time in the right place. Here he was that same wrong man, at the worst possible time, and definitely in the wrong place.

While Cass was trying to regain her composure, Ben came forward, kissed her awkwardly on the cheek, and extended his hand to Darin. "I've heard a lot about you. Welcome to Wells' Springs." He gestured back toward the porch. "My wife, Loretta. Darin Summerhays. And Cass, I'd like you to meet a guest of ours, Brendan Cahill, from Monarch Enterprises in New York. Brendan, my sister—"

Cass cut him off unceremoniously. "I'm sorry to say that Mr. Cahill and I have already met."

Ben stared at her blankly, obviously taken aback by the coldness in her voice. Loretta registered displeasure at Cass's blatant rudeness. Darin picked at a piece of lint on his lapel, ignoring the contretemps. Brendan himself smiled at Cass, seemingly unmoved by her reception, except that now the cynical slant to his eyebrow dominated his expression.

"It's nice to see you again too, Cass," he drawled.

Cass pulled herself together. She was still suffering from a certain amount of shock, but on one level her faculties were in perfect working order. An important piece of troubling information focused itself in her mind: Ben didn't know of her previous relationship with Brendan. He had introduced him to her as a representative of Monarch Enterprises. Had she been flattering herself? Had Brendan come to Wells'

Springs for something more than a personal cause? Something such as business? *Monarch business?*

Her attention moved from Brendan's cynical eyebrow to Loretta's malicious smile of satisfaction and finally to the nervous twitch at the corner of her brother's mouth. They all seemed to know something that she didn't, but she could hazard a nasty, educated guess.

She had no desire to resurrect memories of that night in her apartment weeks before, but Brendan's presence on the ranch gave her no choice. In the privacy of her own home, she remembered with justifiable resentment, she herself had babbled out the information that Ben wanted to sell the ranch. Brendan's tenacious business mind must have recorded that fact and tucked it away for future use. And now here he was, she was sure, to use that information against her. Had he no business ethics? No sense of fair play? Apparently not, she concluded bitterly.

She turned to stare at her brother but, as in New York, he was avoiding her eyes—reinforcing her premonition of trouble. "Ben!" she said sharply. "I want to know what's going on!"

Loretta quickly intervened, her tone solicitous but her velvet claws sharp. "We'll talk about it later, Cassie darling, after you've had a chance to rest. You poor dear, you look simply fagged to death."

Cass was in no mood to play snide games with her sister-in-law. "I want to hear about it *now,* Loretta. And from my brother, if you don't mind." She didn't mince words. "Ben, are you considering selling the ranch to Monarch Enterprises?"

Ben still refused to look at her. His glance skittered past Loretta, Darin, and Brendan and settled on the ground at his feet. "Brendan's made us a good offer, Cass," he muttered, half defiant, half apologetic.

Cass shook her head—hurt, bewildered, incredulous. She had been right. Brendan intended to try and buy the ranch right out from under her. But why? The most obvious answer hurt the worst. He had to know what Wells' Springs meant to her. Buying it had to be his petty revenge for the wound she had dealt his inflated ego.

"You wouldn't, Brendan!" she said miserably. "You couldn't!"

Brendan had no trouble in meeting the pain in her eyes. If he had any feeling left for her at all, it didn't show on his face.

"You're wrong about that, Cass," he answered harshly. "I not only would, but I can and I will."

"Aggie," Loretta instructed the housekeeper, "serve coffee and drinks before you put the children to bed."

"Yes, Mrs. Wells." The elderly woman threw Cass a quick smile and looked heavenward. Aggie Taylor and her husband Will, the ranch foreman, had been a part of Cass's life for as long as she could remember.

"Shall we go into the living room?" Loretta asked. "We'll be more comfortable there."

Cass heard more in her sister-in-law's voice than a simple invitation. There was a steely determination, and Cass guessed that Loretta was planning to precipitate the crisis that had been left pending earlier. Apparently Darin, too, sensed an unpleasant situation in the making.

"Uh, perhaps it might be better if I go out for a walk," he suggested tentatively.

"Nonsense." Loretta smiled coquettishly up into his face, took him by the arm, and personally escorted him toward the living room, her long, beaded caftan of pink silk floating gracefully around her, emphasizing her blond beauty and giving her an undeserved angelic air. "From all that Cassie and Ben have told me about you, Darin, I feel as though you're one of the family."

Cass, watching her sister-in-law and listening to her charm Darin, scowled. Loretta, she concluded, had been born and reared in the wrong century. As a southern belle, she could have made Scarlet O'Hara look like a beneficent wimp.

At the door to the living room, Cass paused, principally to avoid sitting anywhere near Brendan. She had found his presence across the dinner table from her infinitely disturbing. Perhaps it was because the casual western clothes he wore suited him far too well. She would have much preferred to see him looking as out of place as Darin did in his gray flannel three-piece suit, white shirt, and tie.

"Come in and sit down, Cassie love," Loretta called sweetly. With one fluid movement she curled up like a contented cat on the couch next to her husband and preened until she had drawn the attention of all three men. "Isn't this cozy?"

"Very nice," Darin returned with forced joviality. The tension in the room was shaking even his social graces.

"I don't know when we've had so much company," Loretta purred, accepting a glass of liqueur from Aggie. She sought and found Cass, sitting now in a corner easy chair, and her eyes glittered with spite. "So nice that you could visit the ranch one last time, Cassie. It will give you a chance to store up memories for your old age."

"Loretta, please," Ben muttered uncomfortably.

So far, Loretta had orchestrated the day's events to suit herself and obviously intended to continue. She had arranged it so that Ben and Cass had had no time alone to talk. She had hustled Cass and Darin off to their rooms with the warning that they just had time to freshen up before cocktails. Then, during dinner, she had played the role of hostess like a pro, keeping the conversation light and witty and studiously avoiding the topic that was on all their minds—the sale of the ranch. Now, it seemed, she was ready to strike.

"Ben," she said tartly, "Cass already knows how you and I feel about this God-forsaken place. Let's get on with the details of the sale and say good riddance."

"We have to talk this over, Ben," Cass said through clenched teeth. "Now. Alone."

"Not alone, Cassie," Loretta contradicted insolently, her halo slipping. "This little matter concerns all of us."

Her brother threw Cass one apprehensive look, then averted his eyes. He couldn't help being torn, she was convinced, between loyalty to his wife and loyalty to his heritage. She had the sinking feeling, though, that his personal feelings were more inclined toward letting Loretta have her way.

"Well, Ben?" Loretta prodded sharply. "Isn't that right?"

Ben ran a hand through his hair—harassed, miserable, petulent, and stubborn, all at the same time. He had always been weak, Cass considered sadly, willing to let other people make decisions for him. Having a tough, competent, superconfident father hadn't helped any. If he'd married a different sort of woman, he might have toughened himself, but Loretta had moved in and manipulated his life in whatever areas his father had left untouched.

"Loretta's right, Cass," Ben said at last in a voice that was just a little too loud. "This isn't a decision you and I can make by ourselves. It affects Loretta and the children as much or more than it does us."

"And Mr. Cahill, of course," Cass snapped.

"Yes, of course. Brendan came all the way out from New York two days ago with a generous business proposition."

She just bet it was generous! Hadn't she found out the hard way that Brendan was perfectly willing to spend enormous amounts of money to get what he wanted?

"He has a right to know what's going on," Ben concluded.

"And *I* didn't have the same right?" Cass asked coldly. "Brendan must already have been here when I called you yesterday. Why didn't you tell me?"

"Since you were going to be here so soon," her brother muttered defensively, "Loretta and I thought it would be better for us all to sit down together and discuss it in person."

"There's nothing to discuss as far as I'm concerned," Cass announced flatly. "Mr. Cahill is just wasting his time."

The Loretta that Cass had come to know and detest so many years before took charge. "Don't be more of a fool than you can help, Cassie! You haven't even heard the offer yet."

"I don't need to hear the offer to find it unacceptable, Loretta!"

It was Ben's turn to intervene. He hated dissention. "Cass, just listen," he pleaded. "Monarch Enterprises is willing to pay eight hundred thousand dollars, *cash,* for the ranch! Four hundred thousand for you, four hundred thousand for me."

"Even you couldn't be stupid enough to turn down an

offer like that," Loretta interjected sarcastically. "That's more profit than the ranch would bring you in thirty years."

Cass's eyes widened at the sum involved, but at the same time her mouth tightened with anger. Money, money, money—was that all anyone ever thought about? She glared at Brendan, who was sitting back in his chair, listening but saying nothing, watching her face through his thick lashes, his brandy warming between his strong, calloused hands.

"Have you stopped to wonder," she asked Ben and Loretta tartly, "why Monarch should be interested in buying a ranch? This is the first time I've heard of their investing in cattle."

"Brendan explained when he made us the offer," Ben replied uncomfortably.

For the first time, Cass addressed Brendan directly. "You've let everyone else do the talking, Brendan. Now, why don't you explain to *me* why Monarch has suddenly taken such an interest in a comparatively small ranch out in the middle of nowhere? You do know that most of the grazing land is leased from the Bureau of Land Management, don't you?"

"The ranch is just the right size as it is for what I have in mind," he said casually, taking a sip of his brandy.

"And just what is it you *do* have in mind?" she snapped. "I can't wait to hear."

He paused to light a cigarette with his gold lighter, took a puff, and looked at her through the smoke.

"You don't realize what a prime location this is, Cass. It will be ideal for a mountain resort—horseback riding, backpacking, fishing. Monarch will build condominiums, swimming pools, boutiques, all the civilized amenities city people expect. It's private, out of the way, and has a spectacular view. But at the same time it's within easy access to some of the most famous natural wonders and man-made recreation areas in the country—Zion Park, Bryce Canyon, Lake Powell, the rapids of the Colorado River, and the Grand Canyon, of course." He smiled at her wryly. "You see, I've done my homework."

Cass listened to all this with a dismay verging on horror. "Ben? Do you hear what he's saying? He wants to turn Wells' Springs into a *dude ranch!*"

"That's the best part, Cass," Ben told her enthusiastically. "Monarch will keep on all the hands who work the ranch so that no one is out a job. Will can stay on as foreman and Aggie as housekeeper. The ranch house will stay just as it is, for atmosphere. The condominiums themselves will be built higher up, into the mountainside, so that every apartment has a view."

"Doesn't it sound wonderful?" Loretta exclaimed. "And perhaps to show his gratitude," she added shrewdly, "Brendan will commission Cassandra's to do the interior designs. Now that would be an inducement, wouldn't it, Darin?"

Darin grunted noncommittally, unwilling to open this can of worms. He was the only one of the small group who knew how Cass felt about Monarch and their projects, and he was far too shrewd with people either to disillusion Loretta or to anger Cahill. Besides, from what he had heard, he had no doubt that Cass would manage both without any help from him.

"Well, Cass?" Ben asked eagerly. "What do you say?"

"I say . . . I say . . ." Words failed her. When she found her voice, it was all she could do not to annihilate her brother completely. "I say that it looks to me as if you've lost whatever values you were born with, Ben. Can you imagine what Dad would say if he could hear you now?"

"But Cass, I'm not like Dad!" he cried, wounded and pleading. "I'll never be the rancher he was. Consider what it could mean—"

"Ben," she admonished him, more gently now, "no one is asking you to be like Dad. He was one of a kind. But I do expect you to have some sense of responsibility. I *have* considered what selling the ranch to Monarch could mean—which is more than you've done. I won't have any part of it."

Brendan's eyes on her face grew harder. "What would you say if I raise the offer to an even million?"

Even Darin looked startled at this amount. Ben and Loretta turned expectant faces toward Cass. She quickly burst their bubble of hope.

"Mr. Cahill, I wouldn't care if you offered us *ten* million! My answer would still be no. Under no circumstances will I agree to sell the land to Monarch!" Shakily she levered herself to her feet, her face flushed and strained from impotent rage and feelings of betrayal. Deliberately she turned her back on them all. "If you'll excuse me now," she said curtly, "I'll say good night."

"I'll come with you, Cass," Darin offered cravenly.

The men had all risen when she stood. Ben moved now to block her way. "Please, Cass!" he begged.

"Nothing you can say will make me change my mind, Ben," she told him wearily. "Come on, Darin."

She started forward, and reluctantly Ben stood aside to let her pass. Just as she reached the door, she turned back to Brendan for one parting shot.

"I'll say good-bye now, Mr. Cahill. I assume you'll be wanting to leave early in the morning. I can't imagine that you're a man to waste his time on a lost cause."

"When have you ever known me to consider anything I really wanted a lost cause, Cass?"

His voice was deep and husky as he spoke. His hot gaze had followed her across the room, and the expression in his eyes now concealed nothing. He couldn't have made his feelings for her any clearer if he had put them into words and shouted them aloud. Love, desire, anger, and determination all mingled on his lined and rugged face for everyone to see.

Cass saw and was appalled by the sudden racing of her pulse and erratic pounding of her heart. What would it take to dull her senses and rid herself of the foolish, compulsive longing she felt for him? Was she doomed to go through life remembering with such devastating vividness the exquisite touch of his hands, the feel of his soft, expressive mouth, the impact of his hard body against hers?

She was so consumed with her own thoughts, it took her a minute to notice that the room was silent and that every eye was trained on her. Frantically she wondered what her own face revealed. From Ben's open-mouthed surprise, Loretta's calculating frown, and Brendan's expanding, satisfied smile, she could guess that it revealed much too much—far more than she wanted broadcast either to him or to her family.

Why, oh, why had Brendan come to the ranch and made a touchy, complex situation even more difficult and complicated? What on earth did he hope to gain?

Her gaze shifted around the living room of the house where she had spent her childhood years. The portrait of her mother still hung over the stone fireplace. Her father's favorite chair stood to one side, permanently indented from the weight and shape of his large, hulking body. Against the far wall were the rough-hewn shelves, filled with the books she had read and reread as a girl. Her glance lit briefly first on Brendan, then on Ben, next on Loretta, and finally on Darin.

Cass's sense of reality began to warp. Everything was crazy. Loretta and Ben in New York. Brendan and Darin at the ranch. Loretta and Ben at the ranch. Brendan and Darin in New York. Here were people who had existed for her in different worlds, now together, mingling, making outrageous, unthinkable proposals. The evening had suddenly taken on the distorted quality of a bad dream.

"Cass?" Darin muttered in concern. "Are you all right?"

"No," she whispered, sure at the moment that she would never be all right again.

"What is it, Cassie? What are you saying?" Loretta's voice, harsh, strident, cut into their exchange.

"Nothing, Loretta! . . . Darin, get me out of here!"

He took her arm, but before they could move, Brendan was beside them. Cass closed her eyes as he lifted her chin with the tips of his fingers—a touch she remembered all too well.

"Cass? Open your eyes and look at me."

She found it impossible not to do as he asked. Their glances met and held. In the dim light of the doorway, the black flecks had turned his eyes a steely blue-gray. She read his message in their depths before he spoke the words.

"Fight me all you want, Cass," he said softly, "but it won't do you any good. I don't give up easily on anything I begin. And in your case, I don't intend to give up at all."

Chapter 9

JUST AS DAWN WAS BREAKING CASS EASED THE BACK DOOR OF the house closed behind her and stood on the old cement porch. For the first time she saw the contributions Ben had made to the quality of life on the ranch since their father had died.

A new room had been added on, obviously a family room, with sliding glass doors leading out onto a deck that overlooked the farms and valleys below. She was thankful that the addition was a tasteful blending of wood and stone, designed as an integral part of the older wing.

Cass wished she could applaud Ben's taste—or more probably Loretta's, she thought in disgust—on the second addition to the back yard. In space that had once been part of a vegetable garden, the landscape was marred by a gigantic satellite dish. Apparently the long tentacles of television had finally reached out and embraced the Wells' homestead. Cass didn't really begrudge her sister-in-law her television, but the dish was such an eyesore.

Cass shuddered delicately and looked away, seeking more harmonious and familiar sights.

The corral was empty, but from the stables, barns, and chicken coops came the sounds of the animals moving about, aware of the arrival of a new day. The lights were on now in the bunkhouse. Soon the hands would begin the routine of ranch work: the cows to milk, the home-farm animals to feed and water, the new horses to break for sale or use on the ranch. Some of the hands would work near the ranch house and barns, while others would join the wranglers who stayed with the cattle herd on the range.

The work was hard, as Loretta had said, but Cass couldn't imagine that there was a cowboy on the ranch who would have traded his saddle for a desk chair. Just Ben, she thought sadly.

The sound of approaching voices floated along the cool morning air. Will and Aggie were on their way up from their small cottage in the trees. Cass didn't feel like talking with anyone just then, not even her old friends. Silently she slipped around the side of the house and across the dirt track. Almost unthinkingly she sought out the trail that led into the trees, through small streams—water from the numerous underground springs that gave the ranch the last part of its name—and upward to the high plateau.

The climb was easy at first, but soon the trail grew steeper and overgrown with weeds and brush. It looked as though no one had been there since she had come herself nine months before, after her father's funeral. As the climb grew harder, the vegetation became thicker—more pines, aspen, and juniper. At last Cass reached the small outcropping of rock that was her special place, the spot where as a child she had always come for solitude and solace. This promontory gave her a panoramic view of the surrounding countryside. Never had she tired of the sight.

To the west was Dixie National Forest and Bryce Canyon; to the east, Canyonlands and the Colorado River. Directly below her, to the south, lay the town of Escalante, looking peaceful and serene in the morning light. South and east beyond the town stretched a vast expanse of uninhabited wilderness area. There was nothing peaceful, secure, or serene in what Cass saw there, and it suited her mood that morning. The land was awe-inspiring, breathtakingly beautiful and, ultimately, very humbling. As a child, Cass had named this wilderness Lucifer's Playground.

Lucifer's Playground: multicolored stone configurations and isolated mesas, first formed by moving, heaving earth; built layer upon layer by deposits of sand, silt, and decaying vegetation; hardened over innumerable millennia by heat and pressure; and finally carved out by eons of wind, water, and shifting rock. Hidden from sight were enormous caverns, treacherous narrows, deep gulches, and overhanging cliffs. But it was a living land, still in the continuous process of evolution. Often as she grew up, she had wondered fancifully what future generations, children in ages yet to come, would see.

To her the wilderness area had been and still was a wonderful, eerie, magical world where civilization had not yet intruded, where nature played capricious tricks, and where, normally, modern man was alien. But Cass's upbringing had not been normal, and she was no alien to either its delights or its treachery. Lucifer's Playground was a place Cass loved, understood and, above all, respected.

She was staring eastward, lost in reverie, when the sun edged up over the horizon and hit her in the eyes. Everything went dark for a moment as her pupils adjusted to the light. She blinked, and when she opened her eyes again, she saw her beloved country the way Brendan's wealthy, pampered patrons would see it. This strange land wasn't like Yellowstone Park, Yosemite, or even the Grand Canyon. This seemingly barren wilderness demanded a special kind of exploration, knowledge, and appreciation. She could almost hear the tourists' reactions now:

(Shudder.) "Look down there, Wilford. It's so—so *desolate.*" (Whine.) "I wish you'd taken me to the ocean like I wanted. . . ." (Boast, boast.) "Now, that's my kind of country. I drove through the Mojave once, you know. . . ." (Appreciative within limits.) "Isn't that pretty, Frank?" "Let's see if Monarch gives guided tours—on an air-conditioned bus, of course. . . ." (Enterprising.) "Come on, Mildred. We can collect sandstone rocks, doll 'em up a little, and sell 'em as paperweights. . . ." (Practical joker.) "Look at all that red rock, Dolores." "Take some pictures, and I'll tell everybody we went to Mars. . . ." (Most typical.) "Who cares, Delbert?" "It's just another beautiful view. I want to go to Kanab. I heard Burt Reynolds is making a movie there. . . ."

"Ben told me I would probably find you here."

Cass jumped and nearly lost her footing. The voices she was hearing in her head suddenly had substance and that substance was Brendan with his Irish brogue. She swayed, and he caught her by the elbow to steady her.

"I'm sorry, Cass, I didn't mean to frighten you."

"No one usually comes up here but me," she said faintly, pulling her arm away from his disturbing touch.

"I can understand why. That was some climb."

It was indeed a good, healthy climb, and Brendan was slightly out of breath. Too much of the good life, she suspected, and less actual work. Would the callouses on his hands soon soften? she wondered with something approaching regret. But right now there was nothing soft about his rugged face and taut body, and he was staring at her in a very disconcerting way.

"Did you want something in particular?" she asked to break the tense silence.

"You know what I want. My God!" For the first time he looked past Cass to the wilderness area beyond. "My God," he repeated. "What is that? It looks the way our parish priest used to describe hell when I was a kid."

"Maybe that's why I call it Lucifer's Playground," she said stiffly.

"A good name for it!" he exclaimed with feeling. "But this is some view, isn't it? Look. I bet you can see all the way into Arizona."

"I'm afraid we're on federal land now, Brendan," she told him sarcastically. "You can't buy it—unless perhaps you have a senator or two in your pocket."

His jaw tightened, but he didn't reply to her deliberately insulting remark. Instead he turned away, staring out over Lucifer's Playground, his hands stuck in the back pockets of his jeans. If Cass hadn't thought him incapable of feeling such an emotion, she would have sworn that her words had stung him. They stood in awkward silence watching the dramatic play of light and shadow on the land below as the sun rose higher in the sky. Cass was soon caught up in the spectacular light show, but the moment was short-lived. Brendan broke the mood. He obviously didn't share her awe at the uniqueness of the sight.

"Sort of like morning in New York, when the sun comes up and hits the skyscrapers, isn't it, Cass? Only I'd hate to have to find a decent breakfast down there."

Cass flinched. She didn't find his comments either apt or amusing. Casting pearls before swine, she concluded angrily and turned to leave.

"Cass, wait." He caught her by the arm.

"Let go of me, Brendan." She enunciated each word.

"We have to talk." His words were just as clipped, but his hold on her arm slackened.

"We have nothing to say to each other! Now, let me go." She stared silently at his hand until, with a shrug, he let it drop to his side. Cass's every inclination was to leave now that she had the chance, but wisdom told her that if Brendan was bent on forcing a confrontation—which he obviously was—it would be better to quarrel with him there, away from the prying eyes and ears of the family. "All right, Brendan." She sighed. "Say what you have to say and let's get it over with."

"You know what I want to talk about, Cass. About what happened to us. About what made you pick up and leave like that!"

It was her turn to shrug, but she refused to meet his eyes. "It was nothing all that unusual. I just realized a little too late that what we had going for us wasn't the sort of thing that would last. It was better to put an end to it before we were both in over our heads."

"I don't believe a word of it!" he said harshly. "We had something good, really good, between us that night." His eyes took on that steely determination that Cass found so unnerving. "You know how I feel about you, and I can't believe that you don't still feel the same way about me. I can't believe that we can't talk out any problems."

"Is that why you followed me out here, Brendan?" she asked bitterly.

"Yes," he admitted tersely. "And why I made my offer on the ranch. I just happened to luck out and discover that it was also a terrific financial investment. You're sitting on a very valuable piece of property. It can make you a wealthy woman.''

A blaze of outrage flared in her eyes. As though she cared about the money! ''Well, you can take your investment money, Brendan, and spread it around Florida or Arizona or Texas or California or anyplace else you want. Just don't litter my ranch with it! Oh, why don't you go back to New York and mind your own business!'' she finished in anger and frustration.

''Real estate speculation and development *is* my business, if you'll remember.''

''How could I forget?'' she asked sarcastically.

His jaw tightened into a hard, stubborn line. ''I didn't hear your brother complaining.''

''That's because he doesn't know you as well as I do!''

Brendan's eyes slid suggestively over her slim form in her tight jeans, flannel shirt, and denim jacket, and she saw the awakening flicker of desire. ''I certainly can't argue with you there.''

''That's—that's not what I meant, and you know it!'' she stammered and a flush rose in her neck.

''No? Then what *are* we talking about? That's what I'm here to discuss,'' he said huskily.

''I told you in the beginning,'' she said helplessly. ''We have nothing in common.''

''And I thought we had laid that ridiculous notion to rest,'' he came back, the double entendre clear.

''That's all you think about, isn't it! Sex and work, work and sex.''

Brendan threw out his hands in a gesture of frustration. ''I wouldn't have put it quite so crassly, but face it Cass—add eating and sleeping and, reduced to the fundamentals, that's what life's all about.''

''I don't happen to believe that, Brendan—which is what sets us poles apart.''

''Don't believe *what?* We love each other, so we sleep together. We each have our work—''

''Okay! Stop right there. That's what I'm talking about. You don't have any idea how I feel about my work and you

don't really care. And what's more," she added with a new
bitterness, "you have no idea that I find your work absolutely appalling!"

"You find *building* appalling?" he asked in genuine
astonishment. "That's absurd."

"Is it? Well, it's true. What you choose to call development, I consider nothing but a euphemism for exploitation.
You rape the land, and for what? The money. Look what
you've proposed to do with the ranch. Build vacation
condominiums! And don't tell me that the people who
would buy or lease or share them wouldn't have to pay
through the nose."

"We're not a nonprofit organization, for heaven's sake,"
Brendan said in exasperation. "Monarch is a corporation.
Our stockholders expect us to make money."

"And that's what really concerns you."

"I'm president of the company and chairman of the
board. Of course it concerns me."

"But it doesn't concern you at all that you're willing to
take beautiful, unspoiled pieces of land and turn them into
tourist attractions?"

"No," he said tersely. "That's what land is for, for people
to live on and use and enjoy. I help make that possible.
What on earth is so appalling about that?"

Cass shook her head in consternation. He was so obtuse,
so insensitive! "What is so appalling," she explained
through clenched teeth, "is the fact that you have no
consideration or appreciation for the land you buy—other
than the fact that it can make you a handsome profit, of
course. You don't care that a development could devastate
the environment, upset the delicate balance of nature. It
wouldn't matter to you whether or not Monarch preserved
the integrity of the surrounding area as long as it was
bringing in enough money!"

"What is this sudden obsession you have with money and
conservation?" he asked impatiently.

"*I'm* not the one obsessed with money, Brendan. And
there is nothing sudden about my concern for the land or the
environment or the wildlife. We've been fighting battles
with the government for years, trying to keep them from

building new roads through areas that should be protected, to stop them from permitting power companies to pollute the air and destroy natural wonders."

"Who's talking about destroying natural wonders?" he asked in bewilderment.

"I am! You mentioned Lake Powell," she hurried on, her voice thick with remembered rage. "You said you did your homework, but what do you really know about it?"

He shrugged irritably. "What's to know? It's the lake back of Glen Canyon Dam. And who cares?"

"I care!" she snapped. "And I'll tell you what there is to know. The Colorado River was dammed to provide power for southern California. It didn't matter that in creating Lake Powell the government put under water some of the most extraordinary, spectacular places that existed on the face of the earth. Those places are gone forever now. And what makes their willful destruction worse is that even by modest predictions, the lake will be entirely filled in with accumulating silt within a hundred and fifty years, probably even sooner than that."

"This is senseless! I do not build power plants. I do not build dams."

Cass stared at him in growing disillusionment. For some stupid reason, she thought bleakly, she had actually hoped that if she explained how she felt, he would understand. "You really don't care, do you? You don't care if we mortgage the future for generations to come for the sake of whatever's convenient or profitable."

"Will you get off your soapbox, Cass?" Brendan growled in growing frustration. "I don't want a lecture on ecology. I want to find out what in the hell my business has to do with *us!*"

"You made an offer to buy the ranch," she reminded him grimly. "You *chose* to make your business my concern in a very personal way."

His eyes narrowed. "What kind of a number are you doing, Cass? Are you trying to fool me or delude yourself? You walked out on me over a week ago. That had nothing to do with my offer to buy Wells' Springs."

"But it's all part of the same problem!"

"Problem? *What* problem?"

"Working," she said tersely.

"Well, it looks as though we've now come full circle," he said in disgust. "And I'm still unenlightened. I don't have a clue about what the sins of Monarch Enterprises have to do with all this."

"I'm not talking about Monarch now," she said tartly. "I'm talking about you and me."

"Well, that will certainly be nice for a change!"

"I'm glad you think so!" His sarcasm spurred her on to a more cutting explanation than she had intended to make. "You *are* a workaholic, Brendan. Oh, I'm not claiming that you didn't warn me in the beginning, but it took me a while to recognize the magnitude of your obsession with your job and how it would affect me. You made it abundantly clear last week, though, that all you *really* care about is your work, your business. No personal relationship could hope to compete. Love would always run a pretty poor second. Or would it come in third, after money?" she concluded bitterly.

"You're a fine one to talk about love, Cass," Brendan answered with equal bitterness. "From where I stand personal relationships don't even appear on *your* list of priorities. And if you want to talk about obsessions, how else would you describe this fanatical attitude of yours toward the ranch?"

"I just spent the past ten minutes explaining that!"

"You mean you spent the past ten minutes avoiding the real issue! Would you be so indignant about Monarch's wanting to develop around here if we weren't talking about Wells' Springs?"

His accusation took her by surprise. "Of course I would! But the ranch happens to be my *home!*"

"At last we're getting somewhere. Shouldn't you say it *was* your home—a good ten years ago?"

"What are you driving at, Brendan?" she asked suspiciously. She didn't like that triumphant smile on his face.

"You accused me once of trying to evade the past, Cass. Well, it's true, and I make no apologies for that. But it sure as hell beats trying to live your life through old, distorted, childhood memories."

"I'm not!"

"Grow up, Cass! You admitted that I would be an escape for you. But the truth is that I didn't turn out to be a safe enough escape because I asked too much from you. I expected you to act like an adult. I expected you to face your problems and work them out. But you couldn't deal with that, so what did you do? You decided to cut and run, to try and recapture the nice, safe past."

Every word he had spoken that morning had widened the gulf between them, confirmed all her worst fears, and made her decision to leave him all the more sensible. She had known from the first, of course, that they had little in common, but she hadn't realized until that day what a vast difference there was in their outlook on life.

Cass shook her head despairingly. "You really don't understand, Brendan, do you."

"I understand what I see, and everything you've said has confirmed what I've suspected for the past week," he said harshly. "You're obsessed with the past, and I'm not willing to compete with that."

"This is not a competition!"

"You're right," he agreed tartly. "What living man could compete with a bunch of ghosts?"

"I'm not ghost-hunting, Brendan! And I admit—with no apology at all—that I've been dwelling a lot on the past lately—my childhood, my old home, my upbringing. And I did cut and run. I doubt if you'll have a clue to what I'm talking about," she interjected bitterly, "but I guess I do owe you some explanation."

"Don't do me any favors," he snapped. "I'm only your lover!"

"Past tense, Brendan," she snapped back. "You *were* my lover—briefly. And you're dead wrong if you think that I came back here to recapture some idyllic past life. What I intend to recapture are the values and principles I was raised on. Something you would undoubtedly consider a stupid, quixotic gesture," she added angrily, "but to me it's important. My years in New York have warped my perspective and made those values harder and harder to hold onto. I didn't come here to resurrect the past, Brendan. I came back to build a sane future life for myself."

He had heard and in the abstract could understand what

Cass said. But Brendan didn't deal with abstractions. He dealt with reality, and one painful, tangible fact was clear. "What you're obviously telling me, Cass, is that as far as you're concerned, I have no place in that sane future!"

"That's right, Brendan." Considering the nature and bitterness of their quarrel, the words were harder to speak than she would have believed.

"And Wells' Springs has a corner on sanity, does it?" he asked harshly.

"Right now, at this point in my life—yes, it does."

His jaw set so hard that the lines around his mouth turned white. "You're wrong, Cass. And I don't intend to let you stay here and ruin both our lives."

"And just how do you think you're going to stop me?" she challenged him.

"By finishing what I started out to do," he told her ruthlessly. "I am going to buy the ranch!"

Spots of angry color appeared high on Cass's cheeks. "What good do you think that would do?"

"I don't intend to let you run away from me, Cass. I want you in New York—with me—where you belong."

The thought had crossed her mind the day before that Brendan intended to buy the ranch out of sheer revenge. She had been wrong, but his real reason was every bit as bad. Love and hate warred within her until she couldn't tell the difference between the two. A red haze, one that had nothing to do with the rising sun, blurred her vision. She had never been more furious in her life.

"You—you conceited, selfish, arrogant, conniving bastard!" she sputtered. She was so angry she couldn't come up with enough adjectives to express her outrage. "What makes you think you know what's best for me? You don't even *know* me. You have no right to manipulate my life."

"Fool that I am, I love you, Cass!" he ground out through gritted teeth. "And that gives me some rights."

"Love?" she jeered. "That's a joke!"

"Loving you is no *joke,* Cass," he snapped. "Believe me! No woman has ever put me through what you have."

The vision of other women in his arms turned her righteous indignation to pure, feminine, jealous rage. She wanted to strike out at him, hurt him as he had just hurt her.

"What you mean," she cried wildly, "is that I wouldn't throw myself at your feet, wouldn't agree to anything you wanted. I had the gall to turn down your magnificent offer, the honor of being your mistress! I knew that you were capable of doing a lot to get your own way, Brendan, but I didn't really believe that even you would spend a million dollars to soothe your wounded ego! That's sick!"

Brendan's eyes were black with shock. His face was ashen under his tan. "Sick? You really do have a rotten opinion of me, don't you!"

"Is there a single good reason why I shouldn't?"

"Do I need to remind you of a certain night we spent together a week ago? This selfish, arrogant bastard didn't hear you complaining while you shared his bed, while we made love through most the night, while you slept in my arms. If you have such a low opinion of *my* character, where does that put *yours?*"

He caught her hand just before it made contact with his face. Every muscle in Cass's body tensed. If he had retaliated, she could have handled it, but he didn't. He simply held her by the wrist, staring down into her face—not moving, not speaking. She didn't see the pain in his eyes. She only knew that her anger was spent, that her well of adrenaline had run dry. She stared back at him, stricken. Her mouth trembled and her body grew limp. She would have fallen if he hadn't held her.

"Cass, Cass," he groaned. "Oh, sweetheart!" With one convulsive movement, he pulled her into his arms and buried his face in her hair. "I'm sorry," he murmured. "I'm sorry. I didn't mean that, not a word of it."

"Oh, Brendan," she moaned. "Neither did I!"

Contrary to any sensible considerations, she offered no resistance when he sought her mouth and expertly parted her lips. She clung to him breathlessly. The angry words, the bitter denunciations and the harsh accusations, had done nothing to dispel the magic of their kiss. In fact, their quarrel had heightened their senses to an acute degree.

Once again Cass savored the intense, familiar delight of Brendan's hard, tough body against hers, the welcome plundering of his hot, moist tongue in her mouth, and the gentle caressing pressure of his seeking hands.

Why? she asked herself as she willingly gave her heart and soul to the embrace. Why? she wondered dizzily, pressing herself tighter and tighter against him, virtually pleading with him to make love to her. What was there about him that made her love him, when every dispassionate, logical part of her being told her that she didn't even like him? When given the right circumstances, she had even found that she was capable of hating him?

"Brendan!" she cried as he led her off the promontory and laid her down on the bed of tall grass that fringed the rocks.

"Yes, love?" he murmured, pulling down the zipper of her jeans.

"I hate you!" She raised her hips as he put his thumbs in the waistband and tugged downward.

"I can tell," he breathed against her warm, creamy skin.

"I despise you!" She gasped with pleasure as he pulled apart the front of her jacket, undid the buttons on her blouse, and captured the tip of her breast between his lips.

"I'm sure you do," he agreed, beginning to strip away his own confining clothing.

She trembled with excitement as his body covered hers and he parted her thighs with a firm, strategically placed knee.

"Brendan," she panted. "I'm going to fight you every step of the way."

"And you're a worthy opponent," he whispered huskily as he began the search for their mutual joy with gentle, devastating expertise. A moan of pleasure escaped her lips as slowly, surely he insinuated himself into her body. Her words became slower, more slurred as the passion between them mounted.

"I'm not . . . going . . . to sell . . . you . . . the ranch!"

He silenced her with his mouth.

Her cry of ecstatic fulfillment and her stubborn denial came as one.

"I'mmmmm nooooot!"

Chapter 10

CASS TOSSED AND TURNED RESTLESSLY ON THE BED, PUNCHED up the pillow, and tried ineffectually to straighten the sheet and quilt that had twisted around her body—more of the covers now under her than over her. She cast one bleary eye at the clock. Three A.M. Would the new day be as terrible, as soul-wrenching as the one just past? It was no wonder that she couldn't sleep.

With a moan she sank back onto the pillow and closed her eyes, but she couldn't close her mind to the echo of voices ringing in her ears.

Loretta: *"You're a selfish, mean, spiteful, vindictive bitch, Cassie! You don't care about anyone but your own spoiled self!"*

Ben: *"Cass, please! Sell! I—I can't take much more of this. I—I have to get out of here!"*

Brendan: *"Cass, me darlin', I would have thought that you had figured out that I don't love you because of your ranch, I love you in spite of it."*

Cass didn't know which had been the hardest for her to cope with—Loretta's rage, Ben's desperation, or Brendan's passion.

Of the three, it was traitorous thoughts of the early-morning interlude with Brendan that had haunted her memories throughout the entire, horrible day . . .

She had laid supine in the tall grass on the edge of the rocky promontory—lethargic, replete, aware for the first time that what clothes she was half wearing were damp with morning dew. She had watched from under lazy eyelids as Brendan buttoned his shirt, tucked it inside his jeans, and pulled up the zipper.

He had glanced at her, grinned, and dropped down on one knee beside her. "You'd better cover up, sweetheart, unless you're asking for a repetition."

She had struggled up on one elbow and pulled her blouse closed. "We have to get back to the ranch. By now, the whole household will notice that we haven't turned up for breakfast."

"No, it wouldn't do to get caught by a search party," he had drawled, placing a kiss on the side of her neck.

"I doubt if we have to worry about that. The whole family must know by now that there's something between us. They're probably hoping that you're somehow—in some unspecified way, of course," she had added in consternation, "persuading me to sell the ranch." She had turned her head away from the amusement on his face and looked out across the vast expanse of empty land. "I—I meant what I said, Brendan. I won't sell the ranch to Monarch."

"Cass, me darlin', I would have thought that you had figured out by now that I don't love you *because* of your ranch, I love you *in spite* of it." He had given emphasis to his words by pressing another kiss on her softly parted lips. "Toss that over in your mind for the next couple of days."

Finally, she had sent him off down the trail, leaving her lying in the grass, lost in her own thoughts. She had no idea how long she stayed after he had gone, staring up at the clear blue of the morning sky, still exhausted after the violence of their quarrel and the tempestuousness of their subsequent lovemaking.

Cass squirmed in her bed as a rush of remembered ecstasy reawakened the tingling of her breasts and sent a yearning heat coursing through her body. Dear Lord, she had wanted him then and she wanted him now. No, she couldn't think of that. Far safer to dwell on Loretta's vicious attack on her . . .

After dinner earlier that evening, the children had gone to bed and Aggie had returned to her cottage. Ben had taken Darin and Brendan along to the barn. One of the dairy cows had been sick, and he wanted to check on her before turning in. Cass had selected a book at random off the shelf and pretended to be engrossed, hoping that Loretta would leave her alone.

No such luck.

For half an hour Loretta had kept up a constant harangue, accusing Cass of everything from lack of compassion to sheer contrariness to deliberately wanting to ruin her brother and sister-in-law's lives. At first Cass had tried to reason with her, explain her objections, make Loretta understand what she was asking of Cass. Nothing she could say could pierce Loretta's armor of determination. Unbecoming color had burned in Loretta's cheeks, marring her fair complexion, as Cass remained adamant. Her sister-in-law had finally given up, ended the argument, and stomped from the room, trailing behind her a flow of invectives that had turned Cass pale.

"You're a selfish, mean, spiteful, vindictive bitch, Cassie!" Loretta had screeched down the hall. "You don't care about anyone but your own spoiled self! I hope you rot in hell!"

Somewhere in the house a board creaked. Julie or Jacob making a middle-of-the-night trip to the bathroom, Cass guessed. In spite of her anxiety, fatigue, and distress, she smiled fondly at the thought of her small niece and nephew. No matter how she personally felt about Loretta, Cass had to admit, albeit grudgingly, that the woman must do something right. Those children were wonderful, bright, unspoiled kids and their aunt loved them dearly. So did their father. But were Ben's reasons for selling the ranch really out of concern for their welfare?

Her brother had cornered her after lunch the day before. He had deliberately sought her out in the stable where she was looking over the horses. One stallion in particular had caught her eye, a roan that her father had purchased only a couple of months before he died.

"He's a beauty, isn't he, Ben?" Cass had asked hesitantly. "What's his name?"

"Kettledrum."

"Do you mind if I ride him sometime?"

"I don't know why you're asking me," Ben had said abrasively, white-faced, tight-lipped, and barely in control of himself. "He's half yours. And I can't see that you give a damn about what I want or my opinion—on anything."

"Please, Ben," she had pleaded. "Can't we talk this over?"

"What is there to talk over? You've had your mind made up since the first time I even mentioned selling the ranch."

Cass couldn't deny it. "But Ben," she had argued, "I just can't believe that deep in your heart you want to leave here and spend the rest of your career behind a desk."

"If we sold to Monarch, I wouldn't have to," he had replied bitterly. "We could invest the money and live on the interest. But even that isn't what I would do."

"What would you do?" she had to ask.

"Do you remember Tom Brockbank, my friend from college? He's managing a western-wear store in Salt Lake. The owner wants to sell out. I would use the money to go in with Tom."

"If only it weren't Monarch," she had protested.

"Come on, Cass," Ben broke in. "At least be honest about it. You don't want to sell to Monarch or anyone. You're not the one who has to deal with all the problems on the ranch. I really believed that you of all people would understand what it's like to have pressures coming at you from all sides, but what it comes down to is that you don't care that it's happening to me. All you care about is yourself." His composure had crumbled completely. His mouth had twitched convulsively and tears had come to his eyes. "Cass, please! Sell! I—I can't take much more of this. I—I have to get out of here! . . ."

Alone with her conscience, in the darkness of the night, the weight of Ben's accusations struck Cass with new force. She twisted and turned, trying to find a comfortable position. But how could she when the problem wasn't with the bed but within herself?

"All you care about is yourself."

Was she being insensitive and selfish, depriving her brother of the right to make a choice about how he lived his life? She had the right to decide her own future, but in stubbornly holding onto the ranch, was she imposing her values and standards on Ben and his family and tampering with their lives in a way she had no right to do? After all, she had accused Brendan of much the same thing.

It was a painful, sobering thought. Her head tossed back and forth on the pillow as she tried to clear her head. Sleep had never been more elusive. Her eyes wouldn't close. They focused, only half aware, on the yellow glow of light that suddenly shown through the ruffled organdy curtains at her window.

Morning. A new day. And she hadn't come to terms with the last.

Automatically she glanced again at the clock. Ten minutes to four. Her frown turned from worry to puzzlement. Four? It couldn't be. Even the summer sun didn't begin to rise until after five.

A sudden premonition, an instinctive fear, clutched at her. She flung the tangled covers aside and stumbled to the window, a sheet dragging along behind. As she threw back the curtains, a blaze of light shot into the room.

She didn't wait to see any more. She didn't even think to reach for her robe or slip into her sandals beside the bed.

"Ben! Ben!" Her voice preceded her down the hall, through the living room to the opposite wing where Ben and Loretta slept. "Ben!"

The door to their room opened just as she raised her fist to pound. "Cass? What's the matter?" Her brother ran a hand across his eyes and pushed his ruffled hair off his face.

"Ben!" she panted. "The barn! Fire!"

Before he could reply, she turned and ran through to the kitchen and out the door to the back porch, where a large brass bell hung suspended on a metal chain. The pattern of procedure had been instilled in her from an early age, and automatically she responded to the crisis. Four times she struck the bell with the iron bar hanging beside it. She paused for the count of three, then struck it four times again. Before the echoing sound of the alarm had died away, the bunkhouse door flew open and men poured out into the stable yard, still fastening jeans and pulling on boots.

Weakly, Cass sagged against the wall to catch her breath. Through the kitchen window she could see Ben hanging up the phone. He had undoubtedly been issuing orders to Will. The back door slammed as he ran past her, down the steps, and across the farmyard to the burning barn. When she had first looked out her window, only the near end was aflame, but now the fire had spread nearly to the center.

"What's going on?"

Cass turned at the sound of Darin's groggy voice beside her. He was in silk pajamas, tying the tasseled cord of a blue brocade robe. She didn't bother to reply to his question. The answer was self-evident. The fire was lighting up the entire sky. Loretta came up behind them, wrapped in a velour robe, her arms around Julie and Jacob, restraining them from rushing out after their father.

A moment later, Brendan arrived. He pushed through the small group, pausing beside Cass as he finished buttoning his shirt. "Go in the house, Cass," he ordered curtly, "and get into something warm!"

For the first time Cass felt the cold of the cement beneath her bare feet and the chill of the early morning breeze through her thin batiste gown. She shivered and her mind started working again. She turned and fled through the house to return to the kitchen five minutes later, dressed in her oldest jeans and shirt. Loretta, Darin, and the children were where she had left them, standing in the doorway and watching.

As Cass slipped around them, Darin caught her by the shoulder. "Hey, where are you going?"

"To help!"

She pulled free and headed down the steps, ignoring his exclamation of protest. By the time she was halfway across the yard she should see the extent of the damage. In the time she had been gone, the entire structure had been engulfed in flames. Fortunately, the barn was set well back and away from the main house, but the outbuilding housing the farming equipment and several of the storage sheds were close enough to be threatened by the danger of flying sparks.

Within twenty yards of the barn, the heat was so intense Cass had to circle around. At that moment the wind shifted and billows of black smoke enveloped her, totally obscuring her vision. An arm reached out and grabbed her.

"I saw you coming," Brendan growled in her ear. "What in the hell do you think you're doing?"

Cass could hardly see Brendan for the smoke and tears in her eyes, but she probably wouldn't have recognized him anyway. His forehead was streaked with soot and sweat and the lower part of his face was covered with a red bandana. She had no trouble at all, unfortunately, recognizing the electric touch of his fingers on her bare arm or the particular sharpness of his voice in this authoritative mood.

"Will you kindly let go of me?" she snapped.

"Get back to the house!"

She wasn't obeying this command. "It's my ranch, Brendan." She coughed as she took in a lungful of smoke. "You don't give the orders here!" she gasped.

"I don't have time to argue with you," he muttered, taking a firmer hold on her arm and half leading, half dragging her to a point upwind of the fire where the men were working.

They had given up the fruitless task of attempting to extinguish the blaze. Their efforts now were concentrated on saving the other buildings, dousing down the nearby roofs with hoses attached to the pump.

"Well, at least stay here," Brendan commanded, releasing her arm and standing her beside Aggie. Cass was willing. They were part of the bucket brigade, dipping water from the nearby stream and passing it on to the others in front.

Cass's arms felt as though they were going to fall off and her knees were nearly buckling under when Ben finally called a halt. They had done it. The barn was a total loss, but the fire had not spread. Will and several of the men stayed at the sight to watch the smoldering wood and douse any stray sparks they might have missed. The rest of the hands slowly dispersed, to capture what they could of their routine. With Ben and Brendan at her side, Cass trudged up the hill toward the house. They were a sorry-looking trio.

"You know, Cass," Ben said wearily, "if you hadn't

raised the alarm so quickly, we wouldn't have been able to save the livestock. I thank you for that."

The thanks came so grudgingly that Cass couldn't bring herself to respond. She was just too tired.

"How did you happen to see the fire?" Brendan asked as they neared the back door.

She didn't want to admit that she hadn't slept the whole night. "I don't know," she said vaguely. "Something must have woken me."

Darin, Loretta, and the children were dressed now but still waiting for them on the back porch. Cass couldn't help notice that in comparison to the others, she, Ben, and Brendan looked like three tramps. None of them, however, had enough energy left to care. They would clean up later. Loretta had coffee and sweet rolls ready and waiting.

Julie and Jacob received permission from Ben to investigate the damage, and the five adults collapsed around the kitchen table, sipping their coffee and munching on the rolls.

"You took some chance, going out like that, Cass," Darin observed with displeasure.

"Mmmm," she murmured noncommittally. She skirted the thought that Darin hadn't exactly been a great help. But then, Darin's cushy upbringing hadn't exactly made him into the heroic type. He was probably very aware of his own limitations and knew that he would have been more of a hindrance than a help.

Loretta didn't care for the attention Cass was receiving. "Cassie has always liked being one of the boys," she snapped, rising to refill their cups.

The coffee and rich cream tasted so good just then that Cass refrained from retaliating. In fact, she couldn't even think many unkind thoughts about Loretta's lack of active participation in the fire fighting.

A moment of calm prevailed. Ben stretched his legs out in front of him, his boots and pants legs wet, the pocket torn off his shirt, and his denim jacket ruined. Brendan lounged beside him, his clothes in similar disarray.

"Any idea how the fire started, Ben?" Cass asked.

Ben grunted and shrugged. "Faulty wiring, probably. It's

old enough. And with all that wood and hay, one little spark would be all it would take."

Cass opened her mouth to speak and closed it again. She frowned as she attempted to remember as much as possible of the restless night she had spent before the fire. Her mind filtered through the actual events, then sought to dredge up half-remembered or subconscious thoughts and awarenesses. Several points troubled her.

First, she had distinctly heard the sound of someone moving in the house only moments before she had discovered the fire. Second, she was as sure as she could be—given the disturbed state of her mind at the time—that there had been no gradual flow of light into her room. One moment it had been dark, the next she was aware of the bright light, as though the fire had suddenly erupted, consuming the entire end of the barn. That didn't seem the natural course a fire such as Ben had described would take. A third thought. She had been only vaguely aware of it at the time, but when Ben had opened his bedroom door to her, he had been fully dressed. This could mean nothing whatsoever, of course. He could have been as sleepless as she. But still, it was unusual.

Cass tried to shake off her suspicions, but a chilling thought was taking hold in her mind. Was it conceivable that the fire had not been accidental? Was it possible that it had been arson? But to what purpose? And more important, who would do such a thing? It was too ridiculous even to consider . . . wasn't it?

The rest of that day was relatively pleasant and blessedly uneventful. Ben played host—or was it salesman? Cass couldn't help wondering—and after lunch took Darin and Brendan on an extended tour of the ranch in the Jeep. Loretta became so tense and preoccupied after they had gone that she didn't even bother with her usual favorite pastime of baiting Cass. Still, Cass was just as happy to escape from the house and spend her time with Julie and Jacob, exploring their favorite haunts. She was tempted to introduce them to some of those from her own childhood, but she resisted. She knew from her own early experiences that the pleasure of a special place came from the joy of discovering it for oneself.

The men returned just before dinner, and afterward no one seemed inclined to linger in the living room making idle conversation. The events of the day had taken their toll.

What on earth would the following day bring? Cass wondered as she tumbled exhausted into bed, this time to sleep, heavily and dreamlessly.

She found the answer to her question much too early the next morning. Shortly after dawn, she was awakened by shouting in the stable yard.

Not another fire! she thought, her heart pounding as she raced to the window. She leaned against the sill in relief. No fire. In fact, she couldn't tell what was wrong. The sky was cloudy and a light rain was falling, blurring the scene. All she could make out was Ben and Will, arms flying as they seemed to rage in turn at each other and at a handful of men gathered inside the empty corral.

Cass slipped quickly into her clothes, ran a brush through her hair, and went out to the kitchen. There was no sign of Brendan, Darin, Loretta, or the kids, but Aggie was there by the kitchen window, keeping one eye on the breakfast steaks on the grill and another on the argument taking place outside.

"What's going on?" Cass asked reluctantly. Whatever it was, it didn't look good.

The older woman's face creased into new lines of worry. "It's them wild horses. Will was supposed to start breaking 'em in this week. Well, the corral gate was left unbolted last night, and they got away, every blessed one of 'em."

"But, Aggie," Cass protested, "Will always makes the rounds of the corral and stables himself."

"And he did, too," his wife declared stoutly. "Last night just like always." She sniffed indignantly. "But Ben's out there saying Will was careless and didn't check the gate close enough. Like after thirty-two years of locking up, my Will's suddenly lost his wits and doesn't know an unlocked gate when he sees one—"

She broke off abruptly as Ben came storming through the back door, slamming it behind him, unmindful of the mud he was tracking on the kitchen linoleum. "If it isn't one thing, it's another," he muttered.

He stopped and glared at Cass as though she were personally responsible for the missing horses and every other new problem that had befallen the ranch. She understood that look and stared thoughtfully back at him, wondering in growing distress if perhaps he was right.

"Ben?" Cass asked cautiously.

"Yuh?"

"Ben, do you really think the gate was left unbolted by accident?"

He shot Aggie a quick glance. "You mean from carelessness," he said coldly.

"Could it have been done . . . deliberately?" Cass persisted.

He scowled. "Deliberately? Don't be ridiculous, Cass. Who on earth would want to turn loose a bunch of wild horses?"

"I just wondered . . ."

"Well, I suggest you put your mind to better use," he snapped. "Have you thought over what we talked about the other day?"

"I've thought about little else. How could I?"

"And?"

"Ben, please!" she pleaded wearily, knowing it would do no good. "You're asking me to sacrifice my principles for profit."

"Yet you're perfectly willing to sacrifice me!"

"That's not true. But you know how I feel about Brendan's plans for the ranch. I just can't be a party to that. If we had another offer, I—I promise you, I would honestly consider it."

"Yuh, right! We'll never have another offer like this one, and you know it."

She did know it. "I'm sorry, Ben," she said helplessly.

"Save it. I don't need your sympathy." He turned abruptly to where Aggie was hunched over the stove. "Could I have breakfast right now?" he asked sharply. "The ground is soft and the horses left a good trail. I'm taking some of the men to see if we can't round them up before they have a chance to eat their way through half the range."

Cass watched unhappily as he strode out of the kitchen, her expression grave, concern mixed with a lurking fear that darkened her eyes. She didn't even notice when Aggie left for the dining room or when Darin wandered in.

"Morning, Cass."

"Hmmm? Oh! Good morning, Darin."

He looked at the window, pelted now by rain. "I didn't say that it was a *good* morning," he drawled.

"You're right," she acknowledged curtly. "It isn't."

"Something the matter—besides the rain, that is?"

"Yes. Some wild horses got away in the night."

He yawned and stretched. "And that's a big deal?"

"As a matter of fact, it is." His insensitivity to the situation annoyed her, and her tone was sharper than she realized.

"Hey, I'm sorry," he apologized quickly. "Remember, I'm just a city boy. What do I know about wild horses?"

Cass forced herself to smile and say more calmly, "No, *I'm* sorry. I'm upset and I was taking it out on you. You see, wild horses are a problem. They roam the range where the cattle graze and eat what food there is. Some ranchers shoot the horses on sight or have them slaughtered for dog food. My father always insisted that, if possible, they be rounded up and broken for use."

"And the ones that'd been rounded up got away?"

"Yes. The gate to the corral was unlocked. Ben is taking some men to try and find them."

"A lot of work."

"Yes," she replied tersely.

"Relax, Cass," he soothed her. "That's what we came here for, remember?" When she didn't respond, he teased lightly, "I hesitate to remind you, but you're the one who promised me a peaceful, quiet vacation in the mountains. I've spent more restful days in the middle of a bankruptcy. Is it always like this?"

Cass wasn't amused. "No, Darin. It isn't always like this."

"All right, I believe you." He held up his hands in a gesture of surrender and retreated, sauntering off toward the dining room in search of food. "Never a dull moment, that's all I can say. I can't wait to see what happens next."

Cass wasn't sure whether it was this parting shot of

Darin's or her own growing suspicion and anxiety, but she found herself braced through the rest of the day, waiting for what she feared was going to happen next in the string of disasters.

All the wear and tear on her nerves was in vain. Nothing happened.

Or more accurately, nothing tangible happened—if Cass discounted the fact that tempers were noticeably short and tension continued to mount as the day wore on. The rain had become heavy enough to keep them all trapped indoors. Under the circumstances it hadn't been easy, but she managed to avoid being alone with Brendan—which seemed to amuse him more than annoy him. She knew him well enough to realize that he was playing a waiting game, biding his time for the right moment. As for Loretta, short of locking herself in her room there was no way for Cass to avoid the woman and her vitriolic comments. Ben's return midafternoon offered no relief from the gloomy atmosphere. The heavy rain had finally obliterated the horses' tracks and driven the men back home. Once he had changed into dry clothes, Ben sat in the living room with the rest of the party, saying nothing. But his eyes, dark and brooding, followed Cass wherever she went. Coercion through silence.

Darin alone seemed immune to the tension. He maintained his ready flow of idle chatter—the usual witty stories, slightly off-color jokes, and dubious gossip. For once Cass was grateful for his social aplomb. It allowed her to sort out her feelings and perceptions and contemplate the situation at the ranch without having to contribute to the group. It also had the added virtue of putting Loretta in a more pleasant frame of mind, so that by the time Aggie announced dinner, she was again able to look at Cass without snarling.

The grim day in the company of the others had helped Cass reach one decision. She wasn't going to spend another day like it. She made the announcement just as they finished dinner.

"The forecast for tomorrow is for sunshine, Ben," she said casually. "If you don't need Kettledrum tomorrow, I thought I would take him out for the day."

"Alone?" her brother asked sharply.

"Yes."

"Kettledrum? You're joining a band?" Darin quipped.

"Kettledrum is a horse, Darin," she informed him dryly.

"That makes sense, then," he drawled.

Ben frowned. "Where do you intend to go?"

Cass would have preferred not to have told him, but she had no choice. As children they had had the run of the ranch, but her father's standing rule was that anyone going out alone had to leave word where he was going and when he expected to return. In case of an accident, the search party would know when to become concerned and where to look. The precaution had probably saved Ben's life when he was ten. His horse had thrown him down a ravine and he had broken his leg.

"I thought I would leave after breakfast and go up to Coyote Flats. I'll stay there for a good share of the day and be back by five."

"Want company?" Brendan asked. "I've only been on a horse twice in my life, but I imagine you could teach me a few things."

Cass glanced quickly away from the flare of desire she read in his eyes and hoped no one noticed the sudden flush in her cheeks. If Brendan went with her, she had no doubt how they would end up spending the day. She didn't need his presence to confuse her even more.

"No, thanks, Brendan. Wait until you find a place to build your dude ranch and take lessons then."

She hadn't considered the tactlessness of her comment before she spoke. The reminder of Brendan's plans for the ranch put an abrupt end to the conversation and settled an uncomfortable silence over the table. Cass grimaced. Brendan frowned. Ben glowered. Loretta pouted. Only Darin placidly continued to eat Aggie's homemade apple pie and ice cream with relish.

The strain of the day and basic disharmony of the group precipitated another early night. Cass was up and dressed at dawn. She packed herself a lunch before Aggie arrived and went down to meet Will in the stables.

"Anything special I ought to know about Kettledrum?"

she asked her old friend as she saddled the stallion. Will had put her up on her first pony when she was four and over the years had taught her to ride like a pro.

"He's a strong one," the foreman replied, "and needs a firm hand. Watch out for him on a jump. He'll shy away if you give him a chance." He watched approvingly as she tightened the cinch and shortened the stirrup leathers. "Want a leg up?"

"I'm getting old," she said dryly, "but not that old."

He followed as she led the horse out into the cool morning air and swung lightly up into the saddle. She leaned over to pat Kettledrum's neck and murmured a few calming words. Out of the corner of her eye she glanced at Will standing in the doorway, his face wrinkled and leathered from years of exposure to the elements.

"Will?" she began hesitantly. "Could I ask you something?"

"You know you can ask me anything in the world, Cass," he said solemnly, "and I'll answer you true."

"Is there any possibility in the world that you could have left the gate on the corral unlocked?"

A worried frown made his old face look even older. "No, Cass," he replied, without equivocation. "I know that gate was bolted. It stuck a little, and I even remember thinking that I needed to put a little oil on it."

"Do you think someone turned the horses loose on purpose?"

His sharp eyes met hers. "Maybe yes. Maybe no. Maybe somebody went out after me and just forgot to lock up again."

She didn't push him any farther. "All right, Will." She forced a smile. "See you later."

Will had given her a lot to think about, and she had given herself plenty of time alone to think. Unfortunately she came up with a lot of questions and too few answers.

Still, she thoroughly enjoyed her day. It had been years since she had been up on Coyote Flats. The perspective from there was very different from that of the ranch side of the plateau. The view was of less spectacular red rock formations and mile after mile of sand and juniper forest.

She sat, ate, thought, and even napped for a while. At three, she started for home.

Kettledrum was in high spirits after his rest, but Cass kept him firmly under control as they made their way back. Over flat spots she let him break into a gallop, then brought him to a trot again as they reached rocky patches. The final few miles of the trip was through a forest, along a fairly narrow dirt trail.

Once they entered the woods, it took a moment for her eyes to adjust from the bright sunlight. The trunks of the trees cast dark shadows across the path. It was cool and beautiful there after the heat of the July day on the exposed side of the plateau. In spite of the worries that plagued her, she allowed her mind to wander to more pleasant thoughts. Unconsciously her hands loosened on the reins as she slowed Kettledrum to a walk. He snorted and tossed his head restively, as though to remind her of her obligation to him.

"Sorry, old man," she said soothingly and leaned down to pat his neck. "Is the pace too slow for you?"

She clicked her tongue and pressed her knees gently into his sides. Obedient to her command, he broke into a trot and gradually into a canter as he spied the far side of the woods ahead. Cass had returned her attention to the horse, but a movement in the shadows ahead of her distracted her for a second. A coyote, she wondered, or a bobcat?

One minute she was firmly placed in the saddle, feeling the smooth, steady, moving flesh of the horse beneath her. The next instant she felt Kettledrum break stride, stumble sideways, and fall to his knees. She had the oddest sensation that she was flying, held up on one of the puffy cumulus clouds overhead, until suddenly the trail seemed to rise up to meet her.

As if she were falling in a bad dream, she never remembered hitting the ground.

Chapter 11

"Cass! Cass!" From far away she heard Brendan calling her in that authoritative voice she disliked so much. "Cass, open your eyes," he demanded.

"Go away!"

She had intended to shout at him, but her voice came out as little more than a whisper. It definitely hadn't been worth the effort. Her head was already pounding and now she had a rising feeling of nausea in her stomach. For one mad moment she thought that she must be at sea. The bed under her wouldn't remain still. It tossed and rolled in time with the throbbing behind her eyes and the heaving of her stomach. She longed for the oblivion of sleep and thought fleetingly that it was cruel of Brendan to keep her awake.

"Open your eyes," he commanded once again.

"I'll be sick," she mumbled.

"If you are," he said, gently now, "I'm right here. Now open your eyes."

She couldn't resist him when he coaxed like that. Slowly she raised her lids, though they felt as if they were weighted down with lead. She only had them open to mere slits when a sudden chill gripped her and she was trembling in every limb. Quickly she closed her eyes again and moaned through her chattering teeth. The covers over her lifted up and away, and when she reached out frantically to pull them back, Brendan's hand caught hers.

"Just wait a minute," he crooned. "Lie still."

Again she had the feeling that the bed was dipping. But this time, as she felt Brendan slip in beside her and enfold her in his strong arms, she knew that this was reality, not some waking nightmare. He cradled her head against his shoulder and held her gently but firmly against his warm body until the chill left her. In his protective embrace, the world seemed to right itself. Unconsciousness slowly overtook her again, but this time she fell into a more natural sleep.

Her dreams became fitful, and every time she turned her head a piercing pain shot through it. But each time she unconsciously cried out, Brendan was there to sooth and comfort her.

"Cass!" Again Brendan was calling her. "Cass, open your eyes!"

Useless to try and fight him in this condition, she thought crossly. Slowly she raised her eyelids and then had to squint against the light. For the first few moments all she could see were blurred images of color and shape. Gradually the objects in the room came into focus. Her first sight was of Brendan's anxious face looming over her. He looked ravaged—his hair a mess, his complexion sallow, dark circles under his eyes, the vein near his scar pulsing wildly.

"What happened to you, Brendan? You look awful. You'd better sit down." She had spoken faintly but the sound seemed to pound in her ears, echoing back and forth in her aching head, jarring every nerve in her aching body.

A wave of relief flooded Brendan's face, and Cass felt the shiver of released tension that shook him as he perched on the side of the bed. Gradually the color began to return under his tan. A faint gurgle of amusement rumbled in his chest.

"If I look a mess," he said teasingly, "you ought to see the other guy." His voice grew tender. "Would you like a little water?"

"Yes, please."

From the bedside table he poured a half glass of water from a pitcher and shook a couple of tablets from a bottle. "Let me help you," he said when she struggled to sit. "Take these painkillers for your head." He handed her the pills and held the glass for her, supporting her back with his free arm. Even then, the effort exhausted her. "Now," he said, lowering her head gently onto the pillow. "Go back to sleep."

When Cass awoke again it was nearly dark. Experimentally she turned her head. Nothing terrible happened. She raised it a little off the pillow. The sharp pain was gone, leaving only a dull, throbbing ache.

"Cass?"

She turned her head in the other direction and found Brendan sitting in a chair pulled up to the side of the bed. When he turned on the bedside lamp, she could see the difference in his appearance. He'd shaved, combed his hair, and changed his clothes.

"You look better, Brendan." Her voice was stronger now.

"Look up at me a minute." He stared down into her eyes and grunted in satisfaction when he saw that the pupils were once again normal. A twisted smile warmed his face. "I could comment on your appearance, but I'm too much of a gentleman."

"Huh!" she sniffed.

"As a matter of fact, I'd say that you're nearly back to your old self," he drawled. "Want a couple more pills?"

"Please." He poured the water and dumped out the tablets, but this time Cass took them herself. Gingerly she lay back down. "What happened?"

"How much do you remember?"

Cass's brow wrinkled in concentration. "Not much, really. I was on my way home, coming through the woods. That's all I remember. Did Kettledrum throw me?"

"Apparently so. He came back to the stables all in a lather, and Will sent out the alarm. He and a couple of the men found you on the trail. Will said that you must have hit your head on a rock. Nothing broken, but you were concussed." He swallowed at the memory. "I've never been so frightened in my life as when they brought you home. I wanted to go for a doctor, but Will and Aggie said you'd be fine in a day or two."

Cass remembered quite clearly his tender care and concern. "So—so you nursed me."

His jaw tightened. "I'm afraid that Loretta isn't much use in a crisis, and Aggie had her hands full with the kids and the house and the cooking. I volunteered."

"Thank you, Brendan," Cass said simply.

"My pleasure." He grinned and made light of what Cass knew must have been a long, hard, nerve-wracking experience for him. "You see how resourceful I am? If I can't sleep with you one way, I just have to look for another."

It was a full day before Cass was up and about. If Brendan had had his way, she would have stayed in bed another. But Cass had too much on her mind to rest. Details of her accident were coming back to her. On the excuse of wanting to check on Kettledrum, she sought out Will in the stables.

"Well, child," he said, his shrewd old eyes examining her face. "You're looking a whole lot more chipper than when I saw you last time."

"And feeling more chipper too," Cass said lightly. "Thanks for bringing me in."

"What else could I do," he grumbled affectionately, "when my star pupil goes and lets her horse throw her?"

"I—I don't think I did let him throw me, Will," Cass said hesitantly. The foreman glanced at her sharply but said nothing. She smiled at him ruefully. "No, Will. Landing on my head has not done any permanent damage. I know what I'm talking about."

"And what's that?" he probed cautiously.

"I've had two days in bed to think about it," she said solemnly, "and I don't believe my fall was an accident. I was going along the trail at a pretty fast clip, but out of the corner of my eye I saw something move in the trees just before I went down. I think someone had strung a wire across the path, waiting for me to come along."

There. She had finally said it, but it was no relief.

"Why would someone want to go and do something like that, Cass?" It was an honest question, not an expression of disbelief.

"Because someone wants me to sell the ranch so badly that he—or she," she added unhappily, "would do almost anything to convince me to sell. I don't think any of the things that have been happening since I arrived have been accidents, Will. I have reason to believe that the fire was deliberately set. I think someone unbolted the gate on the corral after you made your rounds. And I think someone meant me to take that fall. I don't think whoever planned it really meant me to hurt myself badly," she interjected quickly. "Just bad enough to shake me up so that I would be happy to pack my bags, wipe the red dirt of southern Utah off my feet, and go back to the comparative safety of New York."

Will turned her words over in his methodical mind and grunted but said nothing.

"I can't *prove* any of what I've said, you realize, Will—at least not yet."

"You told Ben?" he asked in his economical way.

"I haven't said anything to anyone but you."

He pondered this for a few minutes while Cass waited patiently. Will was not slow, she knew from long experience. He was just very careful. At one point he shook his head, deliberated some more, and finally pushed himself away from the stack of baled hay against which he had been leaning.

"I think it would still be right smart of you not to say anything to anybody—not just yet. Now, let's take the bandages off and have a look at Kettledrum's legs."

After Kettledrum had fallen, he had regained his footing and taken the shortest way home through trees and bushes and nettles. But in spite of some abrasions on his knees from the fall and the minor scratches he had gathered on his headlong flight, Will and Cass could still see the wound on his right foreleg that could have been caused by a wire.

"Doesn't prove anything, you know," Will said slowly. "He could've run into some old fence on his way home."

Cass's heart sank. "You don't believe me?"

"Now, I'm not saying that, Cass. Think you're feeling up to taking a little ride up to the place we found you? Maybe take a look around, check the trees, see what turns up?"

Cass tried to smile, but it was a poor thing. "Are you just humoring me, or is this your way of getting me back up on a horse before I lose my nerve?"

"Think you could use a little cheering up but no humoring," he said laconically. "The other part isn't such a bad idea. Let's saddle up. You take old Midnight. Nice gentle ride for your head."

Half an hour later Will and Cass found what they had been looking for—two pine trees, directly across the trail from each other, each with a fresh groove gouged into the bark about eight inches from the base. They checked the area around, but there was no sign of the wire. Discouraged, they sat together on a fallen log, surveying the sight.

"Whoever stretched it between them two trees," Will theorized, "must have waited till after you fell, undid the wire so nobody would know it wasn't an accident, and got rid of it for good."

"That means the person must have just left me lying there, not knowing if I was really hurt or not." Cass's head began to pound again, as much from tension as from her injury. Will was quick to note her pale face and the pain in her eyes.

"You okay, Cass?"

"I'll survive." She fished a couple of aspirins out of her blouse pocket and swallowed them with a gulp of water from her canteen. "Give me a few minutes to rest."

He took her at her word. "Nice up here," he commented idly, chewing on a piece of grass.

"I love it. It's so peaceful."

The one comment had exhausted his supply of small talk, and they sat side by side in companionable silence. Only after the aspirin began to do its work and Cass's head started to clear was she struck, not by what Will had said but by what he had not said. He hadn't asked her the all-important question—who she thought might be deliberately sabotaging the ranch.

Perhaps, she decided with a sinking heart, he was as afraid of the answer as she was. If she had her choice, she would have just let the whole matter drop—but she couldn't. Her presence on the ranch was responsible for the damage done, so unless she did pack up and leave, it was her responsibility to stop whoever was doing it from continuing.

"Will?"

"Mmmm?"

"Who?"

He gave her a sidelong glance and looked away from the personal sorrow he read in her face. "I think you have more answers than I do, Cass," he said gruffly.

"I wish I did." She sighed, afraid that wasn't quite the truth.

"Best tell me everything you know," he declared matter-of-factly. "For instance, what makes you think the fire in the barn was set on purpose?"

She told him the sequence of events that night—the noise of someone moving about and the speed with which the fire had flared up. Loyalty to Ben forced her to omit the fact that he obviously hadn't been to bed that night when she saw him at four in the morning.

Will drew the same conclusion she had. "So, what you're telling me," he summed up, as reluctant as Cass to put her suspicions into words, "is that most likely someone in the house is doing all this. Ruling out the kids, that makes it Ben, Loretta, that friend of yours Summerhays, or the man Cahill." He paused, picked himself another long spear of grass, and stuck the end in his mouth. "Which one, Cass?"

Cass passed each in mental review and began with the easiest. "Surely not Darin Summerhays. He wouldn't have any reason."

She didn't go into irrelevant details with Will, but the facts were pretty clear. Darin would undoubtedly miss her when she sold her share of the partnership, but Dee was a distinct asset with her artistic gifts, her years of experience, and the added money she intended to invest in the design house. In the long run he would be ahead financially. Also, Cass discounted any personal motive. She and Darin were and had been nothing but good friends and business partners.

"Loretta?" Will prompted unhappily. "You two never did hit it off, exactly."

Would her sister-in-law go to such lengths to persuade

Cass to give up the ranch? She knew Loretta's malicious, vindictive streak, but her tongue had always been her most effective weapon. Fire and wire traps just weren't her style. Cass shook her head. "I don't think so, Will. Somehow I can't imagine Loretta out in the barn in the middle of the night dumping kerosene on bales of hay."

His face tightened. "But you can imagine Ben doing it?"

Cass flinched. She had shied away from the possibility for several days now, but in all honesty she couldn't discount Ben. Ben was pretty desperate to sell, but was he desperate enough to sabotage his own ranch and endanger his own sister?

"I—I honestly don't know, Will."

Now Will flinched. "I'm not saying that Ben doesn't have his faults, Cass, but he loves you. A kind, gentle man. Until lately, he's never gotten mad, hardly even raised his voice. Even when he was a boy he couldn't stand it when one of the dogs or horses was sick. Can't see him setting a fire and leaving the animals in there to burn."

"True. But Dad's death has changed him," she had to add. "Who knows what can happen to a man when life gets too much for him, when he thinks he's trapped?"

Will considered that, then suggested, "Letting the horses out at night was a blamed nuisance—malicious mischief—but nobody was hurt. Seems to me, though, that it would take a pretty mean or pretty desperate person to do all them other things—setting fire to the barn, risk breaking a good horse's leg, taking a chance on you being hurt bad."

"Mean, malicious, desperate, or . . ."

His sharp glance flew to her face. "Or what, Cass?"

"Or else someone cold, clever, and calculating."

"You talking about Cahill?" he asked bluntly. "I don't see him that way. Me, I like him. He worked as hard as anyone to put out the fire, and nobody could've took better care of you when you was sick. But maybe you know him a whole lot better than I do," he added shrewdly.

Cass stiffened. Brendan's care and concern after her fall couldn't have left much doubt in anyone's mind that something was going on between them. With Aggie in the house, the gossip about the two of them was bound to have reached Will's ears.

"You must know he wants to buy the ranch, Will," Cass said curtly. "And you must know that I won't sell it to him. I guess if anyone has a real motive, he does."

Again Cass gave Will no additional details, but not because the details of her relationship with Brendan weren't relevant. Just the opposite. They were much too relevant and much too personal.

No matter how she looked at it, the person with the most to gain from the sale of the ranch was Brendan. If Monarch bought it, he would achieve both his goals. He would have the land to develop and would, he undoubtedly calculated, drive her back to New York. She knew him to be both clever and ruthless in business, and he had made it clear to her after she arrived at the ranch that his ruthlessness extended to his personal affairs. He was determined to get her back. But she had to believe he felt *something* for her, if not the kind of love and understanding she longed for. The thought that he would deliberately hurt her and then leave her injured on the trail was almost too unbearable to think about. And considering the care and concern he had shown her afterward, she wasn't sure it made sense at all.

"You see how resourceful I am? If I can't sleep with you one way, I'll just have to look for another." Brendan's words. Cass pushed them out of her mind.

No matter how she despised his tactics and his business practices, she concluded miserably, or how contrary it was to every logical consideration or how futile her feeling for him might be, Cass loved Brendan with all her heart.

She was relieved when Will interrupted this painful train of thought and equally grateful for his tact in not pursuing the topic of Brendan Cahill.

"Well, Cass? What now?"

She shrugged helplessly. "I'm not sure, Will. What do you think?"

"First, I don't think it would do much good letting on we know what's been happening. Just make whoever's doing it more careful. And we don't have any real proof that anything *has* been going on—except for the marks on the tree here, and that's not much. Still wouldn't tell us who did it." He paused and Cass waited expectantly. "I think it's time we had some more facts," he continued after a minute. "Like, who-all knew where you were going the day you went up to Coyote Flats?"

"Everyone," she replied with chagrin. "I told them all at dinner."

"Anybody follow you?"

The idea both startled and frightened her. "I don't know."

He thought about this for a minute. "Whoever it was set the trap could've just waited right here for you to come back. But he had to get here somehow. That Cahill know how to ride?" he asked abruptly.

"He says he doesn't—at least, not well."

"Think I'll do some asking around," Will said thoughtfully. "See if any of the boys saw somebody taking some wire from the shed, find out if too much kerosene's missing from the tank, ask Aggie who was home and who wasn't the day you fell, find out who could've taken a horse and gone out riding."

"In the meantime, that's not going to stop more accidents from happening," Cass said unhappily.

"Nope, it won't."

"So, what do we do?"

He tipped his well-worn Stetson back on his head and kicked at the dirt at his feet. "Cass, you still set on keeping Wells' Springs?"

"More determined now than ever, Will," she said grimly.

"No matter how you cut it," he said regretfully, "Ben's got no heart for ranching."

Cass was startled. "Will, are you suggesting that I *should* sell the ranch to Monarch Enterprises?"

"Nope, I'm not saying that at all." He glanced at her shyly and looked away. "I had another idea."

"What?" she asked in bewilderment.

"Well," he began hesitantly, "I was wondering if there was any way you could buy out Ben's share of the ranch."

Sadly she shook her head. "I'm sorry, Will. I thought of that at first, but I couldn't come up with the money to match the offer Brendan made him. I have the bonds that Dad left me, and I'll get a fair amount from the sale of my share of

Cassandra's, but it wouldn't be near enough. With interest rates what they are now, a huge mortgage to make up the difference would kill me financially."

He looked out over the land where he had spent his entire life. "What if I could come up with, say, a couple o' hundred thousand dollars? Would you consider letting me and Aggie go in with you and buy the ranch? Would it be enough?"

Cass stared at him, her mouth open in surprise. "Will! You have that kind of money?"

"Your father left a tidy little sum for Aggie and me to retire on when we wanted, but we've got a lot of good years left in us yet. And living here on the ranch, we haven't had a whole lot to do with our money but stick it in the bank and let it make more money. If we'd 'a been able to have kids, it'd be different. But you and Ben have been like kids to us. I can't stand to see either of you miserable. And this is our home," he concluded simply.

"Oh, Will!" She would have hugged him, but she knew that would only embarrass him.

"You'll think about it then?" he asked diffidently.

"I'll more than think about it!" Her eyes were shining now. "If it's all right with Ben and I can come up with my share, I consider it a deal."

He thoughtfully kicked up more dirt. "Then I'd say the sooner everybody knows, the better it'll be for all of us."

Cass saw his point. Once it was clear that she was determined to stay on the ranch, once it was established that Monarch was not going to be able to buy the land no matter what, and once Ben and Loretta were assured that they would get their money and be able to leave the ranch, there would be no reason for the "accidents" to continue.

Her mouth tightened into a thin, unhappy line, but there was determination in her voice. "I'll make Ben the offer tonight at dinner, when everyone is there to hear."

"Then I'd say it was time we got back down to the ranch. I've got chores to do." He hoisted himself off the rock and righted his hat. "But, Cass?"

She brushed the dirt off the seat of her jeans and followed him to where the horses were tethered. "Yes, Will?"

"Before dinnertime, when everybody hears the news,

don't be wandering off by yourself anywhere. No sense asking for trouble."

With this grim warning very much in her mind, Cass spent the afternoon in her room lying down—with too much time to think. She should have been overjoyed about the possibility of being able to keep the ranch, but the knowledge that this would mean a permanent break with Brendan led to nothing but dejection. She was torn between anxiety, hope, resolution, and depression.

Cass passed up the cocktail hour and when she finally appeared for dinner, Aggie hovered over her like a gingham-clad watchdog. Cass gave her old friend a quick, reassuring smile, wondering how much Will had told his wife. From the mixture of concern and excitement in the older woman's eyes, she guessed he had told her everything.

As the rest of the company gathered around the table, Cass smiled at them coolly. When they were all seated, she said in a tone designed to command their attention, "I have something I want to say." Four pairs of eyes turned on her. "You must all understand by now that under *no* circumstances will I sell the ranch to Monarch."

Her brother swore under his breath. Loretta glared. Brendan said nothing. Darin placed his napkin on his lap.

"Ben," she continued, "I have an alternative proposition to make to you."

His eyes on her face were wary. "What?"

"I'm offering to buy out your share of the ranch for the half-million Monarch would have paid you."

Dead silence fell over the table.

"Do you have that kind of money?" Brendan asked coldly.

She raised her firm jaw at him. "I can raise it. You know that I intend to sell out my share of Cassandra's."

"How much is that worth?"

"I—I don't know, exactly," she admitted.

"Well, what did the last audit show?"

"Last audit?" She turned blankly toward her partner for help.

"We're a partnership, not a corporation, Cahill," Darin

explained stiffly. "Cass, Dee, and I haven't reached the point yet of asking for an outside audit. But the firm's assets are only a small part of the value of Cass's share. The Cassandra name and our established clientele are just as important."

"So you really think she can come up with a half-million dollars from the sale?" Ben asked uncertainly.

Darin shook his head doubtfully and smiled an apology at Cass. "No, Ben. I don't think there's any way."

"What are you trying to do, Cassie?" Loretta interjected bitterly. "Stall for time while you ruin the deal with Monarch?"

"This is a firm offer, Ben," Cass said, stifling her irritation with Loretta. "Besides the partnership, I'm going to sell the bonds that Dad left me. But there's something else. Will and Aggie are going to go in with me. All I'm asking is that you give us time to make the arrangements."

She looked quickly around the table to see how each had taken the news. Brendan's eyes were hooded, but his jaw was tense with suppressed anger. Ben was stunned, Loretta leery. Darin was helping himself to the mashed potatoes.

"How long will it take?" Ben asked uneasily, sending a furtive glance at Brendan.

"I can't give you an exact date right now." She smiled triumphantly at Brendan. "I'm glad you reminded me of the audit. Dee's husband is an accountant, Ben, and he's ready to prepare the books for the sale as soon as Darin and I give him the word. We'll call Dee tomorrow morning and have her arrange it. Frank ought to have all the figures within a few days. Is it a deal?"

"All right, Cass," Ben agreed. The shock was wearing off. He was beginning to look as though a great load had been lifted from his mind. "Yes. All right." He spoke firmly now but carefully avoided Brendan's eyes. "Make the call tomorrow, have the audit done, and then we can go on from there."

The rest of the meal was eaten in near silence. Brendan didn't speak directly to Cass until after coffee, when Darin retreated to the family room to watch television and Ben and Loretta disappeared in the direction of their wing of the house, obviously to discuss this new turn of events.

"We have to talk, Cass."

"There's nothing left to say, Brendan," she said wearily.

"Like hell there isn't! Let's go outside where we won't be interrupted."

Against every inclination, Cass couldn't help but remember Will's warning about avoiding trouble. She repressed her qualms. She didn't want to believe that Brendan would harm her. Still, she followed reluctantly as he led the way out the back door and down to a wooden bench overlooking the moon-washed gullies and farms below.

"I can't believe you're really going through with this," he said harshly.

She couldn't look at him or her resolution would crumble. "Believe it, Brendan."

"Does that mean you intend to leave New York permanently and live here?"

"Yes," she replied bleakly.

He stood and moved away from her, his hands in his pockets. "This last week hasn't made any difference to you at all?"

She hesitated before answering, unsure exactly of what he meant. She had such doubts. Was he referring to the troubles on the ranch or the time they had spent together? "What difference did you expect it to make?" she asked carefully.

With a moan he turned, caught her by the arms, and pulled her into a convulsive embrace. His lips sought her mouth, her eyes, the pulse in her temple, the hollow and the base of her neck.

"I love you, Cass!" he murmured brokenly. "Give up this stupid notion of staying on the ranch. Come back to New York and live with me."

"It just wouldn't work, Brendan," she cried.

"Why?" He groaned in frustration. "Why?"

She tried to pull away, but he held her fast. "I've already told you why, Brendan. You didn't understand when I told you then and you wouldn't understand if I explained it again."

To her it was so dismally clear. After their initial physical hunger had been assuaged, after the euphoria of first love had worn off, what would they have left? She had no confidence that they lived by the same principles, prized the same human qualities in a person, or shared the same fundamental outlook on life. To Cass these were all essentials for an enduring relationship. Brendan either found such considerations irrelevant or, she thought miserably, as had been his pattern, he wasn't looking for a long-term commitment.

"I understand only one thing, Cass, and you may as well make up your mind to it." His fingers unconsciously dug into her flesh. "I don't intend to lose the best thing that's ever come into my life. I won't let you go. I'll do anything—*anything*—to keep you!"

To her hypersensitive nerves his words sounded as if they were both a promise and a threat—primitive, relentless, unyielding, even brutal. Her worst fears about him seemed confirmed. Her heart began to pound in sympathy with the painful throb in her head. The world around her blurred until all she could see was Brendan's rugged face above her, his craggy features accentuated by the moonlight—pools and points, ravines and plains, light and shadow. Lucifer's Playground in microcosm.

"So it *was* you!" she whispered distractedly. "It's been you all along!"

"Of course it's me," he muttered impatiently. "Who the hell else do you think it is?"

His admission was both a relief and a tragedy to Cass. It marked the end of so much. Unexpectedly she laughed, unaware that her voice rang with an hysterical note. It was a chilling sound that rebounded from the hills around them. Brendan's hold eased and he anxiously searched her face in the dim light.

"Cass, are you all right? Is it your head?"

"My head?" The laugh was strangled now. "My head, my heart! What does it matter to you, Brendan?"

He didn't wait to hear any more. "I'm taking you in right now and putting you to bed."

"Oh, that will solve everything, won't it! You end up resolving all your problems in bed, don't you!"

He didn't reply, but his jaw tensed and he took a firm hold on her arm. She had no choice but to let him lead her back up the path. Just before they reached the door, though, she dug in her heels and pulled him to a stop.

"I really didn't want to believe it, Brendan," she said brokenheartedly, suddenly overwhelmed by her disillusionment and grief.

"Believe *what?*" he asked in frustration.

"You know," she cried bitterly. "Fire, wire, desire, acquire."

He shook his head in bewilderment, and the frown in his forehead deepened with his growing concern. "What is it, Cass? A riddle?"

The smile she gave him was twisted and cynical. "Yes, Brendan, a riddle. And you and I are the only ones who know the secret, aren't we?"

Chapter 12

CASS SLEPT DEEPLY AND DREAMLESSLY THAT NIGHT. AFTER A quiet word from Brendan, Aggie had given her a sleeping pill along with the pain-killer for her head. She slept through a thunderstorm and through her radio alarm and awoke only when Aggie gently shook her shoulder.

"Breakfast is nearly ready, Cass, love. Would you like a tray in bed?"

Cass struggled out of her drugged sleep and rubbed a weary hand over her eyes. "Thanks, Aggie, but I have to get up and phone New York. Dee should be in by now."

Aggie grimaced. "I hate to tell you, but it looks as if the storm last night took out the phone."

This news brought Cass fully awake. The telephone lines going down in a storm wasn't an unusual occurrence, but it couldn't have happened at a worse time. "Any idea when it'll be fixed?"

"You'll have to ask Ben. He's out talking to Will now." Aggie threw her a sympathetic smile and headed for the door. "Breakfast in ten minutes."

Cass repeated the question to her brother over the

breakfast table, carefully ignoring Brendan's fixed gaze. "Any idea when the phone will be fixed, Ben?"

He shrugged resignedly and dug into a pile of scrambled eggs. "I don't know. Will's trying to find the trouble now. He's not sure if the lines are down somewhere or whether lightning hit a transformer. I'm afraid there's nothing we can do but wait."

Cass rose from her chair. "Well, there's something *I* can do. If Will doesn't have the phone working by midmorning, Darin and I can take my car down to Escalante and call Dee from there."

"Cass," Darin said cravenly, "I don't think I can face that road again. I'm even planning on having a helicopter fly me out of here when I leave."

He spoke the last lightly, but she heard the underlying seriousness of his words. She suspected that he did intend to hire a helicopter rather than endure the hair-raising ride back down the mountain road.

"All right, Darin," she said soothingly. "I can't see any reason why you should have to go if you'll write out whatever instructions I need to give Dee."

"Please," he pleaded with her. "Wait until the phone's fixed. Give yourself time to reconsider."

"I *have* waited and I *have* considered, and I have no intention of losing another day. Write out the instructions, will you please, just in case?"

"But, Cass . . ." She could hear Ben, Darin, and Brendan all protesting as she stalked from the room.

Cass didn't put in another appearance until just after nine o'clock. She was in no mood for an argument with anyone. She slipped quietly into the kitchen in search of Aggie and information. From one look at the housekeeper's troubled face, she was afraid that the news wasn't good.

"So what did Will find, Aggie?"

"Two of the wires leading into the terminal box were down. One of the relayers is busted. It could be two days before he gets the phone working again."

"That settles it. I'm driving into town."

Aggie sighed. "That stubborn jaw of yours looks just like your pa's when he got some bee in his bonnet. I guess it's no good asking you to wait till Will can go along with you. Him and me don't like the idea of you going down to Escalante alone."

"I'm not just being stubborn, Aggie. And frankly," she added unhappily, "I think I'm safer *off* the ranch than *on*."

She left her troubled friend in search of Darin and found him in the family room watching television. "The phone is still out, Darin," she told him. "I'm driving down to town. Do you have the instructions for Dee?"

"Here they are." Reluctantly he held out a single folded sheet.

Cass opened the paper and read it through. "This is all the information she needs?"

"Yes. The ledgers and journals are locked in the safe in my office. That bottom number is the combination."

Cass studied the list to make sure she could read it all and frowned slightly. "I hope this makes sense to someone. It sure doesn't to me. And what about the stuff in the computer? Do the auditors need access to it?"

"No. I've printed out all the relevant material and put the sheets into the ledgers I've listed. But if Dee's husband has any questions, he can call me here."

"Provided the phone ever gets fixed," Cass reminded him dryly, stuffing the paper into the pocket of her jeans and heading for the door. "I'll see you when I get back and let you know what Dee says."

"Cass!" Darin stopped her, pleading. "Come back to New York with me. Give up this crazy idea of yours!"

"You promised you wouldn't nag me," she reminded him grimly.

"All right, I'm sorry," he apologized. "But I wish you would listen to reason. There's no real need for you to call Dee. The sensible thing for you to do is wait until I get back to New York and arrange the audit myself. I could leave in a couple of days. It would only be a delay of a day or two."

Cass realized that Darin had no notion of the importance of putting the wheels in motion as soon as possible, and she had no desire to explain. Nor was she going to argue with him. "I'm not waiting any longer, Darin. If you're afraid I can't explain it right, you can always change your mind and come with me now."

Darin went pale at the thought. "No," he muttered, "but I don't like your going."

He really was a physical coward, Cass thought affectionately, or else he had a fear of heights that amounted to a phobia. "See you later, Darin."

"Cass?" He stopped her again.

"Yes, Darin?" She sighed, impatient now to be on her way.

"Cass, I'm *sorry!*"

"Never mind. I really don't mind going alone. Honest. No problem."

No problem inside. It waited for her outside. Brendan was leaning against the hood of her rented car. "You didn't really think that I was going to let you go alone, did you?" he asked curtly.

"You're not coming with me, Brendan!"

"And you're not going anywhere alone," he countered unequivocally.

She quelled a moment of panic, wondering what he had in mind now, and declared with equal determination, "Yes, I am. I've driven it hundreds of times by myself."

"Not, I bet, after you've had a bump on the head like the one you got! Let me come with you, Cass." He asked her this time, coaxingly. "You're not well yet. What if you get weak or dizzy? All I'll do is drive, I promise. I won't say a word if you don't want me to."

She wasn't even tempted. If anything, she was more determined than ever to make sure he stayed on the ranch. "No."

He blocked her way as she moved toward the car. "I'm not letting you go alone," he repeated doggedly. "And that's final!"

Nervously Cass bit her lip, her mind racing. Arguing with him obviously wasn't going to do any good, and trying to shove him forcibly out of the way would be like trying to move a brick wall. What she would have to use was brain, not brawn.

"Oh, all right, Brendan." She gave an exaggerated sigh and shrugged in resignation. "If you're going to be like that, I guess there's nothing I can do about it. But I'll do the driving," she informed him crossly. She slipped around him to the driver's side, praying that no one would put in an untimely appearance. "But you had better tell Aggie or Ben that you're leaving or there'll be a search party out looking for you when you don't show up for lunch. In fact," she added testily, "as long as you insist on coming along, you might as well be useful. Aggie's in the kitchen. Ask her if she would like us to pick up anything for her while we're in town."

"You really know how to make a guy feel welcome, don't you, Cass," he said dryly, opening the door for her and bowing her into the seat with mock gallantry. "I'll be right back."

As soon as the front door closed behind him, Cass eased off the brake, gave him enough time to get out of earshot, and started the motor. She restrained the impulse to gun the engine and rip out of the yard. Instead, she quietly put the car in gear and rolled around to the lane. Only then did she apply real pressure to the gas pedal. By the time Brendan returned, she thought with satisfaction, she would be well out of sight.

As Cass began the long climb out of the valley, she checked the rearview mirror. No sign of dust. Brendan wasn't following her. She hummed cheerfully to herself, happy for the moment to have outwitted him. The small victory, however, didn't keep her cheerful long as she began to wonder why he had been so insistent on coming along. He must have intended to keep her from making the call to New York. But how?

That question kept her occupied during the steady climb up the narrow, twisting dirt track, but she focused her attention on her driving as she followed the curving road around the rim of the plateau and began the sharp descent along the side of the cliff toward Rattlesnake Gulch. This was no time for idle thoughts, not with a sheer wall of rock on the far side of the car and a two-hundred-foot drop-off on the other.

As the decline steepened, she shifted into a lower gear and applied more pressure on the brake. It took her a moment to realize that the pedal under her foot was slowly sinking to the floor. The car began to pick up speed, straining against the engine. Frantically she pumped on the pedal, but her efforts were useless. The brakes were failing and the gears wouldn't hold the car back for long. She felt with her foot for the emergency brake pedal and pressed.

Nothing happened.

The car began picking up more and more speed. If it continued on the path it was heading, she realized in horror, a half mile below, around the last bend, it would miss the narrow wooden bridge and plunge straight off into the gulch.

No, no! She couldn't think of that. To panic now was suicidal.

In a split second she considered her options. At the speed she was traveling, there was no way she could make the turn onto the bridge at the bottom. She couldn't open the door and jump. The drop-off on her left was sure death. Her only realistic choice was the mountain. But if she didn't gauge the angle right, if she hit the rock too hard, the impact could throw her across to the other side and over the cliff.

Carefully, carefully, she edged the car to the right. Rock grated on metal. The car didn't slow down, but the contact impeded its momentum slightly. If she only had more time—but the end of the decline was coming much too quickly. She couldn't afford to be too cautious now. She turned the wheel more sharply, crushing in the right side of the car but at least managing to keep it on the road. More bumping, grinding, and a shower of sparks. To her relief, the car slowed, but as she took the last curve she knew that her efforts hadn't been enough to avert disaster. The yawning gulf of Rattlesnake Gulch was visible now, looming closer and closer.

Cass had reached the point where she had to make a decision—whether to risk the left turn onto the bridge or to crash headlong into the wall of rock on her right. She hesitated and, murmuring a fervent prayer, chose to take her chances with the mountain. That decision very probably saved her life. The moment she turned the wheel she recognized a difference in the jolting feel of the road. The edge of the rutted, hard-packed dirt track had given way to a soft shoulder along the base of the rock cliff. A miracle.

Two of the tires became embedded in deep sand. The car lurched, slowed, tipped, and finally rolled to a stop not three feet from a giant boulder on the edge of the gulch.

Cass had no idea how long she sat there while reaction set in. Her hands were frozen to the wheel, her eyes stared straight ahead into space, and every muscle in her body was quivering. Suddenly, as though the wire that had been holding her upright snapped, she slumped back in the seat, her hands dropped from the wheel, and her head drooped forward. The trembling ceased, but she fought a rising nausea. The confines of the car became claustrophobic. With a groan she wrenched the door open and took in great gulping breaths of air.

Another indeterminate period of time passed before she was sufficiently recovered to slide out of the seat and stand, but even then, her legs were still wobbly from the release of tension. She leaned weakly against the door frame for support until she had the strength to push away from the car and begin the long, hot hike up the road toward the ranch.

She had done a lot of thinking right after the accident, and she did even more as she made her way up the steep incline. Halfway, she shuddered and looked away from the signs of her desperate downhill struggle to stop. Broken glass from the headlight and side windows, pieces of mutilated metal from the bumper and fenders, strips of chrome torn from the side, a twisted hubcap, long scrapes in the sandstone wall—mute evidence of a very narrow escape from death.

As she neared the top of the plateau, she carefully examined the ground. Thirty feet down from the last turn she found what she had been looking for. Mixed in with the dust that had settled, she could see the trail of dark liquid that extended on up the road—brake fluid.

Even as she battled for her life, she had known in the back of her mind that this latest "accident" had been as premeditated as any of the others. If she had taken a look under the car, she had no doubt that she would have found that the brake line had been partially cut through. The first time she applied serious pressure on the pedal, the line had broken, leaking out the fluid and leaving the brakes useless.

Slowly she continued the three-mile trek homeward; she was in no hurry to reach the ranch. She had far too much to think about, too many decisions to make, too many plans to formulate.

During the first two miles, she reassessed all the circumstances surrounding the sale of the ranch. She went over each point, every event, every word she could remember speaking. She recalled arguments and reactions, and finally dwelt on everything that *hadn't* been said or done. Facts that she had dismissed as unimportant or irrelevant took on new significance. The conclusion she was forced to reach was staggering, unbelievable, even crazy.

Cass had always heard that a close brush with death could change a person's life, and this one had undoubtedly changed hers—fundamentally, permanently. Even if the near disaster had been an accident, those few minutes careening down the mountainside had made her reevaluate her priorities, reaffirm her values, and basically redefine her goals in life. How much worse it was, though, she concluded bleakly, to know that someone cared so little about you that your life was expendable when it posed a threat.

By the time Cass reached the lane leading to the ranch, she had formed a plan of action. She didn't have time to waste in indecision, eating her heart out, sick with disillusionment—torn apart by love and loyalty, friends and family, and uncompromising conviction.

When she entered the ranch house, the household was gathered in the dining room, finishing their lunch. She glanced at her watch. One o'clock. It seemed almost impossible to believe that only four hours had passed since she had left. She had lived a lifetime in those four hours.

Aggie was the first to see her standing in the doorway. "Cass!"

"Back so soon?" Ben asked, only glancing at her out of the corner of his eye.

Brendan was the one who noticed the scratch on her cheek that was nearly concealed by the streaks of dirt down her face. "Cass, are you all right?"

She smiled at him, a crooked smile. "You always seem to be asking me that, Brendan."

He took a closer look and saw the dust on her shoes, the stains on her jeans, and the small tear in the sleeve of her denim jacket. "What happened?" he asked grimly.

"Car trouble." Her reply was cryptic, but she had no intention of going into the details just then. It would spoil everything.

Brendan frowned in consternation. "You're the one who wouldn't let me come along with you, remember," he growled.

"I remember," she said solemnly.

Now Ben frowned. "What went wrong that you couldn't fix? Dad taught Cass to be as good a mechanic as they come," he explained to a puzzled Brendan.

"I didn't have the spare parts," Cass replied, keeping her tone casual only with effort.

Ben could accept that. "Where did you stall? Shall I send some of the men out?"

"Don't be bothering her now. The car can wait." Aggie spoke sharply, aware that what little color there was in Cass's face was fading fast. She pulled out a chair and shoved it toward her. "Sit down, Cass, before you fall down. I'll get you something to drink."

Only when she sat was Cass aware of her exhaustion, but before she could give in to it, she still had a hand to play. She took a drink of the juice that Aggie gave her, bucked up her spirits, and grimaced wryly at the assembled party.

"I'm afraid that this is the last straw." She sighed. "I had a lot of time to think hiking back to the ranch, and I'm sorry, Ben, but I've had it with this place." She addressed her sister-in-law next. "You're absolutely right, Loretta. This is no way to live. I'm sick to death of the problems and inconveniences." She forced a smile at Darin. "Coping with the wrong bolt of fabric is a cinch compared to dealing with fires and wild horses and broken-down cars out in the middle of nowhere." Lastly, she turned to Brendan. "You understand what I'm saying, don't you, Brendan? If your offer still stands, Monarch can have the ranch. When you get back to New York, draw up the papers and I'll sign them."

"Cass!" She ignored the astonished look in Aggie's eyes and turned a deaf ear to her cry.

"Thanks, Cass," Ben said, smiling. Loretta beamed complacently.

Only Brendan was skeptical. "Do you really mean that?"

"Yes, Brendan, I mean it."

"Does that mean we go back to New York now?" Darin asked hopefully.

"I'm sure Loretta and Ben would be glad to have you stay on, Darin," Cass replied. "But feel free to go back any time you please." Fatigue was getting the better of her, but she still had the final card to play—her trump card. She smiled wanly at them. "I imagine you can all understand that I want to get away by myself for a while. Ben, if you wouldn't mind lending me the Jeep for a few days, I thought I would go down into Arizona, probably stay at the Grand Canyon if I can get a reservation this time in the season. If not, I'll go on to Flagstaff or maybe even to Phoenix."

"Of course you can take the Jeep," her brother replied quickly, all solicitude now.

"You can even take the car, if you'd like," Loretta volunteered handsomely.

"No, thanks, Loretta," she said, declining the offer. "The Jeep will do fine. And you won't mind, will you, Darin, if I take another week or so off?"

"Take all the time you need, Cass," he offered good-naturedly. "Dee and I'll limp along."

"Well, Brendan," she said casually, having difficulty meeting his dark, thoughtful gaze. He was scrutinizing every flicker of emotion that passed across her face. "I guess I'll see you when I get back to New York."

"I guess you will," he said shortly.

She stood on her shaky legs, holding onto the back of the chair for support. "If you'll excuse me now, I think I'll lie down for the rest of the day and go to bed early tonight. I'll plan on leaving at dawn, Ben. Aggie, could I have a tray in my room when you have a chance? Oh, and tell Will that I'd like to talk with him for a minute."

The housekeeper's expression was blank now. "Sure thing, Cass. You just lie down and I'll send the tray in with Will when he comes in."

An hour later Cass was looking out the window when Will arrived with her food. He wasted no time with preliminaries. "Aggie told me what you said in there. Now, you tell me what's going on."

Briefly she told him about her harrowing escape and more hesitantly about the conclusions she had reached. As he listened, Will's mouth thinned until it nearly disappeared from his face, and his eyes burned with anger.

"Will," Cass said when she concluded, "I need your help."

"You know I'd do anything for you, Cass!" he declared rashly and then amended his vow to a more pragmatic, "Anything short of robbing a bank, maybe."

"I won't ask you to rob any banks," she promised, a glimmer of ironic amusement in her eyes. "But how would you feel about being an accessory to a kidnapping?"

Cass set her alarm for four A.M. Fortunately, nearly twelve hours of sleep had brought back her mental agility and stamina. She was going to need them. Wearing nothing but a short silk nightgown, she slipped silently out of her room and down the hall, past the bathroom, past the children's room, to the door of Brendan's bedroom. She listened a moment, but as she expected, all was quiet within.

The door squeaked on its hinges as she opened it, and when she stepped inside, she heard Brendan murmur incoherently in his sleep. By the pale light of the moon through the open window, she watched the shapeless form on the bed toss restlessly, turn, and settle again beneath the covers. The four-poster was massive and sturdy, with a high headboard and footboard, and it wasn't until Cass drew closer that she could see Brendan distinctly. He lay on his side near the far edge, his back toward her. Plenty of room, she decided on an irresistible impulse, for her to slip in beside him.

He murmured again as the bed dipped and she slid under the covers. She moved closer until her smooth legs touched the hair on his and her soft breasts came to rest against his bare back. Now he turned again in his sleep, toward her warmth. His knee hiked up her nightgown and insinuated itself naturally between hers, his tousled head nestled into her shoulder, and his arm curved possessively around her waist.

She wondered with a remembered flame of jealousy just who he was dreaming of, who he thought it was sleeping beside him. It was lucky for her already frazzled nerves that she didn't have long to wait for an answer.

"Cass," he breathed on a long sigh.

She answered with a husky whisper in his ear. "Right here, Brendan."

One minute he was asleep, the next he was fully awake. Cass didn't have to look to tell. The leg between hers stiffened, the arm around her tightened, and she felt the betraying jerk of his head. There was a brief silence; then, "Cass!" he said in disbelief.

She pulled far enough away to see the dim outline of his face and forced a smile. "Surprised?"

"Delighted!" he murmured fervently, trying to draw her near once again.

"Oh, no, you don't," she objected teasingly. "I didn't come here to dally with you."

He ran a hand down her side, from her breast, along the smooth line of her hip, to the bare flesh of her thigh. To his credit—and in an admirable display of self-restraint—he attempted to match her light tone. "Do you always pay your social calls in the middle of the night, dressed in nothing but a very sexy nightgown?"

She raised herself on one elbow and traced his profile with a playful finger. "Only for one very special man."

Brendan caught the truant finger and kissed the tip. "If it isn't . . . uh, dallying you have in mind, what is it?"

"Oh, I had an idea. One," she hinted at suggestively, "that I didn't feel like announcing to the entire family at the time. I told you all that I wanted to get away from the ranch for a while, but the truth is, I don't really want to go away alone." She circled his mobile mouth with the wayward fingertip. "How does a trip to the Grand Canyon strike you?"

"The Grand Canyon with you," he murmured, his voice deep with desire, "strikes me right where I live. When do we leave?"

"Can you be ready in half an hour?"

"Make it fifteen minutes!"

"You're on."

Brendan threw back the covers and made a dive for his clothes before Cass could move.

"Don't bother to bring much," she advised, unable to resist the temptation of watching him for a moment, noting the way the hard muscles in his back moved in such easy rhythm. "Just a few shirts, a couple of pairs of jeans, and a Windbreaker rather than a sports coat. Oh, and bring a hat to keep the sun off your head." She slipped out of the warm bed, stifling a regret that they hadn't spent a little more time in it together, and headed for the door. "Meet you out in front."

She left him throwing clothes into a light bag and went back to her own room to dress. She had packed what little she needed the day before. She smiled in grim satisfaction as she buttoned up a warm flannel shirt and slipped into her own fleece-lined Windbreaker. She had flown over the first hurdle with far more ease than she had anticipated.

Cass was quick, but Brendan had been quicker. By the time she joined him, he was leaning against the Jeep, watching the approach of dawn and smoking a cigarette. He ground it out under his foot and relieved her of her own small bag.

"Would you rather take my four-wheeler?" he asked, casting a skeptical eye at the Jeep.

"No, thanks." She patted the khaki hood affectionately. "This baby drives a lot better than it looks."

With a shrug he tossed their bags in the back. "Want me to drive?"

"No, thanks," she said again lightly. "This trip is on me. The sun will be up soon. Let's go before the whole house hears us and turns out to see us off."

"Ben knows I'm going with you, then?" Brendan asked with interest, climbing into the passenger's seat.

"No, but I told Will, so that panic wouldn't set in at your nonappearance."

The engine sprang instantly into life at the first touch of the starter. Cass shifted gears and smoothly let out the clutch. The Jeep was old and beat-up with use, but it was an army-surplus vehicle, built to withstand rough treatment. Just as well, she thought grimly. It was in for a good deal of abuse that day.

The sun was pushing its way above the horizon by the time they reached the top rim of the plateau. The prospect was for a beautiful day—which suited Cass's plans perfectly. Rain would have been a complication.

As she took the turn and began the descent into Rattlesnake Gulch, she felt a moment of panic. Yesterday's events were still too vivid in her mind. Experimentally she tested the brake pedal. Nothing wrong there. An absurd feeling of relief flooded over her—absurd because she knew that Will himself had checked the Jeep over inch by inch, from tail pipe to fan belt, and had had someone keeping watch on it all night long.

They were rounding the last curve near the bottom of the steep slope when Brendan caught sight of the wrecked remains of her little car. "Cass!" he gasped in astonishment. "That's your car! Look at it!"

"I have," she said tersely, forcing herself not to look now. This was no time to lose her nerve. "Which reminds me. I need to stop in Escalante and tell the rental agency that they're going to need a tow truck to get it out of here."

Brendan was still turned around, looking at the wreck, when they crossed over the wooden bridge. If he glanced down into the gulch, the sight apparently didn't trouble him. He was a much easier companion than Darin had been. Not a word of complaint. In fact, he said little during the entire drive into town, either to allow Cass to concentrate on her driving or else to mull over his own thoughts.

They didn't spend long in Escalante. There was little need. The entire town consisted of a few stores to serve the needs of local ranchers, a couple of gas stations, and what other amenities a would-be tourist might require.

Brendan would have gone into the tiny car rental-cum-insurance agency with Cass, but she asked him to wait in the Jeep while she made her explanations. In his present mellow mood, he gave her no argument. He was even more agreeable when she suggested breakfast at one of the two cafes in town.

She couldn't quell a shiver of apprehension as she watched him polish off a heaping plate of steak, eggs, and hashbrowns, washed down with a tumblerful of fresh-squeezed orange juice and several cups of excellent coffee.

She had no doubt that he would be remembering that breakfast for many days to come.

Shortly after nine o'clock they once again piled into the Jeep and set off on their odyssey. Food and the smooth, undemanding road seemed to have loosened Brendan's tongue, for which Cass was grateful. She had deliberately and confidently headed east on the highway that ran through Escalante. If she could keep him interested and relaxed enough, with luck he would be oblivious to the posted signs and wouldn't notice that they were traveling in the opposite direction of Bryce Canyon and the turnoff south that led to Arizona, the Kaibab Forest, and finally the north rim of the Grand Canyon.

In actual fact, Cass had decided when she made her plans that there wasn't much cause for concern. Brendan's lack of knowledge of the geography of southern Utah was surpassed only by his lack of appreciation. Still, she kept the conversation going with questions about his business, plans for its future expansion, and how the company was faring during his absence. This last prompted him to ask at one point, "How long are we going to be gone?"

"As long as we feel like." She took her eyes off the road long enough to smile at him provocatively. "Does it matter?"

"You must know it doesn't. And I haven't taken a vacation in years. No one will be surprised if I don't show up for a couple of weeks or more."

That was what Cass wanted to hear. "Then if you don't mind, I'm going to take some back roads." She was looking straight ahead again and he didn't see the hard glitter of determination in her eyes. "I have a surprise for you."

"I'm all for it," he told her, his eyes feasting on her clean profile, etched against the blue sky, and the familiar curves of her body, nicely revealed in her fitted shirt and tight jeans. "Especially if it's anything like the one you gave me this morning in bed."

Several miles farther on down the road, some of his enthusiasm dampened. Cass turned off the well-paved highway onto an unmarked graded road. A short time later she turned again, onto a dirt track. This time he couldn't miss the sign meant to be noticed: *Attention! Make local inquiry before attempting travel in this area.*

"What does that mean?" he asked, startled.

"Relax," Cass said casually. "Remember, I'm one of the local people who answer those kinds of inquiries."

"Oh," he replied uncertainly.

As the surface of the track turned into a rutted washboard, Cass picked up speed and Brendan became even more uncertain.

"Aren't you driving a little fast?" he suggested after bouncing and hitting his head twice on the cloth top of the Jeep.

"Just hold on," she advised him. "The trouble is, I'm not going fast enough yet."

He watched her warily, occasionally glancing at the rising needle of the speedometer. Finally, when it hit forty miles an hour, she kept the speed there.

"Feel the difference?" she asked after a minute. To his surprise, he did. The road was just as bad, if not worse, but the ride was relatively smooth. "The mistake most novice drivers make on roads like this," Cass explained, "is that they drive too slowly and the tires hit every bump. At forty, they skim over the top."

She saw him relax and smiled to herself. They were miles and miles from civilization, and this atrocious stretch of road had done its work. Brendan's eyes had never left it. He was so disoriented now that he had no idea in which direction they were heading, let alone where on earth they were.

For over an hour they traveled in silence as Cass kept her entire attention glued to the way ahead. Brendan for his part was more and more puzzled. The landscape around them had changed dramatically. Gone were the sagebrush and sand that had characterized the beginning of their trip from Escalante. Now, high hills, rocky outcroppings, and concealed canyons dominated the scenery. Finally Cass slowed, identified a narrow offshoot from the road they were following, and turned again, onto an even worse dirt track that was classified on the map as only a trail. A few miles on up, even that trail ended. Ahead of them was an opening less than six feet wide, carved out between two sheer rock cliffs.

Here Cass stopped and turned off the engine.

Brendan looked around in bewilderment. For the last two hours, he hadn't been sure what to expect, but he hadn't even guessed at a dead end out in the middle of nowhere.

"Where are we, Cass?"

"We're at one of the entrances to Lucifer's Playground," she said easily.

"Where do we go from here?"

She smiled at him encouragingly. She couldn't afford to have him balk now. "You'll see." She gave two sharp blasts of the horn. Waited. Then honked twice more. "There," she said, pointing for Brendan's benefit to a small side canyon where Will was emerging through the rocks and brush, riding one horse and leading another. Brendan couldn't have looked more startled if a fifty-piece band had suddenly appeared.

"That's Will Taylor, isn't it?" he asked in disbelief.

"Yes. He's brought Midnight and Starfire. You see, we can only get where we're going on horseback." She said this casually, as though it were the most natural thing in the world.

Brendan's voice was faint. "Horseback?"

"The place I'm taking you is beautiful, Brendan," she assured him with the utmost sincerity. "You'll love it." One look at his face told her that he doubted he could love any place that had to be reached on the back of a horse.

"How did Will get here at the same time we did?" he thought to ask once he had overcome his first dismay at the arrangements.

"When you drive, you have to take the long way around. Horses can take a more direct route." Cass's answer was deliberately vague about actual distances. The less specific information she gave Brendan, the better her chances of success. She also failed to mention that Will had taken the horses by truck down to Escalante the night before—partly to ensure that the rendezvous would take place on schedule and partly because she wanted them fresh for the next leg of their journey.

"You made good time, Cass," Will called as he swung

down off his horse, tilted his hat back, and approached the Jeep.

"Yes. Any trouble?"

"Nope. You?" He glanced surreptitiously at Brendan's face and hid his amusement at the consternation he saw there—consternation but no suspicion or anger. Good.

"The last storm made the road a little worse but not impassable." She turned back to Brendan. "Ready?"

Brendan was eyeing the horses warily. "I don't really ride, you know."

"Will's brought Midnight for you," she said airily. "All you have to do is sit on his back and let him do the work."

"Huh!"

Brendan was unconvinced but apparently game to give it a try. Cass relaxed. She had cleared the second major hurdle. While Brendan climbed out of the Jeep, his back to Will, the older man grinned encouragingly at Cass and gave her a conspiratorial wink.

"Do we need anything from our bags?" Brendan asked, eyeing the Jeep he had disparaged earlier with real longing.

"No," Cass replied. "Will has put food in the saddlebags for us. Just bring your jacket and hat."

"Can I give you a leg up, Cahill?" Will asked innocently.

"I think you'd better," Brendan agreed ruefully, watching Cass swing lightly into the saddle and gather in the reins. "I'm a lot more at home on a steel construction beam."

After one abortive attempt to hoist Brendan into the saddle, he was successful and they were off, up the narrow trail. Cass led the way and Brendan followed—or more accurately, Midnight plodded stolidly after Starfire. As they picked their way around rocky outcroppings, through brush, and down and up small ravines, Cass made no attempt at a commentary on the landscape. She had a feeling Brendan was more interested in staying on the loping, swaying horse than on the scenery. Again to his credit, he offered not a word of complaint, and Cass began to feel the first stirrings of hope mixed with a decided guilt.

For the next hour, Cass guided Brendan up narrow canyons, through rocky passes, and along a maze of dried creek beds and washes. Every now and then they would encounter boulders in their path or patches of sand wet from underground seeps. At one point Cass pulled up abruptly. Midnight obediently stopped behind—without a whole lot of help from his rider.

"Wait a minute, Brendan," she called over her shoulder. "Do you see that big stretch of wet sand ahead? It's quicksand. Be careful going around it."

Cass deliberately failed to set his mind at rest by assuring him that Midnight had the good sense to stay far away from the potential hazard without any encouragement from Brendan.

His jaw was tense and the lines in his forehead prominent by the time they were safely on the other side. The noon sun had raised the temperature a good twenty degrees since they started, and he lifted his hat, took out a handkerchief, and wiped away the perspiration that rolled down his face.

"How much farther now?" he asked for the first time.

"Not far," she assured him. "And you'll see that it was worth every minute of the ride."

Ten minutes later Brendan had to admit that Cass had indeed chosen a very pretty spot. They emerged from a rocky, arid canyon into a virtual oasis. And what an oasis. He had never imagined that anything like it could exist in the middle of all the heat, sand, and rock. But there it was—a broad, deep, clear pool, fed by a sixty-foot waterfall, edged on the far side by sheer cliffs and on the near side by cottonwood trees, a patch of tall snake-grass, and bulrushes.

The city-bred part of him found the remoteness of the place daunting. The lover in him saw the potential advantages of such isolation. He glanced at Cass, glowing with health and beauty in the bright sunlight, and decided that he would wait to pass judgment on whether or not the trip had been worth it.

Cass allowed him a moment of speculation, then swung down from her horse and tethered it to a nearby cottonwood tree. "I don't know about you," she said, unbuckling one of the saddlebags, "but I'm starved. Come on down and let's eat."

That was easier said than done. Brendan's descent from Midnight was neither speedy nor graceful, and even though his feet were once again on solid ground, he still felt the movement of the horse in his shaky legs. He was also starting to ache in places that had never had the occasion to ache before.

Out of the corner of her eye, Cass watched him rub his rear end and stare balefully at Midnight who, now free of his rider, had lowered his noble head and was contentedly munching on some grass. Cass felt a flood of relief. If she had had any lingering doubts about Brendan's experience with horses, they were completely dispelled at that moment. He was certainly no horseman.

Both Brendan and Cass had long ago removed their Windbreakers as the heat of the day became more and more intense. She selected a shady spot now, spread her jacket down, and laid out the lunch Will had prepared for them— thick ham-and-cheese sandwiches on Aggie's homemade bread, apples, and a couple of still-cool beers for Brendan. At the welcome sound of Cass opening one of the pop-top cans, Brendan tied his horse to the tree as she had done, sank gingerly down beside her on his own Windbreaker, and gratefully accepted the beer she offered.

"And to think that some people ride horses for pleasure," he said, smiling at her wryly. "I never thought of myself as a coward before, but you're going to have to do some convincing to get me back in that saddle very soon." His smile turned suggestive. "Or maybe I'll convince you that we ought to stay here for a while."

She returned his smile perfunctorily and quickly looked away from the desire in his eyes. "We're in no hurry," she assured him lightly. "We've got all the time in the world."

If Brendan only knew how true that was, she reflected soberly, he would be clambering back in the saddle immediately—aches or no aches.

"At least it's cool here," he observed in relief.

"In a place like this, with plenty of ventilation, there's a thirty-degree difference between being in the shade and being in direct sunlight. You'd do well to remember that when you build houses in desert country," she added dryly.

They spoke little as they ate—Brendan from growing fatigue and Cass from disinclination. She was going to have too much to say as it was before the afternoon was over. As she had expected, though, the explanation wouldn't have to come too soon. The long, physically exhausting day, the heat, the substantial meal, and the two beers all started to have their effect on Brendan. He was half asleep before Cass had cleared away the remains of lunch. As she put the cans and other debris back in the saddlebags, she saw his eyelids droop.

"Why don't you lie back and relax for a while?" she suggested. "Sleep, if you'd like. I'll probably do the same."

She noted with relief that at the moment he was too tired to take her suggestion as an invitation to intimacy. He lay back in the shade of a cottonwood tree, using his jacket as a pillow, and promptly drifted off.

Cass listened as his breathing became deeper and more regular. Her plans were going well, exactly as she had intended, but she could find little satisfaction in her success. She had a pretty good idea of what Brendan's first reaction would be when he awoke—but then what? She shuddered at the uncertainty and suffered a moment of trepidation. Could she withstand his anger? It wasn't too late to turn back. . . .

No! She bolstered her courage and sat down to wait, watching the rise and fall of Brendan's broad chest until she was sure that nothing short of an earthquake would wake him. One arm lay over his head. From it, she slowly, carefully, removed his wristwatch, then paused. He was still sound asleep. Next, from the pocket of his jacket she removed his cigarette lighter.

These tasks successfully accomplished, she rose to her feet, moved to the horses, and stashed the lighter and Brendan's watch, as well as her own, in one of her saddlebags. From the other she removed a canteen, an old army mess kit, and a few packages of dried food. At first she had planned to bring nothing, to live entirely off the land, but she had reconsidered. Brendan was going to have a hard enough time as it was. She wanted this to be an *experience* for him, not a horrendous ordeal.

"There, there," she crooned softly when Starfire grew restive. She patted both horses' noses as they nuzzled her, and fished out a couple of lumps of sugar for them from her pocket. "Good boys. Just a minute now."

She untied their reins from around the tree and looped

them over the horns of their saddles so that the horses wouldn't stumble over them on their homeward trek. She gave each an apple she had saved, a final affectionate pat, and then a sharp slap on its ample rump.

"Off you go now!"

The savvy old trail horses didn't need any more encouragement than that. They snorted, shook their heads, breathed softly down their noses, and whinnied a farewell. Off they ambled in the direction from which they had come. She looked quickly over her shoulder. Brendan hadn't even stirred. By the time he awoke, Midnight and Starfire would be long gone.

Cass moved back to their picnic spot and settled down in the shade beside him, her back braced against the gnarled trunk of the tree. A breeze from one of the canyons ruffled her hair and cooled her heated cheeks. She folded her arms on her bent knees and rested her chin on her forearm, staring at the spot where the waterfall hit the pool.

There was nothing to do now but wait.

Chapter 13

"CASS! WAKE UP!"

She felt Brendan shaking her shoulder, slowly opened her eyes, and frowned. Brendan was hovering over her, silhouetted against the waterfall behind him. Where was she? Memory returned quickly. She and Brendan were in Lucifer's Playground. At some point in the afternoon the waiting had become interminable, and she had lain down beside him and fallen asleep herself.

"Cass," Brendan said more urgently when he saw she was awake, "the horses are gone!"

Slowly she pushed herself up on both elbows and glanced toward the smaller cottonwood tree, its leaves quivering now in the breeze. "Yes, they are."

Brendan sat back on his heels, rubbing a knot of tension in the back of his neck with a frustrated hand. "They must have pulled loose. Do you suppose they're still around here somewhere?"

"Not a chance." She pushed damp strands of hair from her cheek and looked toward the west. The sun was still visible above the far ridges, but most of the pool was in

214

shadow. It had to be close to four o'clock. "My guess is that by now they're nearly back at the ranch."

Brendan stared at her, uncomprehending. "Back at the ranch?"

"Midnight and Starfire are well-trained trail horses, and they've covered nearly every inch of this territory in the past ten years or so. Instinct will guide them on home."

She explained the circumstances as though her major concern was to assure Brendan of the horses' safety, not his own. It took a minute for the implication of her words to sink in. Then, "You mean . . . we're stuck out here?"

"That's one way of putting it, I suppose—though you could always try and hike out," she suggested unhelpfully.

"Oh, right!" he grunted, glancing around, not even really sure which of the narrow washes leading away from the pool had brought them there. "Well, I guess we just wait until someone comes looking for us."

"No one will come looking for us," she told him soberly.

He waved this notion away impatiently. "Of course they will. Taylor will know we're in trouble when we don't show up back at the Jeep."

She disabused his mind of this hope. "No, he won't. By now Will and the Jeep are safely back at the ranch."

The calm, cool certainty of her statement set the hairs on the back of his neck on end. "What makes you think that?" he asked after an infinitesimal hesitation.

"Because those were my instructions."

Again, her cool detachment chilled him. Automatically he glanced at his wrist to check the time and stared in confusion at his bare arm. "My watch is gone."

"You don't need a watch out here, Brendan. Time is relative."

This non sequitur turned his confusion into suspicion. His body grew rigid. "Where's my watch?"

"I took it off after you were asleep and put it in a saddlebag along with your lighter. You'll get them both back eventually."

"And how did the horses get loose, Cassandra?" The new formality spoke for itself.

"I untied them and let them go," she stated flatly.

Even though this was the answer he expected, it still came as a shock. "You *deliberately* stranded us out here with no food or transportation?"

She plucked at a piece of grass, refusing to meet his blue-black gaze. "Oh, there's plenty of food—if you know where to look. And what better transportation than two good legs?"

He stood abruptly, took a quick turn around, and threw his hands in the air, less angry than mystified. "Why? What the hell do you think you're doing?"

"Killing three birds with one stone," she said enigmatically.

He hit his forehead with the palm of his hand in frustration. "Will you cut it out, Cass? I've had it up to here with your riddles!"

She studied his face solemnly. "That's because you didn't get the first one. *Fire, wire, desire, acquire.* You didn't understand that, did you, Brendan. I thought you would, but I was wrong."

He was watching her anxiously now. "Cass," he said more gently. "You're not well. That bump on the head was worse than we thought. You're not making any sense."

"Arson, sabotage, and—" she paused because it was still difficult for her to put the truth into words "—and an attempt on my life. Do they make any sense to you?"

"What?" he asked warily.

"Brendan," she said gravely, "the fire in the barn was no accident. It was deliberately set. Will didn't leave the corral gate unbolted. Someone turned the horses loose on purpose. And Kettledrum didn't throw me by accident. He was brought down by a wire strung across the path."

His face was a study in concern and incredulity. "Cass, that is ridiculous and paranoid."

"Is it? Do you think I imagined the 'accident' to my car?"

This sober question silenced whatever else he would have said. When he remembered the condition of her car as he had seen it a few hours earlier, he went pale. "Cass, your car! What really happened?"

"Someone tampered with the brakes. They gave out on

the ridge of the plateau. You saw where it was, what it looked like. You don't think it was a miracle that I came out of that alive?"

If Brendan had been white before, he was positively gray now. His voice was strangled as he asked, "Cass, surely you can't believe that *I* would do a thing like that?"

She smiled at him wanly. "The knowledge that you *didn't* is the only thing that has kept me going these last two days."

Brendan scarcely heard her. His mind was racing now, and his eyes narrowed. "Your riddle—fire, wire, and so on. You thought that I was the one sabotaging the ranch, trying to force you to sell? You really believed that I was capable of doing such things for a lousy piece of land?"

"At the time, it was the only answer that made any sense. I'm sorry, Brendan," she offered sincerely, but even to her the apology sounded inadequate. He was obviously deeply hurt by her suspicions.

"So what made you change your mind?" he asked harshly.

"I had a lot of time to think after the accident yesterday," she explained, meeting his eyes somberly. "Too many things didn't add up—the fact that you ride so badly, your total lack of knowledge about horses and ranching. But the most important point was that you insisted on going into town with me. You were adamant. If I hadn't tricked you by sending you back into the house, you would have been with me on that trip into town. I couldn't believe that you would demand to go knowing that the brakes were going to fail."

"Well, thanks for the vote of confidence—even if it is a little late . . ." His words trailed off as the sinking sun caught him in the eyes. He squinted, looked around, and frowned—aware again of where they were and the predicament they were in. He threw a sharp, penetrating gaze at Cass, but her expression was unreadable. "If you don't blame me for the accidents, Cass, then what the hell are we doing stranded out here in this God-forsaken place?"

"What do *you* think, Brendan?"

He didn't answer immediately as he thought over all she had told him. He winced once at the memory of her poor smashed car, and then his mouth hardened. "The scene you played at the table yesterday afternoon was all an act, wasn't it? You have no intention of going back to New York or back to Cassandra's or back to me. You have no intention of selling the ranch to Monarch."

"Part of that's true," she admitted unhappily. There was still a lot that she had to explain to Brendan, but they had plenty of time. Harder for him to understand, though, would be the things that he was going to have to discover for himself.

He looked around again in disbelief. "Do you really intend to keep me here?"

"Yes," she told him flatly.

"What good do you think that's going to do?"

"I guess that's something we'll both find out in time, won't we?" she replied enigmatically.

"You can't keep me here forever, you know." Her calm, remote attitude both baffled and infuriated him. "With or without Will's help, I'll be missed in a couple of days, fewer probably, when I don't call into the office."

"No one would know where to look if you *were* missed," she stated matter-of-factly. "You don't know it, but you left a farewell note behind in your room, thanking Ben and Loretta politely for their hospitality and explaining that you decided to go to Arizona with me. As far as the household is concerned, we're at the Grand Canyon right now. I did quite a good job at forgery. It must be the artist in me," she added, with maddening coolness.

"Well, that's certainly something to be proud of," he growled sarcastically.

For the first time the hint of a mischievous smile flickered in her eyes. "Yes, it is, as a matter of fact. For someone who's lived as relatively blameless a life as I have, I think I've done a pretty good job of bringing off my first major crime. Kidnapping is a federal offense, you know."

Brendan was not amused. His stare hardened into marble, and Cass could imagine the number of people who had tried to cross him and had withered at that intimidating stare. In fact, she wondered in amazement that she had ever found the courage to abduct him like this.

Love and desperation, she decided, must bring out physical and psychological resources in people that they didn't realize they possessed. Brendan didn't know it yet, she thought wistfully, but she was fighting desperately for that love and their future happiness. Her prayer was that he would eventually accept her reasons and would be able to forgive her for putting him through such an ordeal.

"It won't work, Cass!" His words were firm and clipped, but there was less assurance in his tone than he probably would have liked.

"I don't have a doubt but that it will," she contradicted him with far more assurance. "You see, in a couple of days Ben, Darin, and your office will receive postcards from us—mailed from Phoenix by Will's obliging sister—informing them that we'll be in touch after we've taken a much-needed vacation of indeterminate length. I can't believe that even faithful Edith will be very surprised or, from what you've told me, even very disturbed. I'm sure that Ben and Darin won't be. Believe me, there isn't a soul who will expect us until they see us."

"I tell you, it won't work," Brendan objected stubbornly, anger beginning to work in his jaw. "All my clothes are still in my room, and the four-wheeler is a company car I drove down from Salt Lake. I wouldn't just leave it at Wells' Springs."

Cass shook her head. "No hope there, I'm afraid. In your—my—note, you also explained that we were taking your wagon instead of the Jeep. Soon after we left, a couple of the hands drove it into a storage shed and covered it with hay. It would be fall before anyone stumbled across it. And by now, Aggie will have packed away the rest of your clothes and ditched them in the cellar. There isn't a trace of you left on the ranch."

Brendan was white now under his tan. "You planned this all very carefully, didn't you, down to the last detail. What I don't understand is why." He shrugged helplessly. "Why? What did I ever do to you, Cass, besides love you, want you, and try to keep you with me? Was that such a crime?"

"No, Brendan," she said gently and had to blink tears out of her eyes. His sincerity was undermining. "The crime was that you were willing to let Monarch exploit this land for profit. I explained all this to you that first day, but words aren't enough. That's why you have to experience what I was talking about for yourself."

He stared at her uncomprehendingly, hurt and bewilderment darkening his eyes.

"Brendan, you don't understand that the greatest danger to this part of the country doesn't come from earthquakes or volcanoes or floods. It comes from human erosion—corporations that want the power or the minerals, developers, windshield tourists who are perfectly willing to spend money but aren't willing to pay the physical price to see and appreciate the land. Don't you see?" she pleaded with him. "This is one of the last, great undeveloped parts of the country. The government has been looking for an excuse to build roads through here, and you would help give them one. You have no idea, no comprehension of what the wilderness means to me. In the next days and weeks I want you to find out."

Brendan glanced around at the waterfall, at the barren red sandstone and buff-colored rock. Nice, but nothing special. In the distance he could see the mesas and buttes in shades of purple shadow, the air above them shimmering with heat waves. He shuddered. He hadn't learned yet that to see their beauty took a special eye. He certainly didn't understand Cass's fanaticism about the place. Nor her purpose in stranding him there. Only one explanation made any sense to him.

"What do you intend to do?" he asked harshly. "Keep me hostage out here until I agree to withdraw my offer for the ranch? Is that it?"

Cass would have been amused by that conclusion if the situation weren't so deadly serious. "No, Brendan. The business of the ranch is only one part of all this. And as you guessed, I had no intention of signing the option papers under any circumstances."

"Then what on earth do you expect to accomplish?"

She had already given him one answer, but he obviously hadn't understood what she was talking about. She gave him another reason, more oblique and much more personal. He wouldn't understand this one either—yet.

"It's not just what I intend to *accomplish*. It's what I

intend to *learn*—about you." She smiled wistfully. "You see, Brendan, I really do love you. I love you very much."

"You'll forgive me if I find that pretty hard to believe right now!"

"You don't believe me now," she said, sighing, "because you never listened to me when I told you that I was worried, that I was afraid we had too little in common to have any kind of future together. Well, right or wrong, I intend to find out."

"Which means what, exactly?" he asked, eyeing her warily.

She shrugged. "Which means that in the next few weeks I intend to find out what kind of a man you really are."

"Weeks!" he echoed faintly.

"That's right. We're going to stay here for as long as it takes."

Brendan stared at Cass in shock, then sat down on a rock at the edge of the pool, gazing into the clear water and considering his situation. The ramifications were just starting to sink in. Cass's behavior was outside the realm of anything he had experienced before, and he didn't know how to handle it.

Time passed and the shadows around them deepened.

They would have to be on their way soon, Cass thought absently. They needed to reach their shelter for the night before it was too dark to see. But she couldn't broach the subject just yet. She had to wait until Brendan had recognized the seriousness of his predicament. He had to be convinced that there was no possibility of rescue. He had to accept the idea that he couldn't find his way out of this hostile wilderness alone. He had to acknowledge to himself that she was fully prepared to carry out her plans and realize the fact that his well-being depended entirely on her.

Cass said nothing, merely waited patiently and watched the variety of emotions that played and replayed in rapid succession across Brendan's face—anger, frustration, skepticism, incredulity and, uppermost, bewilderment. Once he turned, searched her face for some hint of amusement, and asked, "This isn't a joke is it, Cass?"

"This is no joke, Brendan," she assured him solemnly, and she meant it. Her intentions were deadly serious.

As a child her father had taught her the qualities necessary for surviving in a hostile environment. She knew that Brendan possessed some of them already: stubbornness, determination, self-confidence, physical stamina, and endurance. But she was more interested in finding out if he possessed the more subtle qualities, the ones she cared about in a man.

Was he capable of cooperation and compromise, of first accepting a situation and then doing what was possible to make it better? While a survivalist had to be able to endure pain and discomfort, he couldn't be a masochist. Cass had to find out what really drove Brendan, what made a workaholic of him—greed, ambition, the wrong priorities, narrow-mindedness, limited life options—or an ingrained masochism.

Equally important, however, as far as Cass was concerned, were other intangible qualities. She knew that over the years Brendan had become cynical, fiercely independent, and totally self-sufficient. Well, cynicism about life, independence of all people, and a self-sufficiency that excluded her were no virtues in the kind of shared relationship she wanted with him. And they were no virtues in the survival situation she had engineered for him. Survival in the wilderness demanded cooperation and an inherent faith in the goodness of one's fellow men. There were no disposable people here. Would Brendan be willing to put his trust in someone other than himself—her—for his physical and emotional well-being? Was there faith buried somewhere under his cynical veneer? Those were the keys to their future—if he still wanted her after the way she was manipulating his life.

Brendan broke the silence a second time. "You intend to keep me here as long as it suits you?"

"That's right," she said unemotionally. Uncertainty was the real test of endurance. Most people could endure anything if they knew exactly how long the experience would last. Cass didn't really expect to have to keep him there for more than a week or two. In fact, she was sure she would find out more about Brendan in two days in the desert than she had in the two months she had known him in New York.

He fell silent again, glancing vaguely around, the way a space traveler would look at a bizarre, unexplored planet whose natural laws he didn't understand. And in a way, that was the case. He was in an alien environment. His glance returned again and again to Cass's face, as though he expected to find hope in her expression. There was no hope there.

"What do we do all this time?" he asked abruptly.

"As I told you before, I'm going to introduce you to the wilderness, and in the process, I'm going to put you through a course in survival."

"Survival?" he repeated, his voice now edged with hostility.

"That's right. I've already learned," she said dryly, "that you know everything in the book about survival in the business world and self-preservation with women. Now we'll see how you do with nature."

The moment she had been waiting for arrived. His shoulders straightened, his expression toughened, and his voice showed a new sense of purpose. "Okay, Cass," he agreed. "I don't pretend to know why you're doing this, but I admit that you're calling the shots. Fire away."

She rose, removed the few supplies from behind the tree where she had stashed them, and handed the canteen to Brendan. "Here, you can carry this."

"What happens now?" he asked.

Cass studied the lengthening shadows and started toward a mountain of boxcar-sized boulders. "Now," she said, flashing him an unexpected smile, "we climb."

Which they did—for close to an hour.

"This is where we'll stay," Cass said at last, panting. The final twenty yards had been nearly straight up.

"You couldn't . . . have picked . . . a place . . . at ground level?" Brendan growled between pants as he joined her. Then he exclaimed, "My God!" His voice reverberated back and forth from the walls of the huge open cavern.

The overhanging sandstone cliff ceiling was more than a hundred feet above them at the front opening. Inside, it tapered down into darkness, meeting the floor of sand and rocks at the back of the cave, a relatively shallow thirty feet from the entrance. Fifty feet below, from where they had just come, a stream ambled along. Brendan didn't recognize the fact yet, but the combination of a water source, protection from the elements, loose rocks within easy reach, a soft sand floor, and its height above the bottom of the narrow canyon made this cavern an ideal campsite. It had its drawbacks, of course. Firewood, food, and water meant a strenuous climb down the cliff. But physical well-being took precedence over ease.

Cass moved to a spot toward the back of the cavern and untied the sleeves of her wood-filled Windbreaker from around her waist. Both she and Brendan had collected what they would need for a fire before they began the final climb. She poked around in the sand with her foot.

"This will be a good place for the fire pit. Dump the wood here and then gather up a lot of medium-sized rocks."

Brendan did as she asked without comment. Then, "What now?" he asked, plunking down beside her as she lined a good-sized hole in the sand with the rocks. His breathing was back to normal and the hostility was back in his voice.

"Fire first," she replied tersely. No sense wasting time trying to placate Brendan when he obviously wasn't in the mood to be placated. "Then dinner."

"Just what do we eat?" he asked truculently. "Mud pies?"

"Beef stew."

"Oh, right!"

He certainly had every reason to be annoyed with her, she thought wryly, ignoring his bad temper. "I'm spoiling us tonight," she explained patiently. "I brought enough dehydrated food for one meal. We won't start living off the land until tomorrow."

"If you expect help from me, we'll either starve or poison ourselves," he snapped.

"We'll do neither," Cass returned calmly. "Now, let's get a fire going."

"I'd offer you my lighter," he drawled sarcastically, "but some scheming little wench stole it."

"Don't worry," Cass said breezily. "We have a lighter. It just doesn't happen to be gold-plated." And from the wood she had gathered, she selected a flat piece of hardwood and a sturdy, tapering stick about eighteen inches long. "A little more primitive, perhaps, but it works on the same principle."

With a sharp rock she gouged out a notch in one side of the flat piece, inserted the stick, and spun it between the palms of her hands until she had bored a hole. Brendan watched skeptically as she gathered together a bunch of dried moss and thistledown, fluffed it into a ball, and set it where it would catch the spark.

"Now, Brendan," she instructed, "come on the other side of me. As my hands move down the stick, you start twirling at the top like I'm doing. The secret is to keep the stick spinning. Do you or don't you want to eat?" Cass prodded him as he simply stared at her balefully.

"Huh!" he muttered, but he joined her and silently followed instructions.

It took a few minutes, but in the end they were rewarded with a spark. Instantly Cass picked up the ball of fluff and blew. First it smoked and then, a few seconds later, burst into a meager flame. Tenderly Cass nursed it on the prepared rocks, feeding it dried leaves and twigs until the single flame grew into a small but steady fire.

"Who would have thought it?" Brendan asked, unable to conceal his genuine amazement.

His reaction was a small beginning. During the next few days, she would show him many things more surprising than how to make fire. His attitude though, she thought bleakly, was not encouraging.

They ate a silent meal of the dehydrated food, reconstituted with water from the canteen and cooked in the bottom of the mess kit over the fire. Brendan didn't speak until Cass had cleaned away the remains and began banking the fire for the night. He glanced automatically at where his watch should have been and grimaced.

"What time do you suppose it is?" he asked curtly.

"I don't know—nine, nine-thirty. Do you care?"

"Not really." He paused a moment and looked around. "Where do we sleep?"

"Right here by the fire."

"Together?"

Even in the dim glow of the coals, Cass could tell that

Brendan was still glaring at her. She surprised herself this time. She blushed. But then, she had never forced an unwilling, openly hostile man to sleep with her before.

"This time of year," she explained, trying to sound as impersonal and dispassionate as possible, "the temperature won't drop much below sixty. If—if we sleep . . . *next* to each other, with one jacket over our shoulders and the other over our legs, the body heat will keep us warm."

"All right, then," he snapped. "Let's go to bed. I'm tired."

Half an hour later they lay together in their primitive bed of sand, Brendan's arms around Cass. They shared warmth but nothing else. Neither spoke. Neither moved. The dim light of the moon was obscured by the high walls of rock outside. The banked fire, covered with a protective layer of dirt, gave off no light. They lay in almost total darkness, uncomfortably aware of the scurrying sounds of canyon night life and each other's proximity. Neither slept. Time passed very slowly.

Suddenly, high overhead in the upper recesses of the cavern, the whir of wings fanned the air—night scavengers in search of prey. Brendan's body jerked against Cass's.

"What was that?" he whispered in alarm.

"Bats. But you only find them at night."

"You mean they *live* here?"

"Yes. They're on their way to find insects. They'll be back before light and sleep all day in the holes in the rock. There's nothing to worry about, though. These bats are the harmless kind."

She spoke calmly enough to reassure Brendan, but in truth she hated bats—with a primordial, instinctive fear of the hideous flying mammals, she had always believed. She longed to snuggle against Brendan for protection, but his body was rigid and unyielding, repelling her emotionally even as he held her physically in his arms.

More time passed, and Cass never remembered being so uncomfortable in her life. Her nose began to itch, but she couldn't scratch it without disturbing Brendan. His arm around her waist was a heavy weight and as responsive as a log. Her muscles began to stiffen. She desperately wanted to shift position, but she didn't dare do anything to annoy him.

Well, she concluded, with a flash of saving, ironic humor, she had made her own bed, and now she was jolly well going to have to lie in it.

After what seemed an interminable time, Brendan himself finally came to her rescue. "Oh, for heaven's sake, Cass, relax, will you? Let's go to sleep. I don't know about you," he said, sighing as he turned her in his arms and pillowed her head against his shoulder, "but I've had one hell of a day!"

The next few days weren't all that much better.

Brendan leaned wearily against a rock, removed his hat, and wiped the sweat from his forehead. The day was cooler than usual, but he had been working hard, expending pent-up energy in taking out his frustrations and aggressions on the hard, dry ground.

"What's this plant?" he called to Cass, who sat beside the stream in the narrow canyon below their cavern. She looked up from the flat tray of willow and bulrush stems she had just finished weaving.

"My word! That's a sego lily—the state flower. They're rare around here. The roots are sweet and good to eat, but they're in danger of becoming extinct. We dig them up only in an emergency."

"And this isn't an emergency?" he observed tartly.

"No, Brendan," she said patiently. "You've dug up plenty of Indian potato and biscuit-root, and we still have some ricegrass. Here, if you're tired of what you're doing, I brought the fish trap." She held out a narrow, tapering, three-foot-long willow contraption. "See if you can catch a few more trout for dinner while I thresh the sunflower seeds."

Brendan put down the digging stick he'd been using to lever roots out of the red earth. "At least," he said bitterly, nearly snatching the trap from her hands, "we haven't had to resort to the rattlesnakes and lizards you threatened to feed me."

Cass sighed and tried to shake off the effects of his irritability. She knew the past four days hadn't been easy for him as she had taught him the rudiments of survival: how to make rock and wooden implements, how to weave a variety of baskets, how to recognize drinkable water and edible food. No, not easy. But then, the first few days were usually the most difficult for the uninitiated. They had to learn that much of the work of survival was long, hard, tedious and, finally, repetitive.

To Brendan's credit, he had followed every direction Cass gave him with only an occasional grumble. Not as much to his credit, he hadn't spoken a word to her unless the situation demanded it. His cold silence was both discouraging and unnerving. A less determined person than herself, she concluded bleakly, would have given up and taken him back to civilization after the first two days.

Cass was so lost in thought that she didn't notice that the sky was darkening. It wasn't until she had nearly finished harvesting the sunflower seeds, placing them in her flat willow tray, that she noticed that the wind down the canyon was cooling fast and coming in sharp gusts. The beginning of a summer shower? she wondered uneasily. Or worse—the signs of a cloudburst. She looked up. The thick clouds above were moving quickly, and to the north and west the sky was an ominous black. With more haste than care, she dumped her seeds into a woven pouch, slung it over her shoulder, and jumped to her feet.

"Brendan!"

"Shhh," he hissed to silence her. "I nearly got one . . . Damn! The water's getting too muddy to see."

He didn't need to tell her. She had already noted that red mud had thickened the clear stream. "Forget the fish. We've got to get out of here. Rain!"

He looked down at his wet shoes, crumpled clothes, and mangled hat and stared at her incredulously. "We're out here eating weeds, sleeping on dead grass, hauling water fifty feet up a cliff, and you're worried about getting *wet*?"

A flash of lightning and a faint rumble of thunder came from a distance. "Don't argue with me, Brendan! Grab the basket of roots and climb up to the cave as though your life depended on it. Believe me—it does!"

Cass saw Brendan's skepticism, but thankfully he didn't dismiss the urgency in her voice. With a shrug of resignation he matched her frantic pace along the now worn path through the rocks up the side of the cliff. Only a light sprinkle had begun to fall when, out of breath, they finally clambered over the ledge of the cavern and collapsed onto the sand.

"What the hell was that all about?" Brendan panted.

"Listen!" Cass gasped.

Brendan couldn't see any lightning, but he could hear what sounded now like one continuous rumble of thunder. No, not thunder. The sound was more like the roar of an approaching freight train. He looked below. The ambling creek where they had stood such a short time ago was already overflowing its banks with dark red water that nearly covered the canyon floor.

"What's happening?" Brendan asked.

Cass was calm now that they were on high ground and well out of danger. "A flash flood. Watch. You'll probably never see anything like it again in your entire life."

She wasn't exaggerating: Even as she spoke, a ten-foot-high wall of silt, sand, and water came crashing down the canyon, tearing away everything that stood in its path. As it roared beneath them, they could see giant boulders and uprooted trees bouncing off the sandstone walls and off each other, tossed around like children's playthings.

Brendan and Cass watched the fantastic, magnificent, frightening spectacle with all the solemn awe it deserved. At one point he turned to her, his face pale. "We would have been killed if we'd stayed down there, wouldn't we?"

"We wouldn't have had a prayer," she agreed soberly.

"You saved my life," he said slowly.

Cass swallowed and couldn't look at him. "Don't forget that I'm the one who put you in danger to begin with."

He made no comment, simply turned back to stare at the raging torrent below, and a little while later, Cass slipped silently away to build up the fire and prepare their dinner. For the first time Cass allowed guilt and doubt to fill her mind. She had the right to risk her own safety, but did she have the right to jeopardize Brendan's? She knew the answer had to be no.

It was a silent meal, each of them lost in their own thoughts. Every now and then Brendan would leave his food and walk over to the ledge to stare down at the still rampaging water. Evening came before the flood began to subside. Then, almost as quickly as it had risen, the water dropped and the familiar night sounds once again filled the air.

It was Cass's night for domestic chores, and as she scrubbed the utensils with water and snake-grass, Brendan stood on the ledge of their rocky eyrie, the flickering light of the fire just reaching the yawning mouth of the cavern. His pose was the one Cass had seen so often in the past four days—one leg slightly bent, his head back, his hands stuck in the back pockets of his jeans. She watched him out of the corner of her eye as the now soft evening breeze ruffled his hair.

He was looking down the canyon to the stars that filled what he could see of the black sky. The moon was nowhere in sight, but somewhere in the heavens it shone down into the emptiness below, turning the still-swollen creek into a moving sliver of silver and stripping the color from the carved red sandstone wall opposite. He leaned slightly forward, trying in vain to see the top of the wall that rose out of sight, five hundred feet above the canyon floor.

Cass stifled a sigh that she knew would carry to him. Oh, but her heart ached. There were so many things she had wanted to say to him, so much she had hoped to share with him, but the events of that day had changed all that. The decision to stay or leave had to be his—and she had no doubt what his choice would be.

"Through?"

Cass jumped. Brendan was standing above her, casting a looming dark shadow thirty feet tall onto the wall of rock behind him.

"Yes, I just finished," she said faintly.

He squatted down beside her, on one of the mats he himself had woven, and let sand sift through his fingers. "The moon must be full tonight. You can see all the way down the canyon. It's all black and silver. You'd never know there'd been a storm, except that everything smells so fresh. It's amazing."

Cass didn't know how to respond to that, so she sat quietly, staring into the dying embers of the fire. Brendan didn't seem to notice her silence.

"Do you know, Cass," he continued soberly, "as I watched the flood today and as I stood on the ledge just now, I realized that never in my thirty-six years have I ever felt so small and puny and insignificant. It's a very humbling feeling." He stopped, drew a breath, and poked at the fire with a stick. "Is that what you've wanted to do these past few days, Cass?" he asked harshly. "Humble me? Because if it is, you've succeeded."

"Brendan, no," she said gently. "I would never want to see you humbled—not in the way I think you mean."

He shrugged. "What other way is there?"

"Not lowered or diminished. But there's nothing to be ashamed of in a humility that helps keep things in . . . well, in perspective. Nature does that. You said so yourself. But I don't believe that means we shouldn't take pride in what we do. Not when we do things for the right reasons." She saw him looking at her in a new and strange way and was suddenly embarrassed. "I'm—I'm sorry. I must sound awfully self-righteous."

"Not self-righteous; just very passionate about how you feel."

"Well, you see," she said diffidently, not quite able to meet his eyes, "I came to a few realizations myself today. Brendan," she continued when he didn't speak, "I'm sorry. I—I had no right to do what I've done to you. I had no right to kidnap you and bring you here, to try and force my opinions on you. We'll go home tomorrow. All I have to do is light a signal fire for Will in the morning. He'll have the horses here by noon."

There was a long pause before Brendan replied. Then, "What if I don't want to go?" he asked thoughtfully.

"What?" she gasped.

He didn't reply. Instead, he leaned over, fed another piece of wood into the fire, and sat back to watch as the uneven flare of light cast fascinating shadows on Cass's face, contouring her chin and high cheek bones.

"You look so lovely, Cass," he said unexpectedly, irrelevantly, his words deep and resonant in the hollow space. "More beautiful than I've ever seen you."

She stared at him uncertainly, not really sure she could trust what she was hearing in his voice. "You can say that after all I've put you through? All—all I planned to put you through?"

His mouth twisted in an ironic smile. "I can't believe that anything you have left in store for me could be any worse than what you've put me through already! Oh, I don't mean the work of the past few days. I mean that from the first moment I met you, you've battled me at every opportunity, turned my thinking upside down and inside out, forced me to question every opinion I've ever held, wounded my ego, made terrible inroads into my self-esteem, and basically disrupted my entire life. Then, to top it all off, you subject me to the indignity of sticking me on the back of a miserable horse and letting me ride in blissful ignorance to my own abduction!"

His words were the most unloverlike imaginable, but the glow of love in his eyes was setting Cass on fire. "Do—do you hate me, Brendan?" she asked breathlessly.

He took her by the shoulders and pushed her ungently back into the soft sand. It felt like weeks instead of days since he had touched her like that—with purpose, with desire. Every nerve in her body sprang instantly into hungry, pulsing life. Her mouth opened, her arms encircled him, and her legs twined with his.

"You made me feel like a fool," he murmured against her lips, then slid down to her throat. "Sleeping with you night after night. Despising myself for wanting you so much and being too stubborn to do anything about it."

He pulled apart the front of her blouse and tugged at the zipper on her jeans. Slowly he finished undressing her and then rid himself of his own bothersome clothing.

"You don't feel like a fool at all!" she gasped moments later as his fingers delighted in the arousal of her most sensitive curves, her heated flesh, the moist warmth of her body.

"How do you suppose it makes me feel right now . . ." he began slowly.

"I *know* how you feel right now!" she cried, as with one hard, quick thrust he entered her body.

"How do you suppose it makes me feel," he teased, holding her motionless beneath him, prolonging the moment of fulfillment, denying them the release they both needed so badly, "to realize that even after all the agony you've put me through, I love you more than I thought it was possible to love any woman?"

"Oh, Brendan," Cass cried impatiently, struggling to move against the strength of his hard body. "Please! Show me!"

Chapter 14

Cass stood poised for a moment on the rock before she did a clean dive into the pool. The water was wonderfully cooling on her heated flesh. That morning she and Brendan had made the long, hot, dusty hike up to an isolated sandstone double arch. Ultimately the view had been well worth the effort, but it felt good now to soak off the fine sand that coated her skin and sifted through her hair. She swam under the waterfall and let the spray cascade down over her, wishing it could wash away her trepidation about the future as effectively as it did the dirt and grime.

Since the decisive night of the flood over a week before, the time she and Brendan had spent together in the wilderness had been nearly idyllic. Every doubt she had had about him had vanished. Her love for him had deepened with every passing day. And she had to believe that he felt the same.

But their days were coming to an end. She couldn't run away forever, and soon, too soon, she and Brendan would have to face all the problems that awaited them in the outside world.

A pair of hands grabbed her ankles and pulled her under the water. A pair of arms encircled her body. A pair of lips took hers in a searing kiss that not even the clear spring water could cool.

"Brendan!" she gasped as they surfaced. "I didn't even see you!"

He grinned. "That was the idea."

They played happily in the pool for the better part of an hour—diving, splashing like children, but stopping now and then to kiss, touch, and enjoy each other in a thoroughly adult fashion.

Finally, they swam reluctantly to shore and lay side by side in the tall grass, their nude bodies drying quickly in the heat of the midafternoon sun. Cass closed her eyes and drifted in and out of a light sleep. Brendan lay on his back, his hands pillowing his head as he allowed himself to be hypnotized by the swaying limb of the cottonwood tree above. His murmur of contentment reached Cass and she smiled.

Brendan had immersed himself in the pleasures and dangers of Lucifer's Playground with more enthusiasm than Cass could ever have hoped for. He was like an inquisitive child, insatiable for information, and Cass taught him everything she knew—about the Anasazi Indians, the original settlers of this land who were farmers, probably driven out of the area by a long drought; about the Navajo sandstone that retained water; about the formation of their wonderland—its geology, geography, and anthropology.

Brendan had been fascinated by the Indian cliff dwellings, intrigued by nature's engineering of the sandstone arches, and overwhelmed by mesas that in places dropped a thousand feet or more to canyons below. His love of the place now matched, if not exceeded, her own.

"Do you know what?" he had confessed one night. "I had never slept out of doors before you brought me here."

"Never?" Cass had asked in amazement. "You never went camping, not even when you were a kid?"

"No. We didn't have the money. I always worked during the summers."

That explained so much to Cass. Brendan had traveled

the country as an adult, but that wasn't the same as learning to love nature and the out-of-doors with the curious, wondering awe of a child.

Brendan turned his head now and allowed himself the pleasure of letting his eyes rove over Cass's relaxed, golden-brown body. Cass felt his gaze and smiled. The female form, she reflected happily, was one of the glories of nature he *had* learned about as a young man, and he had learned his lessons very well.

"You're awake," he noted, resisting the impulse to appreciate her body more intimately, more physically—at least for a little while.

"Mmmm."

"Want to see what I caught for our dinner tonight?"

"It had better not be a snake or a lizard," she murmured suspiciously. Out of necessity for his safety but against her better judgment, Cass had taught him how to deal with snakes. Her instincts had been right. A couple of days before, like a mischievous little boy, he had surprised her with a rattlesnake he had caught and killed. Cass wasn't charmed. She had become reconciled to snakes at a young age, but they were only a notch below bats on the list of her ten most unfavorite creatures.

"Nope," he announced with pride. "A rabbit."

Cass opened one eye and arched her eyebrow in doubt. With all her experience, she had seldom been able to catch a rabbit. There weren't all that many in the area where they stayed, and those that were around were speedy, cautious, wily little animals. "Are you serious? How did you do it?"

"I built a new kind of lair."

Now she believed him. Once she had introduced him to the tools, weapons, and useful articles to be made from various plants and rocks, his imagination had gone to work. With a natural genius for creating gadgets, Brendan had devised numerous inventions to make their life easier—not the least of which was a pulley, made from a stone and a woven rope, for hauling wood, food, and water up to their cavern. In all, he had simplified daily living to the point that they had had plenty of time to explore.

"We," he continued, "are going to have real meat tonight." He sighed again in contentment and continued his contemplation of the fluttering cottonwood leaves. "This is the life, isn't it, Cass? I could stay here forever. I know now just how Adam must have felt."

Cass echoed his sigh, but there was no contentment in the sound, only regret. The time had come to say all the things she had avoided saying, even thinking, in the past two weeks.

"Brendan," she began quietly, "I'm afraid that every Adam has to have his Eve."

He ran a loving finger down her soft cheek. "Do you think I don't know that? This would have been no Eden without you."

She caught his finger and kissed it. "Brendan," she continued unhappily, "I'm afraid that it's time for your Eve to feed you the apple. Tomorrow morning we have to signal Will."

Brendan stiffened and drew his hand away. Then slowly he relaxed on a long sigh. "I guess I've known for the past couple of days that we couldn't go on like this much longer." He smiled at her ruefully. "It was too good to last, wasn't it, Cass." Not a question but an admission that reality had intruded into their paradise.

Brendan leaned up on one elbow to watch as she reached over and pulled her clothes toward her. She didn't speak until she'd slipped into her blouse and fastened her jeans.

"Can we talk for a few minutes, Brendan? I—I need your advice. I don't know what to do."

"About the ranch? Cass, you must know now that I'd never go through with the plan to turn Wells' Springs into a tourist resort." He sat up and looked around at the now familiar, awe-inspiring landscape with newly acquired appreciation and respect. He smiled at her ironically. "You knew it was a rotten idea from the beginning. And Sweetheart, you do have one hell of a way of proving a point. Next time I'll listen to you the first time."

His words were all Cass had hoped they would be when she first planned this mad adventure, but still she searched his face. "You aren't really sorry I brought you here, are you?"

He leaned over and kissed her tenderly. "You know better than that." Suddenly he grinned. "And if you want the truth, I'd better tell you that by the second day, I figured that I could hike out of here myself by following the stream. It had to empty out somewhere near civilization.''

He was right, of course. "But you didn't go," she said in amazement. "Why? You were furious with me!"

"Well, yes, I was," he agreed. "Furious and hurt. But I knew that in spite of that, I still loved you and I had to believe that you loved me. If you were willing to go to all the trouble and risk of kidnapping me, I thought I'd better stick around and find out why."

"And did you?" she asked lovingly.

"It took me a while," he admitted. "By the time the storm hit, I had just about recovered from the first shock and nearly gotten rid of my frustration and anger. The flood clinched it. As you promised me that night, things came into perspective. I realized pretty soon how much I was learning —not just about survival, but about you. If that was true for me, it had to be true for you. That's when I knew what you had hinted at the first day.''

"And you've really forgiven me?"

"There's nothing to forgive, love. I've had the most wonderful two weeks of my life." He punctuated his assurance with another kiss on her soft lips and added solemnly, "I don't believe that I'll ever be quite the same person again. You've opened new worlds for me, Cass, and I'm very grateful."

Her response came from the heart. "Thank you, Brendan. I love you so much. You know that."

He would have asked for an even more satisfying, tangible assurance, but Cass stopped him as he reached for her. "Brendan, I have this problem. I need your help so badly."

"What?" The worry and sadness in her eyes both concerned and alarmed him.

"I think I'm going to find myself in a terrible position when I go back to New York."

"You're going back?" he asked in surprise.

"I have to," she said simply.

"You don't have to do it for me, Cass," he told her soberly. "If you want to stay out west, we can work it out. Your happiness is more important to me than anything in this world."

She believed him, and tears flooded her eyes. She tumbled into his arms and for a few precious moments let his love and strength soothe her.

"This is something different, Brendan," she said at last, drawing away reluctantly. "Remember, I told you when I first brought you here that someone had deliberately sabotaged the ranch and tampered with the brakes on my car?"

Brendan shuddered at the thought of what she must have gone through plunging down that cliffside, but at the same time he was obviously skeptical.

"I've thought about what you said, Cass," he said gently, "and the more I've thought about it, the more improbable it seems." He took her hand in his and stroked it. "That was a hard time for you. You still weren't well. You were tired and confused and under a lot of pressure. It doesn't make any sense that someone would go to such lengths to force you to sell the ranch. Who would do it and why?"

She hesitated. Out there in the wilderness, so far from civilization, all her fears and suspicions seemed absurd, but she knew they weren't and she couldn't dismiss them.

"The who, I think I know," she said sadly. "The why, I can only guess at."

"Do you mean Ben?" He considered the notion and shook his head. "I've seen that kind of desperation before in a man, but I can't believe he'd actually do anything to hurt you. In his own way, he loves you."

"No, not Ben—though I admit I thought it might be him at first. But by the time the brakes were tampered with, he had no reason left. He was going to get his money."

"Loretta?" Brendan asked, even more skeptically. "She had no reason left either—except sheer spite." He grimaced as she glanced at him sharply. "No, her antagonism toward you didn't escape me. You undoubtedly threatened her royal reign on the ranch from the first minute she arrived. But I can't see her fiddling around under a car, messing with the brakes, for any reason."

Cass half smiled at the vision his words created, but she sobered quickly. "No, Brendan. Definitely not Loretta."

"Then who?" he asked, perplexed.

She realized she was stalling for time. She genuinely

hated to put her suspicions into words. "The last person in the world I would have thought of," she said sadly.

"Come on, Cass," he said impatiently. "Out with it. Who?"

"There's only one person it could have been. Darin."

He was stunned. "Summerhays? Impossible! Ridiculous!"

"Brendan," she asked sadly, "how did you know I was leaving Cassandra's? Who told you Ben was looking for a buyer for the ranch? How did you know I was coming to Utah before I had even told Ben? Only two people knew— Dee and Darin. Dee would have had no reason to tell you. That leaves only one person. Darin."

"You're right," he said slowly, grimly. "Summerhays called me a week before you left New York."

"Do you see?"

"But it doesn't make any sense, Cass," he protested. "Why should he care about Wells' Springs? He obviously doesn't know anything about ranching and doesn't care to."

"No, nothing about ranching, but he was raised with horses. He owned his own thoroughbred. He rides as well as any jockey. He could easily have followed me to Coyote Flats that day without my knowing it. He would know what a wire would do. And cars are a pet hobby of his. He wouldn't have any trouble stripping down an engine, let alone a simple thing like cutting a brake line."

"But *why*, Cass?" Brendan asked, incredulous. "Why should he care whether you bought or sold the ranch?"

"That's why it took me so long even to consider Darin," she said unhappily. "I couldn't see that he had any reason at all."

"And he did?" he asked, still only half believing.

"It took me a while to figure it out. After the fire was set and the horses were let loose and the wire was fixed to bring down Kettledrum, I assumed that someone was trying to force me to sell the ranch to Monarch—"

"Myself being the most likely suspect," Brendan said dryly, no rancor in his voice. Cass squeezed his hand in silent communication. They understood each other now.

"But after the car wreck, when I knew it couldn't have been you and that Ben and Loretta had no reason to stop me, it dawned on me that maybe the accidents had nothing directly to do with my either buying or selling the *ranch*. Maybe they were meant to stop me from selling *Cassandra's*. Think, Brendan. I was on my way into town to arrange for an audit of the books."

"My God!" he exclaimed, pieces of information beginning to click together in his mind. "Summerhays admitted that the books had never been audited before by an outside accountant. It would be the easiest thing in the world for him to juggle them any way he pleased. He could have been embezzling from you for years without you ever knowing it."

Cass grimaced. "That's what I was afraid you'd say."

"You never thought that his methods were a little . . . unorthodox?"

"I don't know anything about bookkeeping, Brendan. I—I just found out recently about some of the things he was doing—like overcharging clients without telling me. I had noticed that even though we split the profits equally, he always seemed to have a lot more money than I had. He told me he bet on the horses."

"And you believed him, I suppose." Brendan sighed.

"I didn't have any reason not to. How was I to know? Though I probably should have thought something was wrong," she admitted ruefully, "when he urged me to either raise prices or cut down on quality and started pushing me to take on more and more work, arguing for expansion and bigger commissions, saying we needed the money to meet the cost of higher overhead."

"With all that, you never even suspected that maybe something funny was going on?" Brendan asked incredulously.

"I thought he was my friend," she replied simply, as though that explained it all. "I trusted him."

"No wonder you were going crazy," Brendan said grimly, "worrying yourself sick, working yourself nearly to death. You've just explained one hell of a lot. And I was sure a great help, wasn't I?" he concluded in disgust.

"It wasn't your fault that I was so trusting," she said. "And I don't really have any proof even now. So far, it's all just conjecture." She shook her head miserably. "But when

I thought it through, Darin and the sale of Cassandra's were the only explanation that made any sense out of all the so-called accidents. And it wasn't just the threat of this audit. He couldn't afford to have me sell out for any reason—whether it was to move to the ranch or . . . or enter a convent. With Dee's husband an accountant, he couldn't keep on embezzling from her the way he had from me. He was bound to get caught at it." She winced. "I was the goose that laid the golden eggs."

Brendan didn't need any more convincing. Cass thought she had seen him angry before, but never like this. His eyes blazed and his hands clenched into fists. Darin ought to have been thankful he wasn't there at the moment.

"So he tried to convince you to leave the ranch and go back to New York," Brendan said harshly, "and when that didn't work he tried to kill you."

Cass shivered at the bluntness of his words. "Maybe he wasn't really trying to kill me," she offered hopefully. "Maybe he was only trying to stop the audit, give himself time to get back to New York and fix the books."

Brendan thought that over for a minute. Then he said grimly, "I think you could be partially right, but I can't help wondering, Cass. Do you know what provision there is in your partnership agreement about the rights of survivorship?"

Cass's eyes grew wide as she realized what he was suggesting. It was horrible, unthinkable. But her voice when she answered was thick with dawning awareness, increasing disillusionment, and pain.

"Oh, my God, Brendan!" she cried. "If either of us dies, the surviving partner automatically inherits the other half share. If I had been killed, Darin would have been sole owner of Cassandra's."

His face had become a hard mask of rage. "That's what I thought."

"What on earth do I do now?"

Brendan took her hand and cradled it in his, her need to be comforted greater at the moment than his wish to vent his anger.

"You didn't mean a word of what you said, did you, Cass, about going back to work at Cassandra's after a rest?"

"You must know I didn't mean it. It was all I could think of to say to stop the accidents from continuing. And I knew that I had to get away from the ranch before . . . well, before something else terrible happened."

"So far, love, you've done exactly the right thing," he said thoughtfully. "*I* believed you meant it, and if I did, surely Summerhays did too. I can't believe that he suspects a thing. He's had two weeks to think that he's safe, that everything is all right."

"So what do I do now?"

"Not you, Cass—we. As soon as we can arrange it, we fly back to New York and have a look at Cassandra's books for ourselves."

Cass and Brendan took a taxi downtown from his apartment to the loading dock behind Cassandra's. They had landed at Kennedy Airport just before midnight five hours earlier, stopped to rest, clean up, grab a bite to eat, and wait until the janitorial service had finished its work and gone. They didn't want any witnesses to Cass's unexpected return.

The building looked old and tired in the predawn light, but no older or more tired than Cass herself felt as she punched in the security number at the back door. At Brendan's suggestion, they had brought a flashlight with them. No lights downstairs to give them away.

Cass led the way through the storage area, across the showroom, up the stairs, and down the hall to Darin's office. The oak door with its translucent pane and Darin's name scripted on it in fancy black letters was locked, but Cass had a master key. There were no windows inside the office to betray their presence to the outside world, and she flipped on the indirect overhead lighting. Everything was just as she had seen it last, three weeks before. Piles of papers, a letter organizer, and half-filled "in" and "out" boxes cluttered the top of the desk. The computer terminal stood as usual on its table—dark, silent and, to Cass's imaginative eyes, slightly sinister.

From her purse, Cass removed the slip of paper Darin had given her at the ranch. She overcame the compulsion to whisper as she handed it to Brendan.

"This is the list of ledgers he gave me and the combination to the safe." She didn't add the frightening thought that Darin had never expected her or anyone to use that combination and see those books.

"Why don't you get them while I take a crack at the computer? Unless I'm very much mistaken, the real figures are around here somewhere, probably stored on disks. We're going to need to compare the data." He tugged at the drawer of a locked filing cabinet. "What's in here?"

"I don't know."

"Hand me a paper clip, Cass, will you please?"

"What are you going to do?"

"Pick the lock," he told her bluntly.

"Can you do that?"

Brendan's grin held little humor. "I didn't grow up a street rat in a tough section of Baltimore for nothing." A couple of seconds of probing and one quick flick of the wrist, and the filing cabinet was open. "Success," he muttered, lifting out a plastic container of computer disks.

"You can make sense out of those?" Cass asked uncertainly.

"Given enough time and the right touch, yes. I've been playing around with computers for the past ten years, and if I do say so myself, I'm a wizard."

Wizard or not, it still took Brendan more time than he had anticipated to figure out Darin's system, break his code, and search out the incriminating data he had very cleverly concealed among a lot of factual entries and assorted trivia. Cass became more and more nervous as time passed.

"You're finding a lot?" she asked periodically.

"Too much," was his inevitable reply.

"Will you be much longer?"

"What time is it?"

Brendan didn't look up as he continued extracting bits and pieces of information, punching in new combinations, copying data files onto clean disks, and printing out various results.

"Ten after six."

"Mmmm." And he made notes on a pad of paper beside him.

Cass wandered aimlessly back and forth between the desk

and the door, wishing she could do something more useful than listen for sounds downstairs. "How much longer?"

"What time is it now?"

"Nearly seven-thirty," she told him anxiously. The staff came in at eight, sometimes earlier if they were behind on a big job.

"All right. You can hand me that blue ledger now, the one for the last fiscal year."

Cass's face had become increasingly pinched and drawn as the magnitude of Darin's crime became clear, even to her. "You have it all then?"

"Everything but the final, combined totals." Brendan's own face was haggard now and lined with the fatigue of concentration as he bent over the books, comparing entries.

"And?" she prompted when he finally threw down his pen and slammed the book closed.

"It will take a professional auditor weeks to sort it all out," he said grimly. "Darin has been very clever and extremely careful. But if the ledgers give a factual list of all the accounts and record the actual credits and debits, we're talking about a couple of hundred thousand dollars he's channeled out of the firm and into his own pocket. The first year looks all right. Then for a while the discrepancies are relatively minor—only irregular, smaller sums. It looks to me as if most of the money was siphoned off in the last year and a half."

Which coincided with the increasing pressure Darin had put on her, during the past year in particular. Still, Cass was staggered by the amount. "And it's all there on the computer disks, Brendan? Why on earth would he keep such incriminating records?"

"The way he's duplicated some of the entries and juggled amounts is very ingenious," Brendan said thoughtfully, "but it's complicated too. Some of the data are so interwoven, he couldn't just get rid of it all. And I'm not sure how you run your firm, but I would think that you have a certain number of companies that you do business with regularly with repeat or similar orders, and you must have repeat clients. Summerhays would have to know—sometimes in a hurry—what he had charged who for what, what entries were sheer fiction, what accounts and invoices he had padded and for how much—"

He broke off abruptly at the sound of laughter out in the hall. Quickly he turned off the desk light while Cass made a dash for the switch near the door.

"That's Dee and the sewing-room crew," she whispered. "I checked Darin's desk calendar. His first appointment is for nine-thirty, but he could come in any time now. What do we do?"

Brendan's face hardened. "Now," he said as he spread the damning papers before him on the desk, "we call the police."

"Brendan, wait a minute," Cass exclaimed as he reached for the phone. "Isn't there some other way?"

He saw the grief in her face and shrugged. "I guess that's a decision for you to make, Cass."

"Then, I—I want to wait and talk to Darin first."

They didn't have to wait long.

Darin's whistle heralded his approach. They watched him silhouetted through the glass as he inserted his key in the door Cass had relocked. She tensed as the knob turned and the door swung inward. Darin paused for a minute to toss his briefcase onto a nearby chair before he turned on the lights. Even then, it took him a moment to notice that the office wasn't empty. He saw Brendan first, leaning back in the leather swivel chair. Next he caught sight of Cass, perched tensely on the edge of the sofa.

"Cass! Cahill! You're back!" His smile of welcome was broad and beaming until he noticed the litter of computer print-out sheets strewn across his desk. The smile faded fast. "What the hell's going on here?"

"Oh," Brendan said coldly, "at a rough estimate, I'd say about a quarter of a million dollars worth of embezzlement."

"Is this some kind of a joke?" With an effort, Darin dredged the smile back, but it didn't reach the cold blue of his eyes as they darted from Brendan's hard, rugged face to Cass's grim expression.

"It's no joke, Darin." It was Cass who answered, in a voice Darin would never have recognized. "No more than it was a joke to set fire to the barn or string a wire across my path. I didn't laugh a whole lot either, when I found you had cut the brake lines on my car."

Darin's face flooded with color, then quickly faded to an ashen gray. "That's crazy, Cass! You—you don't know what you're talking about!"

"Oh, yes, I do, Darin! You'll be happy to know, though, that I can't prove any of it. But Brendan isn't going to have any trouble at all proving that you've been robbing me blind for years now." Her eyes filled with pain. "Why? Why, Darin?" she asked sadly. "What did I ever do to you? I trusted you. I thought you were my friend."

He had enough conscience to wince momentarily at her words, but that was his only show of remorse. He made no attempt, though, to deny the accusation.

"You never understood the social world I live in, Cass," he muttered harshly. "You never did, and you never could. The Summerhayses have been leaders of New York society for six generations."

"Well, I'm sure all those illustrious ancestors must be really proud of you now!"

"I tried to tell you, tried to explain, Cass," he went on, self-pity his dominant emotion, "but you couldn't understand what it was like, losing all your money, being poor after you'd always had everything you wanted. You had no idea what it was like to have old friends turn their backs on you. 'I'm sorry, Darin, but I'm afraid we're really going to have to cut the connection,'" he mimicked bitterly. "'It would just be an embarrassment for all of us.' Or worse, to have your friends pity you! 'Poor Darin! Darling, let's invite him out for the weekend, cheer him up a little.'"

"You're right, Darin," Cass said coldly. "I've never had *friends* like that."

He scarcely heard her comment. He was too self-absorbed. "Then you came along with the idea for Cassandra's and gave me a new chance, a new status. I tried at first, Cass, I swear. But I was going into debt. There was no way I could keep up my social position on my share alone. I *had* to have more money!"

Cass shook her head, incredulous. "And you think that justifies what you did?"

"Don't you see?" he pleaded. "Everything I did, I did for

Cassandra's. How else could I mix with the right people, go to the right parties, bring in the right clients? *You* are Cassandra's, but *I've* made it what it is today. You never could have done that without me. You've told me so yourself, over and over." He flicked an uneasy glance at Brendan, who was sitting silent, grave, and unyielding behind the huge desk like a judge on the bench. "I *deserved* everything I took, Cass. I'd earned it. You can see that."

Cass studied his face solemnly. She noted the puffiness around his face, the slight bags under his eyes, the faint flush of alcohol abuse that was beginning to tinge his fair complexion—signs betraying dissipation and overindulgence. He would look like an old man before he was thirty-five, she concluded, sad at the thought of a life wasted.

"You understand, don't you, Cass?" Darin asked in his most cajoling tone, flashing his most winsome smile.

Cass was neither cajoled or charmed. She looked at him again and saw in his face the more familiar character flaws—weakness, selfishness, moral cowardice. Always in the past she had tried to overlook Darin's faults, forgive him his failings. She couldn't this time.

"Yes, Darin," she said soberly. "I understand, more than you realize."

His face brightened. "Then everything's all right?"

She disabused him of that absurd notion with a grim twist of her lips and shake of her head. "Nothing's all right, Darin. And it never will be again. I could forgive you the money. I could forgive you all the mental and emotional pressure you've put on me. I could even forgive the damage you did to the ranch. But what I can never forgive—or forget—is how cold-bloodedly you did it all. I can never forget the fact that you cared so little about me as a person that you would rather have seen me dead than have to give up that social position of yours."

"That's not true, Cass! I swear! I never meant to hurt you. I just had to stop you from selling Cassandra's, from having the books audited. And you're all right. Nothing happened—"

"Maybe you can say that about Kettledrum throwing me," she interrupted harshly. "It was bad luck I happened to hit a rock. But only a miracle saved me from plunging into the gulch. You had every intention of killing me when you let me drive that car off the ranch."

He would have tried to brazen it out, but he met her steady gaze and the cold fury there defeated him. Weakly he sank into a chair.

"What—what are you going to do?"

Cass looked toward Brendan. He was again reaching for the phone. "The police?" he asked.

Slowly Cass shook her head. "No, I don't think so." Darin—mistakenly—began to look hopeful. "I don't want a public scandal if I can help it, Brendan. I want my own private, poetic justice."

Darin's face fell, and she studied him thoughtfully, with speculation. He slumped lower in his chair, as though to hide his hand-tailored silk suit, Gucci shoes, and emerald signet ring.

"You owe the firm a lot of money, Darin," she said at last, pronouncing her judgment on him, "but I'll take your share of the partnership in lieu of repayment. Our attorney can draw up the papers for you to sign before you leave town tomorrow."

"Leave town?" he asked startled. "For where?"

"I think . . . yes—California."

Darin couldn't have looked more horrified if she had suggested he emigrate to Alaska. "You mean you want me to leave New York for a while?" he asked uncertainly.

"I mean I want you to leave New York *permanently*. You'll give up that social position you prize so highly and those so-called friends of yours. I'll grieve for my partner— the man I trusted, respected, and thought I knew," she said sadly. "But the man you really are I never want to see or hear of again. As long as you stay away, I'll keep your embezzlement confidential, but if you try to come back to the city, I'll tell the story to every newspaper in town. I'll create a scandal you'll never live down."

"You—you wouldn't do that," he said faintly.

"You know I would," she told him coldly. "As far as I'm concerned, you can give your friends any reason you like for leaving, but you'll always know the truth. You'll know what *I* think of you—that you're a weak, disloyal, sniveling, cowardly little snob who must be making your Summerhays ancestors turn in their graves. Poor Darin," she mocked him. "You're going to have to live the rest of your life with that thought!"

The waterbed in Brendan's room undulated fiercely, reached its maximum sway, then slowly calmed to a gentle, soothing, rocking motion.

"Mmmmmmm." Cass sighed happily into Brendan's shoulder.

He nuzzled the soft flesh of her neck just under her ear. "Mmmmmmm," he hummed in agreement, sending teasing vibrations down her spine.

"It's a good thing neither of us gets seasick," she murmured.

He turned his head and met one drowsy eye. "Do you want to buy a boat?"

She kissed the bridge of his crooked nose. "What would we do with a boat?"

"Oh, I don't know," he said lazily. "Sail the Caribbean when the weather turns cold up north, maybe. I'll teach you to scuba dive."

"You know how to scuba dive?"

He ran a titillating finger around the tip of her breast. "Love," he murmured huskily, "I have talents I've only begun to show you." He leaned down to kiss the hard little nub. "It's going to take a whole lifetime."

"What about your work?" she asked, half teasing, half serious.

"To hell with my work!" He raised himself up to smile lovingly down into her face. "There's more to life than building empires—and don't tell me that wasn't one of the things you wanted me to learn down there in Lucifer's Playground."

She returned his smile with a mischievous grin. "I won't even try."

"Maybe you taught me more than you bargained for," he said softly.

"Oh?"

"You taught me how terrible it would be if I ever lost you

again," he said huskily. He placed his fingers under her chin and lifted her face to his. "Marry me, Cass."

"Is that what *you* want?" she asked, searching his eyes, looking for answers to the questions that not all their time together, not even his hungry lips, had answered. "Marriage?"

"I don't ever want to live without you," he said simply—and those simple words were more convincing than any long declaration of love could ever have been.

"What about *my* work?" she asked, more seriously this time.

"To hell with your work too! Do what you want with your life—as long as you do it with me!"

"And the ranch?"

"While you were talking with Dee, I was on the phone to Ben and Will. If you agree, the Taylors and I will buy out Ben's share of the ranch. The three of us will own it together. After we're married," he said temptingly—as though she needed tempting, "we can spend part of our time in New York and part at Wells' Springs."

His thoughtfulness deserved more thanks than words. She pulled him down to her once again and let her mouth speak silently for her. Brendan accepted her gratitude with all the appreciation she could have wished. His fingers were once again deliciously nimble, his body elegantly agile. Just before their passion replaced all practical considerations, Brendan whispered against her lips:

"The ranch will be a wonderful place to raise children, Cass. We'll teach them all about the wilderness, just as you taught me."

"There is one thing I never had to teach you," she breathed, beginning to move more and more impatiently beneath him. The bed again undulated in countermovement to her desire, creating an exquisite wave of sensation. "One thing," she whispered, "that *you* taught *me*."

Brendan took pity on himself and her, picked up her rhythm, and added variations of his own. "What was that?" he whispered back, trembling against her.

"Your own unique talent," she cried as their passion mounted higher and higher. "How to soar like an eagle!"

WIN

a fabulous $50,000 diamond jewelry collection

ENTER

by filling out the coupon below and mailing it by September 30, 1985

Send entries to:

U.S.
Silhouette Diamond Sweepstakes
P.O. Box 779
Madison Square Station
New York, NY 10159

Canada
Silhouette Diamond Sweepstakes
Suite 191
238 Davenport Road
Toronto, Ontario M5R 1J6

SILHOUETTE DIAMOND SWEEPSTAKES
ENTRY FORM

☐ Mrs.   ☐ Miss   ☐ Ms   ☐ Mr.

NAME   (please print)

ADDRESS   APT. #

CITY

STATE/(PROV.)

ZIP/(POSTAL CODE)

RTD-A-1

RULES FOR SILHOUETTE DIAMOND SWEEPSTAKES

OFFICIAL RULES—NO PURCHASE NECESSARY

1. Silhouette Diamond Sweepstakes is open to Canadian (except Quebec) and United States residents 18 years or older at the time of entry. Employees and immediate families of the publishers of Silhouette, their affiliates, retailers, distributors, printers, agencies and RONALD SMILEY INC. are excluded.

2. To enter, print your name and address on the official entry form or on a 3" x 5" slip of paper. You may enter as often as you choose, but each envelope must contain only one entry. Mail entries first class in Canada to Silhouette Diamond Sweepstakes, Suite 191, 238 Davenport Road, Toronto, Ontario M5R 1J6. In the United States, mail to Silhouette Diamond Sweepstakes, P.O. Box 779, Madison Square Station, New York, NY 10159. Entries must be postmarked between February 1 and September 30, 1985. Silhouette is not responsible for lost, late or misdirected mail.

3. First Prize of diamond jewelry, consisting of a necklace, ring, bracelet and earrings will be awarded. Approximate retail value is $50,000 U.S./$62,500 Canadian. Second Prize of 100 Silhouette Home Reader Service Subscriptions will be awarded. Approximate retail value of each is $162.00 U.S./$180.00 Canadian. No substitution, duplication, cash redemption or transfer of prizes will be permitted. Odds of winning depend upon the number of valid entries received. One prize to a family or household. Income taxes, other taxes and insurance on First Prize are the sole responsibility of the winners.

4. Winners will be selected under the supervision of RONALD SMILEY INC., an independent judging organization whose decisions are final, by random drawings from valid entries postmarked by September 30, 1985, and received no later than October 7, 1985. Entry in this sweepstakes indicates your awareness of the Official Rules. Winners who are residents of Canada must answer correctly a time-related arithmetical skill-testing question to qualify. First Prize winner will be notified by certified mail and must submit an Affidavit of Compliance within 10 days of notification. Returned Affidavits or prizes that are refused or undeliverable will result in alternative names being randomly drawn. Winners may be asked for use of their name and photo at no additional compensation.

5. For a First Prize winner list, send a stamped self-addressed envelope postmarked by September 30, 1985. In Canada, mail to Silhouette Diamond Contest Winner, Suite 309, 238 Davenport Road, Toronto, Ontario M5R 1J6. In the United States, mail to Silhouette Diamond Contest Winner, P.O. Box 182, Bowling Green Station, New York, NY 10274. This offer will appear in Silhouette publications and at participating retailers. Offer void in Quebec and subject to all Federal, Provincial, State and Municipal laws and regulations and wherever prohibited or restricted by law.

SDR-A-1

If you enjoyed this book...

Thrill to 4 more Silhouette Intimate Moments novels (a $9.00 value)— ABSOLUTELY FREE!

If you want more passionate sensual romance, then Silhouette Intimate Moments novels are for you!

In every 256-page book, you'll find romance that's electrifying...involving... and intense. And now, these larger-than-life romances can come into your home every month!

4 FREE books as your introduction.

Act now and we'll send you four thrilling Silhouette Intimate Moments novels. They're our gift to introduce you to our convenient home subscription service. Every month, we'll send you four new Silhouette Intimate Moments books. Look them over for 15 days. If you keep them, pay just $9.00 for all four. Or return them at no charge.

We'll mail your books to you *as soon as they are published*. Plus, with every shipment, you'll receive the Silhouette Books Newsletter absolutely free. *And Silhouette Intimate Moments is delivered free.*

Mail the coupon today and start receiving Silhouette Intimate Moments. Romance novels for women...not girls.

Silhouette Intimate Moments

IMIM-R-A

READERS' COMMENTS ON SILHOUETTE INTIMATE MOMENTS:

"About a month ago a friend loaned me my first Silhouette. I was thoroughly surprised as well as totally addicted. Last week I read a Silhouette Intimate Moments and I was even more pleased. They are the best romance series novels I have ever read. They give much more depth to the plot, characters, and the story is fundamentally realistic. They incorporate tasteful sex scenes, which is a must, especially in the 1980's. I only hope you can publish them fast enough."

S.B.*, Lees Summit, MO

"After noticing the attractive covers on the new line of Silhouette Intimate Moments, I decided to read the inside and discovered that this new line was more in the line of books that I like to read. I do want to say I enjoyed the books because they are so realistic and a lot more truthful than so many romance books today."

J.C., Onekama, MI

"I would like to compliment you on your new line of books. I will continue to purchase all of the Silhouette Intimate Moments. They are your best line of books that I have had the pleasure of reading."

S.M., Billings, MT

*names available on request